Where Has Summer Gone?

MELINDA CROCKER

Cover art and design: www.jamesfaecke.com

Cover photograph: Stacy Hamilton

ISBN: 1519762402
ISBN-13: 978-1519762405

DEDICATION

Mike: Love you Always.

Christina Eanes: best coach and editor ever

Jim, thanks for the great art!

Katherine, Sandi, Alyssa & Linda - constant support and edits!

All the rest of you (you know who you are)

I am forever grateful for the encouragement

"Golden slumbers kiss your eyes,
Smiles await you when you rise.
Sleep,
Pretty baby,
Do not cry,
And I will sing a lullaby.

Cares you know not,
Therefore sleep,
While over you a watch I'll keep.
Sleep,
Pretty darling,
Do not cry,
And I will sing a lullaby."

-Golden Slumbers

Traditional, Written by: Thomas Dekker

CHAPTER ONE

Scrape…click…scrape.

A noise.

Summer jerked awake. She cocked her head to one side and listened. A dream? Had she actually slept long enough to dream?

Tap, tap. Click…scrape.

It wasn't a dream. She was fully awake. Summer leaned forward and cupped her ear.

Click…click.

Metal against metal.

It was something coming from the darkness and not just in her head. She tried to stand, but hit her head on the low ceiling. "Damn!" she said, then clamped her hand over her mouth and froze. No more movement or sound. The noise had stopped. No. No. No.

She leaned her back against the wall. How long had she been here? It might have been days, or only hours. Summer Mahoney Reynolds was lost. Lost to time and place. Lost to the world.

She might not know the location of her prison, but she knew every stinking inch of her cell. A dark, windowless pit, with four rough walls, a low rock ceiling, a dirt floor, and a single tiny, wooden door. A door just big enough to crawl through in a crouch—if it wasn't locked from the other side. She couldn't even pace the dirt floor without walking in a weird half crouched position.

Summer bent her petite frame at the waist and pulled her thin jersey shirt away from her back. The cold, damp wall, or a sore back? Guess the wall wins. So her back found the wall, and she allowed the dampness to seep through her shirt.

She shivered and hugged her knees. The soggy shirt and mud-soaked jeans did little to shield her from the frigid air. She yawned and rubbed her numb hands together. Her body craved sleep, but she refused to lay on the dirt floor. The thought of some creepy, crawly thing as it moved over her in the darkness was enough to create permanent insomnia.

Where am I? There it was again. The thought kept surfacing like a line in the Sunday New York Times Crosswords that she couldn't quite solve. With the dirt floor, rock ceiling, and damp, foul smelling corners, it had to be somewhere subterranean. Where? How? Why? She rubbed her forehead and mumbled, "Think."

Her memory was Swiss cheese. Not her distant past. That was crystal clear. Every tragic and joyful moment played easily when her mind reached for it. Her recent memories were the ones that wouldn't come. How she arrived in this black pit was gone. Vanished. Just like her.

Her last recent memory was of a road trip with Shelly. After that, things got murky. She distinctly remembered a bump and hard jerk of the steering wheel before she told Shelly to stay in the car so she could check it out. Next she remembered feeling the crisp, cold mountain air as she got out of the car to look at the flat, black puddle of rubber that used to be her rear wheel. As she bent over the tire and poked her finger inside a large rip, she could remember turning to look behind her, but why? A noise? Then only a faint memory of a strange smell, a gray fog, and then nothing. And now here she was, lost in the dark. A subterranean hell hole. Summer snorted. Maybe she had died and this actually was hell.

The familiar bolt of lightning hit hard. It had the same impact each time she tried to remember what happened.

"Shelly. Where is she? Where is my daughter?" she whispered as she choked on a sob.

Summer took a deep breath. "Stop it! Don't go there. You have to think this through," she said through clinched teeth. But the familiar panic and need to protect rose from the pit of her stomach and spread throughout her body. Her hands clinched in a need to punch something. "Stop it!" she shouted as she hugged her knees and pressed her head against them.

Scrape.

Louder this time, then a sound like something moving in the dirt floated through the darkness. Summer's head snapped up.

"Mom?"

"Oh, my God!" Summer yelled as she scrambled onto her knees. "Shelly? Honey, is that you?" she called as she scooted toward the locked door. It was still bolted, but now some sunlight and air filtered through the narrow slats. Light, real light and air!

"It's me, Mom. Are you okay?"

The cross slats of the rough wooden door had enough separation to see a little of the other side. It wasn't wide enough to get her fingers through, but as Summer pressed her face against the door, she could see her daughter's soft blonde hair flowing around a very pale face. Summer's voice trembled as she said, "I'm fine, Sweetheart. What about you? Are you hurt?"

"No, uh, I'm okay." Her daughter leaned in and whispered, "but, Mom, I don't know what to do. This is so insane!" Summer caught a whiff of the girl's recently shampooed hair. It smelled like lemons. Her stomach clinched. They didn't have lemon shampoo.

"What do you mean? Do you know where we are? How did we get here?"

"I'm not sure where we are? Somewhere close to Grandma's house, I think, but Mom, I'm really scared. This place is so strange and the people are like something out of a movie; not a good movie either, the kind of movie you won't let me watch." Her daughter's voice rose shrilly as she continued, "I just found out you were here. The girl told me. When I first woke up it was all weird, and I thought I was alone, and you were, were, just gone…" she said as her voice trailed off.

Summer shoved hard on the door, but it didn't budge. "Oh, Sweetie; I'm so sorry. Can you open this door?" she said as she pressed her hands flat against the rough wood. She could feel the warmth of her daughter's hands as they pressed back from the other side.

"I haven't found the right key. This key only worked on the outside door and the others I've tried don't fit." She held up her hand and shook a set of multiple keys dangling from an iron ring.

Behind Shelly was a much larger outer doorway that was flooded with sunlight. The vestibule inside the open door had a curved rock ceiling and wooden walls to shore it up. The rusted metal hinges on the open door appeared buried in the rock sides of the arched doorway. Blood pounded in Summer's ears and her palms began to sweat. A formidable prison carved out of rock. "Try the rest of them, Honey. There has to be one that works!"

A shadow loomed into view and eclipsed the sunlight. The shadow said, "Angel-3, what do you think you are doing?" The shadow moved forward and developed definition. A blonde girl of about fifteen or sixteen. Summer had to blink at the older carbon copy of her twelve-year-old daughter. "You can't be here. It isn't allowed," the teen sounded frantic as she whipped her head around, then she surged forward and yanked Shelly away from her. Within seconds, her daughter disappeared behind the outer door as it slammed shut. Back to total darkness.

"Wait! Wait, please. Uh, listen, don't go!" Summer yelled as she heard the snap of a padlock. She pounded on the door and rammed her shoulder against it when she heard the muffled cries of protest from her daughter.

"No, no, no! Please don't hurt her! Please?" Summer yelled.

The response was utter silence, as if the interruption never happened. Summer dropped her hands to the dirt floor as she began to cry.

She turned and crawled back to her spot against the wall. "This is not happening," she said as she pounded closed fists against her legs. "Please, let this stop!"

Summer screamed. A deep primal scream that developed a life of its own, and got louder with each breath. Her hands found their way to her ears as it echoed in the empty cell. Her screams stopped as abruptly as they started, and her body went limp, but her thoughts churned and bounced off each other.

Angel-3? Why did she call Shelly that? What the hell does that mean? Who is that girl? Why does she look so much like Shelly? Where the hell are we?

So many questions, but no answers. It was too much. She sighed, then began to sing, softly at first, then stronger and louder.

"Sleep; Pretty baby; Do not cry; and I will sing you a lullaby." A favorite tune when Shelly was little.

As the tune floated in the air and wrapped around her like a blanket, she thought, "I might just be losing my mind." The song turned into a low hum, then silence as she fell into a shallow sleep.

CHAPTER TWO SATURDAY

Four Days Earlier

"Shelly, please, we're going to be late!"

"I'm coming."

"You've been saying that for the last fifteen minutes. Now let's go. I mean it, Shelly!" Summer yelled as she placed the last dish in the dishwasher and wiped down the kitchen counter.

"When did I turn into such a shrew? Wait, I know, when my daughter was taken over by a strange pod person, because I certainly don't know that creature living in her bedroom," she mumbled. "I hate this."

"Okay, okay. It is Saturday, you know Saturday's are supposed to be a free day!" Shelly yelled from her room.

"Shelly!" Summer responded as she thought, "Free for whom? Certainly not for me."

The girl appeared in the doorway. Uncombed hair stuck out in wisps as if she had just jumped out of bed. Blue jeans and a wrinkled t-shirt adorned her thin body. She was still all arms and legs but the promise of a woman's body was peeking through. The slogan on the t-shirt: "I'm annoying." Ratty sneakers with holes in the toes completed her outfit. Summer glanced at her watch, then sighed audibly and pointed in the direction of her only child's bedroom.

Shelly turned and trudged down the hallway, but not before she displayed a pronounced eye roll.

Could she move any slower? "Shelly," Summer's voice held a note of warning as she moved in behind her daughter and placed a firm hand on each shoulder. She applied just enough pressure to speed up the girl's step.

Once in her bedroom Shelly stood in front of her closet as Summer pulled out a dress and leggings. "No way!" the girl shook her head. "Not a dress," she said as she stomped one foot.

"No arguments. I'm not in the mood and I'm really tired of the way you live up to the slogan on your shirt. Now change!" Summer shoved the clothes at her daughter.

Shelly pulled off her shirt and gazed at the slogan while she mouthed the words, then looked up and said, "Moooom."

Summer cocked her head to the side and said, "Really? You put it on and didn't even know what it said?" She shook the hangers in her extended hand.

Shelly accepted the clothes and silently shucked her jeans then pulled on the outfit. She stood in front of the mirror and frowned as Summer combed her long blonde hair and pulled it up into a ponytail. "Ouch!"

"If you had taken care of your hair on your own, you wouldn't have to put up with this, so be quiet."

"But it hurts."

"Please—" Summer stood back and said, "Much better, now to the car, Mz Drama Queen. Tyler is already at school, and the concert has probably started."

"It's not even my class. It's for the high school kids."

Summer sighed, "Shelly, we are a family now, and that means we support Tyler's projects, and he supports ours. Now, let's go."

The ride to the school was filled with a silence Summer was not about to break. When she pulled into the school parking lot, it was full. "This is what being late gets us," she said as she thought, "I sound just like my mother. When did that happen?"

SUV's and pickup trucks surrounded the small Texas town's only high school, but Summer found a spot three blocks away and squeezed into it. "Let's go, kid. We need to sprint if we want to make it before the intermission."

They were both out of breath once they entered the darkened auditorium. They stood just inside the door until their eyes adjusted to the dim lighting, then they slipped in with some other late arrivals who stood against the back wall.

It was a short wait to intermission, and when the lights went on, they were the first to spill out into the reception area. At least there was some benefit to being the last to arrive.

Folding metal tables in the lobby were covered with white plastic cloths and laden with homemade goodies. Summer took in the baked goods with mouthwatering envy. She loved sweets, but to create them was not one of her talents. She had learned that the tasty morsels were something of a duel for the small town moms. Hierarchy was established by the elaborate and delicious donations. Summer readily accepted her position at the bottom of the ladder. Her idea of homemade was to slice and bake a tube of cookie dough instead of breaking open a package of Keebler's.

One of Summer's darkest secrets made her cheeks burn every time she saw the array of cakes, pies, and sweet treats at a community benefit. She once resorted to cookies from a bakery in the city, which she displayed on her mother's hand-painted platter. It was the one time the town queen bee raved about her contribution. God help her, she had never admitted her sin, not even to Tyler, and hoped it would follow her to her grave.

Most of the parents flocked to the tables, while nicotine addicts headed for the nearest exit. Summer had no interest in either tonight, so she scanned the crowded lobby until she spotted Tyler on the other side of the room. She still felt a tingle when they locked eyes. Electric.

He moved in their direction, "Hey, how are my girls?" He gave Summer a hug and tugged at Shelly's ponytail, "I see your mom managed to corral you into a dress." He smiled, shook his head and winked, "Sorry about that, kiddo."

Shelly grinned as if she had won the lottery as she gave her mom a withering look. She turned toward Tyler, "It's okay, Tye. I don't mind, really. You've got some pretty cute guys in your orchestra."

Summer's jaw dropped, then she gazed at Tyler over her daughter's head and mouthed "What?" A smile passed between them. "Why don't you go hang with your friends? I see them by the cookies," she said aloud.

"Really? Cool." She gave her mother a quick peck on the cheek, gave Tyler a squeeze, and then rushed to the tight group of tween girls.

As she watched her daughter move away, Summer called, "Not too many cookies, we're going out to dinner after the concert." She turned back to her husband, shrugged her shoulders and said, "Wow, Doctor Jekyll and Mz Hyde comes to mind. She gets a little more impossible every day. Where has my sweet baby gone?"

"That's why God created teenagers, so you don't mind as much when they head off to college."

"College? She's barely twelve!"

"She's precocious, what can I say? Besides, I hate to break this to you, momma, but twelve is a teen and college days will follow before you know it."

"I thought basic training was tough. To raise a strong willed girl makes it seem tame," Summer said. She looked Tyler in the eye before she continued with, "I heard my mother in my words today. That's something I swore would never happen."

Tyler raised one eye brow, "Whoa! Slow down. You're a great mother and, no offense, nothing like your mom. You know Shelly gives you grief because you two are close. That's the rule; the closer you are, the harder they have to pull away. Not to mention she is a lot like you. It's inevitable you two would butt heads." He smiled and leaned in close, "Have you told her yet?"

Summer cringed visibly, "No. She's going to be impossible when I do, so I'm waiting for a non-combative moment." She glanced in Shelly's direction and then back to Tyler. She mumbled, "If it ever comes. These days whatever I say, she says the opposite."

Tyler laughed, "She may surprise you and welcome the news." He put his arm around her waist, gently touching the small bump in her otherwise flat belly, "A little brother or sister might bring out her maternal instincts."

"I plan to tell her on the way to Mom's. We'll have hours alone in the car and we don't seem to find much to talk about these days." Summer gazed at her daughter. A group of senior boys walked past the tight group and the girls turned away and giggled. Shelly flipped her ponytail and said something to the group that made them all laugh harder. "That's if I can manage to get her to take out the ear buds, or stop texting for a few minutes to actually listen to me."

"Do you still want to leave tomorrow? We break for the Thanksgiving holiday on Wednesday. I could get everything ready around the ranch Tuesday night and we could all go early Wednesday morning. We both have the rest of the week off, anyway." He moved even closer and whispered, "We could tell her and your mom together."

Summer smiled, "Noooo, as tempting as that sounds, I want to tell Mom alone." She placed her hand on Tyler's arm and said, "You know how she frets and worries about us. I would rather she do her usual gloom and doom predictions without you there to hear it."

Tyler said, "I know how she can be, but I don't want you to take it alone. Both your mom and Shelly's reactions at the same time may be a lot of uh, unnecessary stress, and after all, I had a part in this," he smiled.

"No—but, thank you." She squeezed his arm, "I'm used to mom, and I learned a long time ago that all her blustering is her way of saying 'I love you'. Let her get it out of her system. She will be ready to celebrate by the time you get there. Honestly, it won't be that bad. She is really excited about having us visit, so she is already in a great mood. I'll tell Shelly on the way, and I can tell mom over dinner. I have her favorite wine to soften the blow. Of course, she will know immediately when I don't pour myself a glass." Summer sighed, "Maybe sooner, if Shelly is ticked off enough, she will blurt it out as soon as she walks through the door just for shock value."

"Are you sure you want to do this alone?" Tyler asked.

"Yes, very," Summer smiled and said. "But thank you. It means a lot to me that you want to help."

"Okay for now, but that doesn't mean I am through with my pitch." Tyler glanced at his watch, "It's almost time for me to get backstage. Have you spoken to Richard?"

Summer nodded, "Yeah, much as I hated to do it. He'll pull me from outside duty as soon as I get back from mom's and put me on a desk for the duration."

"I'm sorry. I know you love to climb those damn telephone poles,"

He laughed and Summer grinned. "My wife, first boots-on-the-ground Army, then the telephone line person. I think there might be a country song in there somewhere."

Summer laughed and said, "I'm not sorry." She rubbed her stomach, "It's totally worth it, but get ready for me to be pretty bitchy without my usual adrenaline drain at work."

Tyler laughed again, "I can handle it. Maybe we can think of other ways to drain your energy." He gave her a quick kiss and glanced at his watch again, "Whoops, better run. They'll think the concert is so bad that I've jumped ship." He gave her a squeeze and headed toward the exit.

Summer watched him make his way through the crowd. He greeted each person with a smile, nod, or light touch of his hand before he moved on. She thought about how lucky she was to have met and married a man she loved, not once, but twice. So few people got even one chance at happiness with another human being. She had it twice.

∞

Summer pushed the pillows and a blanket into the backseat of the car and slammed the door. She stood straight and rubbed her lower back. The pregnancy had barely begun, and this child already played havoc with her body.

To carry Shelly for nine months was a breeze, even after the day her world changed. Shelly was not much more than a clump of cells in her womb when two soldiers in dress uniform knocked on her door one early spring morning. A roadside bomb on another side of the world had ignited and Phillip no longer existed. Summer had turned into ice that day, but when Shelly appeared a few months later, the ice melted.

Summer put both hands on the car and stretched her back, then reached toward the ground. She couldn't quite place her hands on the grass from a standing position. She raised up, placed her hands on her hips, and frowned. It was twelve years since she was pregnant with Shelly, and her body certainly wasn't in the same shape as when she was Army tough, but good grief, this was ridiculous. She bent at the waist once more and this time felt the blades of grass tickle her fingertips. Better, but she vowed to find a pregnancy yoga class as soon as she got home.

She walked to the front of the car and watched Tyler checking the oil. Satisfied, he closed the hood and wiped his hands on a towel.

"Am I getting fat and out of shape?" she asked. Tyler laughed and she felt her face flush, "Okay, I know I sound like a pregnant woman, but I am, so humor me."

He said, "Why do I feel like there is no correct answer to that question?" Summer crossed her arms over her chest and frowned, so he sighed and said, "You are as beautiful and as strong as the day we met."

She smiled broader, "Right answer."

He put both hands on her shoulders, "You will watch the gas?"

Summer rolled her eyes and replied, "Yes, dear." She gazed at him, "Will you ever let me live that one down?"

"Probably not," he laughed.

"Geeze, Tye. I was just a little distracted."

He laughed again and put his arms around her shoulders, "Yeah—how distracted were you?"

"Well—a lot!"

"At least I got to see you before our vows. It was worth it to drive twenty miles to pick you up." He ran a finger over her cheek, "Now the crowd of folks who waited for us were not as amused. They thought you stood me up."

"You know it's supposed to be bad luck seeing the bride before the wedding."

He kissed her, "No bad luck here, Baby"

She kissed him back then pushed him away, "We need to get on the road. Where is that girl?"

"There she is—oh, my."

Summer turned and gasped. Shelly had her arms completely filled with stuffed animals. She walked past them and struggled with the back door before she carefully placed each one on top of the bedding.

Once her furry charges were safely tucked into the back seat, Shelly gave Tyler a hug, then got into the passenger side of the car. She fastened her seat belt, lowered the window on her side, and then looked at her mother. "What?" she said, but didn't wait for an answer before she stuck her ear buds in and faced forward as her head began to bob to the music.

"Oh, yeah, this is going to be fun," Summer mumbled before she turned and gave Tyler a quick kiss and headed for the driver's side. She said, "Bye, Babe—Call you from the road, and when we get there."

"Be careful—Love you!" he waved and stood in the middle of the driveway. She watched him continue to wave until he appeared to be a small dot in the rear view mirror. Summer gazed at her daughter and shook her head as they headed toward the main highway.

CHAPTER THREE MONDAY

The sun peeked above the flat West Texas plains with an oily orange glow. Birds chirped as crickets and toads got busy singing down by the creek. It all seemed like a typical fall morning, except it wasn't. Summer was gone.

Where was she? What happened? It was as if she drove down the road and just disappeared.

Tyler kicked off the blanket and sat upright as the aluminum chaise lounge squeaked in protest. Same noise it had made every time he moved during the long night. He rolled his neck in a circular motion and the birds got quiet as it cracked with each roll. He stared at the sunrise, then at his right hand still clinched around his cell phone. As he opened his hand it felt sore, and red lines outlined where the phone rested. He glared at the rectangular window to the world. No missed calls. No voice messages. No text messages. Nothing. The damn thing remained silent. Not even a chirp. The fricking birds and crickets put it to shame. He pulled it close and squinted at the tiny battery symbol on the top of the screen. There was still some power left, but he better go inside and plug it in. He needed the hope of a

100% charge, not the excuse of a dead battery.

“Where the hell are you, Summer?” Tyler grumbled as he stood up from the flimsy chase. As he spoke, Jake perked up his ears and turned solemn eyes toward him, the Blue Healer was tense and poised, ready for action.

“No buddy, no cows today.”

Since the dawn caught him wrapped in the wool blanket on the chase lounge, sleep must have stolen at least a few hours. The chaise was pulled close to the fire pit, but the fire was just ashes now. Last night it was a refuge from the house. The empty wine bottle perched on the ledge of the pit explained why he had finally found sleep and the wild dreams that still floated in his head. He couldn’t quite grasp them as daylight turned them into wisps of smoke.

“Geeze, Tyler, don’t you do that. Don’t dive into a bottle. Not this time,” he said as shook his head. Summer wasn’t like his first wife, Bethany. She would not just take off on a whim. Booze was not the solution then, and it wasn’t now. He would not go down that road. Jake whined and he rubbed his head, “It’s okay, buddy. I haven’t lost it.” He stretched and said, “Not yet anyway, the jury is still out on that one.”

The fire was just ash, but the smell of burning mesquite still clung in the air. Tyler poured the bucket of sand he kept by the pit over the coals, then picked up a stick and poked them until he was satisfied the fire was completely out. “Okay, Jake. Let’s go.” The dog jumped up and matched his master’s pace as he shuffled across the yard toward the rambling ranch house.

They entered through the kitchen door and Tyler froze in his tracks. The smell of freshly brewed coffee tickled at his nose. “Summer?” A quick glance around the kitchen, then his shoulders slumped. Of, course. The usual 5:30am setting had automatically started the brew cycle. He had set it up himself the night before. It was as if the world had not shattered and time was not interrupted, but he knew better. Summer was gone.

He poured himself a cup of the dark brew and headed through the house toward the bedroom. Our bedroom. "Oh, Summer," he whispered.

He passed Shelly's room, then returned to the doorway. The white iron bed was neatly made with a wild purple bedspread. Posters plastered every available wall space. Everything from Disney to the latest boy band. Tyler could never remember their name. Something about a direction? Dark, plumb curtains hung across the wide windows. A teenage heaven of a room. It smelled of sweat and perfume. Tyler moved across the room and pulled the curtains back. The sun bathed the room with light. Summer hated those curtains, but hung them anyway when Shelly insisted. Tyler turned to the bed and touched the solitary stuffed bear that leaned against the headboard before he left the room. The house was so damn quiet it made him want to shout.

The door to the master bedroom was closed. He stared at the door knob a long moment before he twisted it open. The bed was a mass of jumbled covers, and for one heart-stopping moment, he thought he saw her asleep under the heap of blankets, but what he saw was simply a result of his restless night before he gave up and fled the house. His imagination tried to change reality once again.

It was just that she liked to do that sometimes; roll herself up in the warm bed he had just left, hug his pillow and sleep until he finally teased her out of the tangled blankets.

Summer's love of sleep amused him. The sun was his alarm clock. It was a remnant of all those years on the family farm, that is, if you could call that barren piece of crap a farm.

What a childhood. Memories of the pre-dawn hours of back breaking work before school. Not pleasant, *Father Knows Best* memories. More, *This Boy's Life*, with a skinnier, hardened De Niro as his father.

A hard life, but he learned he had a talent. The ability to fight and survive. A talent that both served and cursed him. He didn't always like himself when in flight or fight mode, because fight was usually his first choice.

Not much remained of that kid. Maybe the tangled mass of curls when he forgot to get a haircut, but now the curls were as much gray as blonde. The smooth apple cheeks were gone; replaced with a road map of the years spent in the field under the relentless West Texas sun.

Life was strange. These days he worked the ranch just as hard and still rushed off to school, but now it was to teach music. He laughed. His dad would have hated that. Sissy work. His schedule wasn't that different than when he was a kid, but it was his ranch, and Summer and Shelly were here instead of his old man - somehow those distinctions made all the difference.

Tyler snapped out of his memories. Summer's smell floated in the bedroom air. A peculiar mix of soap and lavender lotion, it curled around him and teased his imagination.

He plugged his cell into the charger and stared at it as the battery symbol lit up. "Damn, Summer, call me!" he said as he sat on the edge of the bed. Jake turned his furry head to one side. His dark brown eyes were solemn. "I know, boy. I, know."

The clock read 6:10 AM, but he decided to make the call anyway. Maybe she couldn't sleep either. As he held the phone close to his ear he heard hope in the fragile voice that sounded so much like his wife's, "Hello? Summer?"

"No, Jennifer. It's me, Tyler."

"Oh," she said in a voice thick with disappointment. "No word?"

"No. Nothing on your end?" he clutched the phone so hard he thought it might break.

"No."

"I'm coming." He sat a little straighter with the decision made. Out of the corner of his eye he saw a framed picture on the bedside table. He felt his chest tighten, so he looked away.

"Are you sure? What if she comes home?" Her voice rose a little with each word.

He reached out and flipped the picture frame face down. "Jennifer, I can't just sit here. I was supposed to join her in a couple of days, anyway." He tried to keep the anger and frustration out of his voice, but it snuck in anyway. Tyler closed his eyes, took a deep breath, and continued, "I'm taking a personal day today, and I'll ask for another one tomorrow. They'll understand," he opened his eyes and rose from the bed and paced the length of the room as he spoke, "School's out after that for the Thanksgiving holiday. I have my neighbor's son to tend to the stock, so the ranch is good. I'll come by the same route they took and make inquiries along the way. Maybe someone has seen them, or maybe they just took a scenic detour and are out of cell range—but my gut tells me something just isn't right."

"Tyler, do you think maybe she did it on purpose? I mean, uh, she could have panicked." He froze, unable to speak. She whispered the last words in a voice so low he could barely hear her. They were both silent a moment, then she cleared her throat and continued with a stronger voice, "You've only been married a few months, and, uh, she was on her own for so long. Well, ever since Phillip died it's been just her and Shelly." Another pause, then she lowered her voice to a whisper again, "Maybe she simply needs some time to think; you know, be alone, maybe take a little vacation?" her words trailed off.

Tyler found his voice and said, "No way." He shook his head violently. "No, that's not the Summer I know. She would have said something first, she's too damn honest to do something like that." He stopped and stood in the middle of the room as he felt a sudden chill that rocked him to his core, "Jennifer, did she say something to you about us?" He closed his eyes and whispered, "Did she say something about being unhappy?"

"No. Actually, I don't think I have ever heard her sound happier…"

she said as her voice trailed off.

Tyler expelled a held breath and moved to the bed. He sat on the jumbled covers and smiled. He made a quick decision and said, "Jennifer, she has news for you."

"What news?"

"We are expecting." His voice lifted, "You will be a grandmother again. Shelly will have a new baby brother or sister."

"Oh, oh, my!"

Tyler could hear her begin to cry. He squeezed his eyes shut and mumbled, "Shit." He stood and said, "Jennifer, I'm sorry, Summer wanted to tell you herself." He gazed around the room, swallowed, blinked rapidly, and then continued, "I should have waited, but somehow I thought it would help. I just had to share the news. I, I…" He coughed and cleared his throat, "Well, anyway, I'm on my way. I should be on the road within the hour."

"Okay," her voice was even lower, almost childlike. "Maybe you're right. I'll wait for your call. Oh, and Tyler, I am very, very happy with the news, really. It's just, well the timing, not knowing, you know. If we just knew they're safe," she said as her voice broke once again.

"Jennifer, stay strong. Please. They need us to be strong. Uh, I need you to be strong." He searched his mind for the right words. His head felt as if it were full of cotton. This was so strange. Then a clear thought broke through, and he said, "Why don't you contact the police department on your end? I called John Henry last night when I didn't hear from Summer. John is the police chief here. He said there isn't much they can do officially just yet, but John is a neighbor, and a friend, so he is going to check it out anyway. Maybe your police department might have some suggestions."

"That's a good idea! I'll head down there now."

"You have my cell number, so we'll keep in contact. Let's talk every two hours."

"Tyler, please be careful, and don't worry about me. I'll keep the faith."

He smiled as he disconnected. The woman was still a full-fledged, liberal-hearted, freedom-loving Hippie. She lived as if it was still the sixties. The thought made him laugh aloud. Some things never changed. Even his wife's name, Summer Breeze, was from the Seals and Crofts song so popular in that era. How strange life could be. Summer was completely different then her mother. She would still be active duty Army if Shelly's dad had made it home from his deployment.

What an amazing woman he had married. She did not give in to grief, instead, she left her dream career without hesitation. She moved in with her mom until Shelly was born. How hard was that? As soon as she could, she moved to Texas for the best paying job she could find, a telephone line person. Incredible. She didn't know a soul in her new town, but that didn't stop her.

Tyler buried his face in his hands as he thought, "She has to be okay, whatever happened. She's good under pressure. Really good. She has military training. She is strong. Wherever she is, I know she can handle it."

He picked up the picture he had turned over and gazed at it. A snapshot of the day they were married. They held Shelly between them and they were all smiles. Shelly's arms were encircling both of their necks, and she was pressing their heads together. A wonderful day. The best day of his life.

Tyler set the photo down and threw some clothes and toiletries into a duffle bag. He was headed for the door, but stopped, swiveled, and crossed the room in three strides, grabbed the picture, and tucked it under his arm before he headed out of the bedroom.

Shelly's room was his next stop. He snatched the tattered bear off her bed, then put it in his bag, and eased the picture in next to it. One more glance around the room, then he headed for the door with Jake tight on his heels. He had a mission and this was one he would not fail.

∞

Idalou, Texas was quiet. Not unusual for early on the Monday before Thanksgiving, actually, not unusual for most Monday mornings. Tyler thought as he pulled his pickup into the dirt lot in back of the police department. Jake gazed at him, "Stay." The dog flopped down on the seat and placed his head on his front paws, then whined. "Stop your bitchin. I won't be long," Tyler said. He lowered the window on the passenger side, "There. That better?" The dog thumped his approval with his stubby tail.

The wind had a bite to it. Winter was coming fast this year. Tyler pulled his jacket collar up and headed for the door. It was unlocked, so he went inside as he called out, "morning, Chief."

"Tyler, I was expecting you might be by."

"Yep, on my way out of town. Heading to Summer's mom's place in New Mexico. Thought I'd see if you found anything?"

"Sorry, Tye, nothing." The Chief of Police stood and enclosed Tyler's outstretched hand with a dry, firm grip. He was a couple of years ahead of Tyler in high school, but they met and bonded on the football field. Their time in college had overlapped, but the Chief played college ball while Tyler became a music major. Their bond remained tight in spite of their separate paths. Tyler was a music teacher and now John Henry wore a baseball cap with a Texas Tech emblem on it instead of the Idalou PD cap that sat on his desk, but he was a cop through and through. "Checked with Lubbock PD, State Police, hospitals, even checked in New Mexico with Roswell PD, called everyone I could think of, but no one has seen anything, or reported any accidents."

"John Henry, I do appreciate it. Guess that's good news in a way,"

Tyler said as he shook his head, “I can’t just sit around anymore, though or I’ll wind up bonkers, so I’m off to Noisy Water. I’ll take the same route they took. I have a picture of the girls and will show it at each place they might have stopped for gas or food.”

“Not a bad idea, Tyler. You have your cell, so she can reach you if she makes contact.” He sat on the edge of his desk with one long leg touching the floor and his arms crossed over his barrel chest, “How long do you think it will take you?”

“Well, usually takes about five hours, but with all the stops, maybe six or seven?”

“Okay. I have to meet the wife at church in a few, or she will skin me for sure. We’ve got that setup for the Thanksgiving play the little ones do on Wednesday, but I’ll head back here after and see if anything pops up. Call or text when you get there. I’ll have my cell on vibrate in church, but will have the ringer on for the rest of the day and night.”

“Thanks, John Henry. I’ll report in regularly and you let me know if you hear anything.” Tyler shook his hand again and headed for the door, but stopped, turned and asked, “You put the word out with Billy Ray and the boys?” Reference to the five officers the Chief had to reside over the 2,000 plus citizens of Idalou.

“Did that first thing.” He stood and shoved his hands in his pockets, “Take care, Tyler. We’ll get them back, you’ll see.”

“I know John Henry, I know.” He headed out the door as he mumbled, “We have to.”

CHAPTER FOUR
MONDAY

The mini-mart appeared empty. A deserted parking lot, dark and dusty plate glass windows, and the last possible stop before Noisy Water was a disappointment. Tyler's last hope. Another dead end.

The familiar "You are entering Noisy Water" roadside sign was just around the bend, and this store was only a few miles from Jennifer's house. The road trip produced only one clerk who recognized Summer and Shelly, and that was at a truck stop one gas tank into the trip. What did it mean? Did they even make it out of Texas?

Obviously the girls were on course yesterday and headed this way. But with no sightings after the Texas/New Mexico State Line, had they headed in another direction, or did something evil on the highway happen?

Tyler shoved the truck into park and gazed at a solemn Jake, "I can't lose focus. If there is somebody actually in there, and they give me another one of those blank looks, I will not buy whatever booze they have for sale to make the pain go away." Jake whined and stared at him. "I know," Tyler said and reached into the glove box and found a bottle of aspirin. He popped several in his mouth and downed half of his water bottle, then he poured the rest into a bowl and watched as Jake lapped it up.

Tyler slipped out of the truck, stretched, and then opened the door wide and whistled. The dog jumped to the ground and headed for a bush at the edge of the parking lot. He relieved himself, then pawed the gravel rapidly with his back legs before he strutted in a tight circle as he sniffed at each patch of grass or clump of weeds.

"Yeah, looking pretty sharp there, Jake." Tyler felt a tug at the corner of his mouth, then snapped his fingers. The dog returned and leapt up on the bench seat of the truck. "Sorry Jake, won't be long this time, buddy." He slammed the door of the pickup and said, "Promise. Keep your paws crossed, buddy." He left both windows on the truck all the way down. It was cool in the mountains, but still too warm for a closed cab in a fur coat. Besides, Jake wouldn't make a move to leave the truck without his approval.

At the door to the mini-mart Tyler paused, took a breath, then reached for the handle and tugged. The glass door was unlocked and buzzed as he opened it. Once inside, the store was quiet except for a low hum from the refrigeration unit.

The unit covered the entire wall that faced the door and held dust covered bottles of milk and very clean beer bottles, lots of beer bottles. Tyler turned and sailed past it through the aisles until he spotted a twenty something girl who manned the cash register. He smiled, squared his shoulders, and moved in her direction.

She sat on a tall stool behind the counter and was hunched over a glossy magazine. She glanced up as Tyler moved toward her, then back to the magazine.

As he approached he could see the colorful pages filled with movie stars in bright, flashy clothing. The girl sighed as she gazed at a full page photo. The crew from one of the latest young adult sci-fi flicks. Shelly had a poster of the same group. What is so sexy about kids forced to kill or fight other kids? Tyler just didn't get it. He eased the framed picture on the counter beside the magazine, "Have you seen these two?" He tapped the glass that covered the photo as he pointed to Summer and Shelly.

She gazed up at him instead of the framed picture. His eyes tried to stay with hers, but they drifted to the small stud protruding from her nose. The skin surrounding it was red and puffy. It looked like one of her many pimples, but with a silver head. He couldn't seem to take his eyes off of it, but he forced his attention upwards.

She frowned and glanced at the picture, then her eyes squinted… recognition? Tyler's leaned in and gripped the counter. The girl grabbed the frame and studied the trio. Although his first instinct was to snatch the picture back, he forced his hands to his sides and stuck them into his pockets. The picture was the last link to his family. He held his breath. She pointed at his image with a nail painted dark blue, "You?"

"Yes."

"Is this your wife and daughter?"

"Yes." He pointed at the picture, "This is my wife, Summer, and this is our daughter, Shelly."

She looked at him again and said, "You all look happy here."

"Yes, very happy. That was the day we were married." He let the girl take her time. "Did you see my family yesterday, or even earlier today?" he finally asked.

Dark eyes with thick black liner and dark brown eye shadow studied him in a blink-less stare. After a moment her eyes narrowed again, "Wedding picture? Then you mean stepdaughter, right?" She frowned as she said, "If you are all so happy, why don't you know where they are?"

Tyler caught the first reply that sprang to his mouth and swallowed it, he took a sharp breath and said, "Yes. Shelly is my stepdaughter, but I think of her as my own." He crossed his arms over his chest and leaned back on his heels, "Yesterday they were on their way to my wife's mother's house in Noisy Water, but never got there. They've vanished without a trace." The girl gasped, but didn't interrupt. He continued with, "Her mother hasn't heard from her, and neither have I. This is my last stop before I get to her mom's house, and my next stop is the Noisy Water Police Department. So far, no one remembers seeing them since they left Texas." He leaned forward and placed his palms on the counter, "Can you help me?"

She was quiet a moment then said, "Vanished? Man, that's sketchy." She shifted on her stool. "They were here, yesterday, late morning I think, or maybe mid-day. They got gas and used the bathroom. Oh, and she got the kid some chocolate milk." She pointed to Summer's image, "Wow, that's creepy! You mean she just disappeared? Just like one of those shows on cable?"

Tyler grabbed the picture and held it in front of the girl as he pointed at the image, "You're sure? You saw them yesterday?"

She leaned back on her stool as she replied, "Yeah, Man, that's what I said. Like, we don't get that many tourists this time of year, once skiing starts it gets busy, and the summer, of course." She smiled and he could see the youth under all the heavy makeup, "uh, your wife has a very cool name, by the way."

"How were they?" Tyler's voice cracked, "I mean, did they seem okay—not stressed out or anything?"

She cocked her head toward her right shoulder and said, "Like, uh, yeah, they seemed fine." She frowned and said, "Pretty happy, actually. Except the kid was a little pissed she couldn't have candy." The girl snorted, "The mom, uh, your wife, said no way that it was too close to lunch time." She giggled, "Man, that kid had some attitude." She shook her head and said, "Man, I talk like that to my mom, I get a wakeup call across my face." She leaned back some more and almost fell off the stool, so she grabbed the counter top, and steadied herself, before she continued with, "You're telling me they disappeared right after they were here, in this store?" She shivered visibly, then tapped Shelly's face in the picture, "What about her dad? Could he have snatched them? That's usually who it is in the movies or on TV."

Tyler frowned at the girl, "Her dad was a war hero killed in Afghanistan."

"Whoa! That's messed up, man." She shook her head and said, "Like, really, that is totally uncool."

Tyler relaxed. Even with the piercings and makeup, this girl was just a kid, not much older than the teens he taught. He smiled and said, "I know, you're right, it is, uh, really messed up."

"Hey, Man, what could have happened?"

"I don't know, but thanks to you I know they made it this far by lunch time yesterday. Thank you so much! You have no idea how much this helps." He turned the photo around and gazed at the smiling images in the picture as he stifled an urge to grab the girl in a big hug. One step closer to his family. "I'll have the police contact you as soon as I talk to them. Now, at least we know which police department is responsible.

"Whoa, really?" she sat up straighter, "Sure, sure, have them call, or stop by." She glanced up at the ceiling, "The camera don't work, not for years if it ever did. I don't know why they leave it up there, unless it's to make people think they are being recorded. Pretty lame if you ask me, especially since everyone knows it don't work. The owner is a stingy old coot and won't get it fixed. Maybe now he will." She gazed at Tyler and said, "Hey, I didn't say that about the owner, ok?" She winked at him.

"Sure, sure, all I am interested in is your statement about my girls."

She grinned and said, "You bet. I can tell the police they were here. Just like on those cop shows. Hey, maybe they will put this on TV—you know, that crime stoppers thing—maybe they will want to interview me for the show? Wow!"

Tyler frowned, "Well, maybe." He held the picture against his chest and sighed, as he allowed his shoulders to relax. "Thanks again, someone will contact you," he said, then turned and sprinted out of the store without a sideways glance at the beer in the cooler.

When Tyler reached his truck, he jumped in and said, "We got them Jake!" He shoved the gears into reverse and backed out onto the highway. When the town sign came into view, he slapped the steering wheel and said, "Damn! They made it this far. I feel like we are on their trail at last!" Jake barked once and stared through the windshield as they roared down the road

∞

The pickup truck skidded to a stop in a cloud of dust in front of the rustic log cabin. Summer's mom's house was shrouded in tall pine trees to the point of invisibility from the road. Tyler flipped the key and the truck engine quieted. As silence filled the yard the screen door on the front porch burst open and his mother-in-law bounded down the cabin steps two at a time. The screened porch ran the length of the cabin, and when the sun was bright, it acted like a two way mirror. Jennifer must have hovered there since his last call an hour ago. Poor lady.

"Tyler," she said as she stood by the pickup and rubbed her hands together. He jumped out and grabbed her in a fierce hug. She first felt like an iron rod in his arms, then he felt her melt into sobs against his shoulder. He knew just how she felt. Jake scooted to the edge of the seat and whined, but stayed inside the cab.

"It's okay, boy," Tyler said as he gazed easily over the older woman's head, "Come." The dog scampered out of the truck and scouted the driveway and yard as he marked his new territory.

Tyler patted her back as the sobs subsided and said, "Jennifer, good news, the clerk at the mini-mart on the highway remembers them! They made it almost all the way here."

Jennifer pulled away as she sputtered, "Wha—what?" She placed both hands on his chest and the blood drained from her face, "Tyler—What could have possibly happened to them between there and here? What?"

Tyler shook his head, "I don't know." He felt moisture gather in his eyes. He took a deep breath and said, "But, they were alive, well and happy yesterday, and they were here, right here in Noisy Water. I can't think beyond that, I just can't."

Jennifer Warrenton burst into tears again.

"Jennifer. Please don't," Tyler pulled away and edged back to the truck as he gave a slap to his thigh. Jake heard the slap and ran to the vehicle, making a smooth jump into the truck before settling in the center of the bench seat. "I know you spoke with the police, and you said they told you there was nothing they could do yet, but now we have proof they were in this area. I want to talk to them myself."

Jennifer swiped at her red and swollen eyes, then ran around the truck and climbed up into the passenger seat beside Jake, "Let's go. I want you to give that small town Napoleon who calls himself a police chief a piece of your mind. He was absolutely no help— And he treated me like a crazy woman."

Tyler climbed in, shoved the truck into reverse and placed his arm across the seat as he backed down the rough driveway, then he swung it around and headed for town. "We'll see about that," he said through clinched teeth.

CHAPTER FIVE
MONDAY

Tyler glanced around the police chief's inner office at the Noisy Water Police Department. Some office. Windowless, and not much bigger than a closet, it was jammed in a corner of the rectangular building. Tyler eyed the fake wood paneling and the flimsy door. The structure was termed as 'pre-fab,' but in reality, it was a double-wide trailer. It made the small brick Idalou PD look formidable by comparison. Tyler sighed. The offices didn't exactly instill confidence. Jennifer told him on the way over that the 'temporary' building had been the department's home for just over ten years, and Ralph Anderson had been Chief for nine of those years.

The Chief squeezed into the office, shut the door, and eased into the swivel chair behind the desk. The chair protested with a grinding sound along with a whoosh of the seat cushion. Chief Ralph Anderson tapped the file folder on the desk between them and said, "Folks, it's not that I don't believe you, I do, but there isn't much I can do." He edged his chair back from his desk but bumped against the back wall. He looked surprised, as if the space was new to him, then he turned toward Tyler, most likely to avoid Jennifer's glare, and said, "My officers are on alert, but, unfortunately, without some idea of where your girls went, or another reported sighting, there simply isn't much more we can make happen."

Tyler glanced at the file folder. His stomach clinched and he swallowed hard. The label read "Summer Breeze Mahoney Reynolds and Shelly Caitlin Mahoney." He glanced away and remained quiet.

Chief Anderson placed both hands across his ample mid-section and said, "I'm glad you got the information from the girl at the mini-mart, Tyler, and I'll interview Cocheta Chato. I have to warn you, though, the girl loves to embellish a story, and isn't the most reliable person in town." He raised one eyebrow and lowered his voice, "She loves the spotlight a little too much, if you know what I mean. It's possible that she simply wanted to be a part of this, and never saw Summer or Shelly."

Jennifer lunged forward and spat, "Ralph, she saw my daughter and granddaughter at the mini-mart yesterday." She placed both hands on the edge of his desk and her voice rose almost to a shout as she continued, "You can't tell me she made it up. Don't you dare! We know they were in town. This is now your responsibility, so what are you going to do?" He jumped back as if she had slapped him and his chair hit the back wall again.

Tyler placed his hand on Jennifer's arm. She quieted, moved back in her seat, and let go of the desk, but she continued to glare at Chief Anderson. Tyler almost felt sorry for him, almost. He cleared his throat and gazed at the Police Chief as the man shifted his weight. Tyler asked, "Chief Anderson, any suggestions? We want to do whatever it takes to get them back. What about Search and Rescue, or an Amber Alert?"

The Chief raised both hands, palms up, "Where would we send Search and Rescue, Tyler?" He dropped his hands into his lap, shook his head as his shoulders slumped. "This doesn't meet the criteria for an Amber Alert," he mumbled.

"How could it not meet the criteria? Shelly is a child and she is gone. Abducted. Abducted, Ralph, along with her mother," Jennifer's voice cracked as she clutched both hands into fists in her lap. Tyler reached over and rubbed her shoulder, she turned and glanced at him, then she pulled a tissue out of her pocket and turned her head away as she dabbed at her eyes.

Chief Anderson gazed at her as his expression softened. He spoke in a low voice as he said, "Jennifer, an Amber Alert is just a tool for law enforcement. You need certain things to make it effective. For instance, if we had a report of them being forced into a car, or a reliable witness who said they saw them followed, or anything pointing to a third party, and I mean anything, just to indicate they didn't leave on their own. Summer isn't suspected of an abduction of her own daughter, and, sorry, but the child's father is not in the picture." He turned toward Tyler and said, "I am sorry Tyler, but you know what I mean—since her biological father is deceased."

"For God's sake, Ralph, don't be condescending. We know he is dead, and they didn't leave on their own. Summer didn't abduct Shelly. She didn't!" Jennifer said. She clasped her hands together with such force, the nails dug into the skin on the back of her hands. Tyler was afraid the woman was about to lose it. He patted her arm again, but this time she remained tense, and gazed at him with wild eyes, "This is ridiculous, Tyler. They have to do something." He thought back to the remark she made to him earlier in the day. At least now she seemed certain Summer had not left voluntarily. Good. They needed a united front. It was hard enough to get some action out of the police without evidence of an abduction. Abduction. Tyler gasped as the word floated through his head as if shouted instead of thought.

A large shadow appeared at the door to the office, "Chief, I just got a call from the Dawson's. Another bear sighting in the upper canyon. They said it's a big one. Their dog chased him out of the yard, but then he turned on the dog, so they ran inside and called us. While they were still on the phone to dispatch they could see that the bear had climbed into the dumpsters. They can't see the dog, though. Probably a goner."

"Jennifer, Tyler, this is Officer Jeffrey Brandon."

The officer touched a finger to his forehead, then stuck his hands in his pockets, "Uh, pardon me, folks—didn't mean to butt in, but this bear is close to the middle school. A lot of those kids walk home."

The Chief gazed at his officer, "Okay, Jeff. Make sure Fish and Game is notified. They will most likely have to relocate him. You go on out there and keep an eye on those kids. Be sure to have your shotgun. You don't want to be stuck between an angry bear and a bunch of kids with only a hand gun."

He turned his attention back to Tyler and Jennifer as his officer left, "Wish he hadn't killed that dog. Damn shame, if he did. Uh, sorry, Jennifer, pardon my language." She waved her hand in the air as if she swatted at a fly. He looked at Tyler and continued, "Not just a tragedy for the dog, but it complicates things. The relocation alone will put that bear in a bad mood, especially after the dumpsters provided such an easy food source." He leaned forward, "Dumpsters are like grocery stores to these animals. If he killed the dog, he will be empowered and ready to draw blood more easily the next time."

"Ralph we don't care about the damn bear." She snorted and said, "Pardon my language."

One of his eyebrows shot up, then he smiled and said, "Folks, my point is that is usually the extent of what we have to deal with here: some wild animal encounters, petty thefts, and a few drunk and disorderliness. This disappearance of your girls is pretty unusual, that's all I'm saying." He rubbed his face with both hands, "Okay. It will very much surprise me if there is 'foul play' involved."

"Ralph," Jennifer began.

"Wait," he held up his hand, "That being said, I believe you when you say this is totally out of character for Summer, and besides, I know her, and I have to agree with you. Again, there is not a lot to do yet." He reached out his hand toward Tyler and said, "Tyler, let me scan that picture. At least I can get it to the police departments statewide, and put it on the national web site of missing persons." He reached for the photo then asked, "Would you mind if I take it out of the frame?"

"Of, course, here let me," Tyler said.

As they watched him remove the back panel and ease the photo out, the Chief said, "At the very least we will have more folks on the lookout for them."

Tyler handed him the photo and said, "Thanks, Chief Anderson. Any help is appreciated." Jennifer turned away from both of them and studied the wall.

"Please, it's Ralph," the Chief said to Tyler as he gazed at Jennifer, "I've known Jennifer a long time and this sickens me. I just wish there was more I could do."

Jennifer didn't say anything, but Tyler noticed her shoulders relax a little and her hands were loose in her lap.

The Chief placed the picture on the scanner and pushed some buttons, as it started to hum he turned and spoke to them again, "Uh, maybe you could make some posters and post them around town? You can put the word out on Facebook. The folks up here love their social networking. Something about the mountain isolation I recon, but I have to say, word in a small town travels fast, so everyone probably already knows anyway. Most of the locals know Summer, and they'll send up an alert if they're spotted. Believe me, the news will have spread like a wildfire. I'm sure we'll hear if anyone spots anything remotely suspicious. But, still, it would be good to get the information out as much as possible."

"I made some calls this morning, but I'm not on social media, Ralph," Jennifer said.

"I am, Jennifer," Tyler turned toward Chief Anderson. "I'm even on Twitter, but not Instagram or any of the others. A teacher has to at least try to keep up with the kids, but some sights just aren't meant for older folks. I'll put it out there, Ralph," Tyler said.

"Good. And for the record, Search and Rescue is a great idea, Tyler. They are always ready to roll, but we simply have to have somewhere to point them. As soon as you get off the main highway, you have the whole mountain range and the Rez," He glanced at Tyler, "Uh, the Apache Reservation, Tyler."

"Okay, that's reasonable," Tyler said, "I know about the 'Rez', Ralph. I've been coming up here a while now."

"Oh, sure, sure, sorry," Chief Anderson said as he removed the scanned photo and handed it to Tyler, then he snapped his fingers, "Hey, don't know why I didn't think of it before now, but that mini-mart is actually real close to the Reservation." He grabbed the phone, "I'll call the Tribal Police and see if they've heard anything. They're a small department like us, but do a great job." He glanced at Tyler again and said, "I will also check with BIA, uh, that's Bureau of Indian Affairs. It's under federal authority since the reservation is treated as if it's another country." After a quick conversation, he hung up.

"Well?" Jennifer asked as she leaned forward in her chair.

"Nothing from the Tribal Police, but I'll still check with BIA. It will most likely be the same story, though. Both would have called if they heard anything." He held the phone in his hand as he said, "Of course, unless a native is involved, or it happened on the reservation, the Tribal Police, and the BIA for that matter have no jurisdiction, and in this case, we don't even know if a crime has been committed." Jennifer started to speak, but the Chief held up his hand to silence her and said, "Since we live in a small mountain community, and everyone is connected or related in some way or another, the Tribal Police still would like you to go to the reservation station. Bring this picture. Their officer, Maggie Littlejohn, is on duty and will take a report."

"I know Maggie; she's good people." Jennifer stood, "Let's go, Tyler."

The men stood also, and the Chief said, "Would you like me to come along?"

Jennifer said, "No, I know the way. We wouldn't want to inconvenience you, Ralph."

"Aw, Jennifer," he said as his shoulders slumped, "Okay, I'll call BIA and give you a ring immediately if I hear anything."

Tyler reached out and shook his hand, then smiled and shrugged. His mother-in-law was already at the door, so he followed her out of the office. This time he did feel sorry for the man.

∞

Officer Jeffrey Brandon scanned the sides of the two lane highway as he maneuvered his cruiser into the upper canyon. The trees were so dense that the bright day turned instantly into dusk, and he strained to see any movement in the thick foliage. He drove the SUV slowly, as he looked for big, dark shadows.

"Shit," he mumbled as he squinted through the dirty windows. The cruiser hadn't been washed in a while, and visibility was poor. He lowered all the windows and the cool, pine scent washed over him.

It was a tight squeeze behind the steering wheel. Jeff was used to that, though. At 6'4" and 245, he was a formidable figure. The shotgun was on the seat close beside him. It was loaded and the safety was off. The Chief would skin him if he found out, but there was something Jeff feared more than the Chief, and that was bears. Jeff just hated bears.

Not many of God's creatures were that much bigger than Jeff and lived in the same community. And bears were so darn unpredictable to boot. A vivid memory from childhood colored his bear phobia. It was his tenth birthday. A glorious day. His parents had agreed he could have a dog. He had begged for one for years and they finally gave in to his constant pleas. Anxious to choose his long awaited companion, he got his dad to drive him to the Humane Society early that morning. They arrived just after an old, sick bear had attacked the outside pins. He could never forget the carnage the old guy left before an attendant had been forced to shoot him. Never did get that dog.

Jeff realized his fear sprang from that ten-year-old boy as he stood by the massive bear carcass. He could still see the blood that covered the animal's gray snout and his huge teeth and claws. The memory made him shutter. The self-awareness did nothing to stop his fears.

This animal wasn't old and sick. The report was of a young, lively specimen. He managed to avoid contact all these years. Now here he was, thirty years old, headed straight for a big, angry bear.

"Officer Brandon! Officer Brandon!" Jeff's head swung around toward the excited voice. A young boy ran toward the cruiser, "There's a bear in the dumpster!"

What is this kid's name? He remembered him from one of his calls, oh yeah, the one who sold illegal firecrackers to the other kids in his class. A real little pistol. His dad had Jeff haul him in and put him in a cell for a couple of hours. It must have worked. Jeff didn't see the kid again until now, "Where is he, Mike?" That was it —Michael Causby.

"At the end of the cul-de-sac." The boy was out of breath, "I was almost home and I heard him in the dumpster. Man, I couldn't believe it when I saw him. Good thing he didn't see me."

"What did you do?"

"I ran!"

"Smart boy, now get on home and stay inside."

"You bet!" The boy turned and ran to his house. The door slammed and Jeff saw the blinds pull open. He laughed. Bet that was worse than the 'jail time.' Poor kid, he would have a lot of fears to deal with when he grew up, maybe even more than Jeff.

At the end of the cul-de-sac one of the dumpster's metal lids was wide open and it had long claw marks down the side. The dumpster beside it had a closed lid, but it had a big dent in it. He must have jumped on it before he climbed into the open one.

Garbage was everywhere, and as Jeff got out of the cruiser, he noticed it smelled like rotten meat. He ambled toward the open container with his shotgun held high.

As he got closer, a huge swarm of blue flies appeared and surrounded him. He swatted at them and almost dropped the shotgun. He covered his mouth and nose with one thick arm and kept the gun in the other.

The dumpster remained quiet. He edged close enough to peer inside. Just garbage.

Thank you God!

The flies seemed to be thicker around the back of the dumpster, so Jeff eased around the side.

He saw the trail of blood first. Dark brown slashes in the tall grass. He followed the slashes and found a mass of bone, blood and fur. He turned away, then swallowed, tried to breathe through his mouth, and looked again. A German shepherd, and it was a big one, maybe 140 pounds worth of mangled dog. "Damn."

Jeff moved back to the cruiser as Fish and Game rolled up. He tasted bile, but swallowed and moved over to the truck, "Bear's gone but left a trail I think you can follow pretty easily." He gazed over his shoulder and could see the school red roof in the distance through the trees, "There's a dead dog back behind the dumpster. Has a collar on, but the owners were the ones who called it in, the Dawson's. They said the dog chased the bear out of their yard. Guess it didn't end too well for him."

"Bummer," the man shook his head.

"Yeah, shame. Looks like he was a beauty, too. But, I have to say, I'm glad it was the dog and not the owner that got in the way." Jeff gazed at the house to the left of the cul-de-sac and saw an older couple emerge and gaze in their direction.

"You got that right. Most of these animals don't bother with anything but the garbage and run off when people are around, but this guy has been giving us some grief for a couple of weeks."

"Yeah, the Chief figured you would have to relocate him. I don't envy your job." He stood back as the couple got closer, "Looks like the Dawson's are on their way over here. I'll give them the notification, but I need to get to the school to make sure he doesn't double back. You be okay on your own?"

"Oh, yeah," He got out of the truck, pulled out a dart gun and loaded it, "Rodney is on his way and will bring the truck with the bear trailer on it. I understand this one's big and young."

"That's what the reports said, but honestly, they all look big to me."

The man laughed deeply, "You have a point, Officer, you do have a point.

CHAPTER SIX
MONDAY

Maggie Littlejohn backed her police cruiser up the narrow drive until it rested behind a thick grove of trees. The hood faced the highway and the keys remained in the ignition as she slammed the door. The SUV was always ready to roll. It was safe in the driveway; locals wouldn't touch it, and strangers couldn't see it.

She trekked up the dirt drive toward her cabin. The house perched at the top of a hill on a plateau that overlooked the highway in the front, and a mountain range in the back. When she passed the empty single-car carport next to the house, she smiled. The empty spot belonged to her partner's Subaru wagon. The reserved space was one of the few arguments they had, and even rarer, one Maggie always won.

Elsa saw right through her argument of emergency readiness for the cruiser, and railed at the preferential treatment, but they both knew the truth: Maggie liked to spoil Elsa, and Elsa loved the special treatment.

She gazed at the sky. It was a sunny day, but the sky wasn't the usual clear crystal blue; it was hazy and the air held a chill. It wouldn't be long before the first snow.

She rounded the corner of the house, but paused at the back door, not ready to go inside just yet. Her entire day was spent at her sub-station desk. An unusual day. She loved her job because a lot of it was spent roaming the vast mountain reservation. But today the window in front of her desk was nothing but a constant tease. The forest and solitude beckoned, but she was too busy to respond. Now as she gazed over the horizon she gave thanks. The panoramic mountain range seemed to stretch forever. God, she loved that view and their isolation. She was indeed blessed.

With a sigh she turned and entered the back door. No need to unlock it; locks only kept honest people out. If someone wanted in the cabin, they could make as much noise as they wanted with the nearest neighbor miles away. A locked door meant a broken door or window and missing treasures. Insult added to injury, as her Shichu would have said. Besides, the only thing she really valued was Elsa, and maybe her own life, not things.

Maggie shook her head. Elsa came to the reservation all the way from Scandinavia. What were the odds? A world away to someone like Maggie, who rarely left the reservation.

What could Elsa possibly see in her that made her want to stay? Whatever it was, Maggie was not going to question it. Then she laughed, because that was exactly what she did, and probably always would.

The gun safe was her first stop, but the kitchen was next. She grabbed a cold beer from the fridge, popped the top and took a long swig of the brew. What a day. She carried the beer and a bag of chips into her office and turned on her laptop.

She munched on the chips as the thumb drive transferred files for the missing mother and daughter. What could have possibly happened to those two? She wiped her hands on her jeans, then opened the file and stared at the scanned photo of Summer, Shelly, and Tyler

Reynolds. The mother and daughter were last seen near her territory, and then they simply vanished. It made Maggie crazy to think someone might have snatched them from right under her nose, even though logically she knew she was not responsible.

"Maggs? You here?"

"In here," she called.

Elsa peeked into the office, "Working?"

She nodded, "A serious one."

"Jennifer's missing family?

Maggie frowned, "How did you know?"

"The town gossip mill is alive and well, even at the reservation school." Elsa stepped the rest of the way into the office. She still wore her jacket and boots and her checks were flushed, either from the cool air, or excitement, "Just makes me sick. What do you think happened to them?"

Maggie swiveled in her chair to face Elsa and said, "I can't imagine. If they broke down, someone would have seen them, unless they went off into a ravine, but I'm sure someone would have noticed a break in the trees, or skid marks on the road." She picked up her beer and sipped it again, then handed it to Elsa and said, "It's like they just vanished into thin air. Maybe someone passing through from the city grabbed them?"

Elsa took a delicate sip then handed the bottle back and flopped down in a chair to tug off her boots, "I got to know Jennifer when we worked on the school fundraiser. She donated some of her sculptures and carvings, she is a fabulous artist by the way. Her work made a lot of money for school supplies and she personally donated a bunch of art supplies. I just can't believe her family is missing; she must be going crazy."

"She is. I met with her and her son-in-law, Tyler Reynolds, and they're understandably devastated." She turned the laptop so Elsa could see the picture of the family, "Look at them, they look so happy."

Elsa pulled out her reading glasses and stared at the image. As she leaned over the desk, she took a chip and placed it in her mouth. When she spoke she sprayed a crumb, picked it up and said, "Sorry." Maggie smiled and Elsa continued after she swallowed, "You know, I knew Summer years ago. We skied together, but that is the first time I've seen her daughter." She leaned forward and stared at the picture, "They don't look anything alike do they?"

Maggie laughed and said, "Kind of like you and me. Summer is dark and Shelly is a blondie."

Elsa leaned in closer and Maggie could smell her perfume—lilacs, "The girl looks enough like Felix's girl to be her sister."

Maggie bolted upright and pulled the screen forward as she scrutinized the photo. Felix Alvarez Lea, "Damn, why didn't I see that?" Her smile disappeared as her eyes narrowed and jaw tightened. "Felix," she said in a low voice through clinched teeth. Then she picked up the phone and called the Chief of Police.

"Ralph, have you given any thought to Felix Alvarez Lea?" she paused as she listened, "Well, he has that isolated, guarded compound, and Shelly looks just like his daughter, and you know how strange he can be." Another pause, "I know it's pretty thin, but Ralph, you know the gossip. That child has been home schooled for years and she just appeared one day. No one really knows if she is actually his kid." A long pause as her cheeks reddened, "Yes, I understand. I know we need more than 'a hunch' or wild guessing." Maggie rolled her eyes at Elsa, "I just wanted to share a thought with you." She frowned and shook her head, "Yeah, right, right. I will call you if I have anything concrete. Good bye, Ralph."

Elsa said, "Well, it is just an idea."

"And a good one, given he doesn't have diddly. He could have at least said he would do a little research on Felix." Maggie pushed her beer to the side, scooted up to the desk, and brought up a police search engine up on her screen, "I know it isn't my jurisdiction, but if he won't even check him out, I will."

Elsa sighed, "I know that look, it's puzzle-solving time. Want me to bring you something to eat?"

"Hmmm, what?" Maggie was flipping through websites and jotting notes as she went.

Elsa laughed, "Never mind. Oh, and don't wipe your hands on your jeans. I see the streaks. I can't get the grease out when you do that. We do have napkins, you know?"

Maggie felt a peck on the top of her head, "I'm sorry; I won't—old habits." She turned in Elsa's direction, "And, uh, sorry, what did you ask before that?"

Another laugh, "Never mind; you just better eat whatever magically appears at your elbow."

"Thank you. You know me much too well."

"Truer words were never spoken," Elsa tossed as she left the room and Maggie turned back to her virtual world.

∞

"Felix apparently didn't exist until he bought his mountain retreat," Maggie said as she took off her empty gun belt and hung it in the closet along with her uniform. She pulled on a t-shirt emblazed across the front with the Tribal Police logo, let down her long hair, and padded barefoot into the bathroom, "Oh, thanks for the burger, it was delicious."

"You're welcome, glad you liked it," Elsa scooted higher on the pillows. "Aren't we lucky? About Felix, I mean. So honored that when he appeared it was here," Elsa replied with a yawn.

Maggie stuck her head out of the bathroom and gazed at her. A book lay face down on her chest and her short, white blonde hair stuck up in tuffs around the top of her head. Maggie pointed her toothbrush at her as she said, "Sorry, I woke you."

"No, no. I was reading; took a little nap, that's all." Elsa smiled and patted the bed, "Come, tell me more."

Maggie disappeared into the bathroom for a few moments then returned and jumped into bed. Elsa laughed, "You smell like mint toothpaste. Now tell me what you found out?"

Maggie reached for her lamp and turned it off, "I searched all the records in New Mexico, then branched out nationally—nothing. Seriously, I mean nothing. I'm pretty sure Felix re-invented himself before he came here." She stretched and pulled the comforter up to her chin, "You sure you're okay with the window cracked?"

Elsa frowned, "Have you forgotten where I'm from?"

Maggie laughed, "You have a point."

"How will you check him for priors if he has a new identity?"

Maggie turned to Elsa and smiled, "Look at you! Priors?"

"Hey, I listen. Besides, all your cop stuff is much more exciting than when Martin Silver tried to eat a grasshopper today."

"You're kidding?"

"Nope. The kids dared him, and I caught him as he had the poor creature almost over one of the Bunsen burners. Saved it just before it was toast. I imagine the poor thing is happily hopping around the school yard, and very grateful for the reprieve."

Maggie laughed, "Geeze, and I thought my job was tough. Here you are saving lives."

"Ha, Ha, very funny," Elsa elbowed her, but smiled, "Now all the kids call Martin, *Grasshopper.* I bet that will stick to him the rest of his life."

Maggie snorted a short laugh, then sobered as she thought of her own nickname as a kid, "Twin Spirit Girl." At the time, she did not find it funny, even though it was accurate. Twin Spirit was an early tribal reference to gay people, and today the Twin Spirit organization took great pride in the meaning. She and Elsa were actually members. Time and perspective does seem to change all things.

Elsa closed her book and placed it on the bedside table, then turned off her light, "Okay, Maggs, so tell me, what's next?"

"Well, I'll run some more computer searches for missing persons with Shelly and Summer's physical descriptions. I'll go nationwide with it. I have a hunch Shelly might be the target, not Summer, especially if Felix really is involved. A mother, daughter disappearance without a family member being involved, is not the norm." Maggie paused to yawn, "Now you've got me doing it. What worries me, is if this is a 'stranger' abduction, no matter which one of them is the target, it makes the other one expendable."

"What about Felix's kid? Do you think she may not be his?"

"It's possible; I searched state records for two years around the time she would have been born, and there is no birth record, at least that I can find. Even with a mid-wife and a home birth, there still should be a birth certificate. And I can't find any mention of a wife, or baby momma linked to Felix. Even a common law marriage would show up somewhere. Since his girl is homeschooled, and Felix isn't employed anywhere, it's going to be tough to dig up more information on him. There have been no complaints that I can find, or any reports to child services."

"I have faith in you, Maggs." Another yawn, "Will you tell Jennifer about your suspicions?"

"I'm not sure—I don't think Chief Anderson would approve—and neither would my boss."

"When has that ever stopped you?"

Maggie laughed, "You're right about that—as usual, you know me. Let's leave that decision for later and see what else I can dig up."

"Okay, but Jennifer is a friend, and I really think we should share with her. I could do it on the sly; she needs to know something, even if it is pretty thin. I would certainly want to be informed."

"True—but give me a little more time. I don't want to stir up something if we are wrong, and I don't want to give them false hope."

"Right now they probably need anything to think about besides their worst fears."

"I know, I know. Just be patient, and please don't say anything on your own." Maggie rubbed her hands over her face, "I'm going to have to get creative, but it can be done." She was quiet a moment, then said, "I may do some surveillance and interviews on the sly. The Chief is actually right, technically Felix's property isn't part of the reservation, it just borders it, so it's out of our jurisdiction, and gossip isn't enough to hone in on someone, or we would all be in trouble." She gazed at Elsa and lightly touched her hand, "I mean it. Promise me you won't say anything to her, or anyone else about this, and keep that pretty nose to yourself."

"Okay, okay. I promise." Elsa shrugged, then said, "Oh, Maggs, if you're right, and Shelly is the target, does that mean Summer might be, uh, expendable?"

"The same thought occurred to me, but let's not go there, at least not yet. Another reason to hold off with Jennifer and Tyler. We don't want them to make that leap, either." She patted Elsa's arm, "Let me check out more on Felix's first, we may be completely off base."

"I doubt it. The man is guilty of something if not this, maybe even if he doesn't have anything to do with the girls, you can bust him for something."

Maggie laughed, "I can't 'bust' him for being an asshole, Elsa."

"True, if that were the case your jail would be full."

"Our community is small enough to recognize the spirit of the law rather than the letter of the law, so I think I will be forgiven if I step over the gray line a little, but I don't want to abuse my authority, either." Maggie stifled another yawn.

Elsa rolled over and mumbled, "Okay, I understand, but keep me informed."

Maggie smiled, yawned again, then patted her on the back, before rolling in the opposite direction and mumbled, "You know I will."

CHAPTER SEVEN
TUESDAY

Rodney eased the truck to the right side of the road and cut the engine. It was the first place that had been wide enough to safely pull the truck and trailer off the road since entering the National Forest. As he sat in the cab he could hear the bear wail, then the truck rocked as the animal threw himself against the side of the trailer. The tranq must be wearing off.

He chuckled, rolled down the window, and pulled a joint out of his pocket. Lighting it up, he took a long drag, then held his breath and leaned back in the seat. He closed his eyes as he exhaled enjoying the cool breeze floating through the open window. Another wail and an even harder bump.

Rodney shook his head and said, "Okay, okay, you poor bastard." He slipped out of the truck, and hitching his jeans up, he sauntered to the back of the trailer. He gazed through the open air grate at the bear, "Take it easy, buddy. I can't hit you with another dart yet. I know it's still a long drive, but we're too close to the drop off spot. You're too big for me to drag your sorry ass out of this trailer. I need to be on top as you jump out and run away. You can't do that if you are sound asleep in la la land." He leaned forward and said in a low voice, "Soon you will have a whole new mountain to explore. Maybe even some hot bear babe to pursue." He smiled and took another deep drag, but this time he blew it through the grate at the bear, "Mellow out, my big friend."

Normally this was at least a two man job, but the holiday provided a chance for Rodney to volunteer to do it alone. Time and a half pay and a little Rocky Mountain High. Not too shabby. He could feel the boss's hesitation. Rodney knew he thought of him as a screw up, but no one else stepped forward, so here he was. Free, and getting paid for it.

Dense forest surrounded the forest service road and it was still a long drive to their final destination through more areas just like this. The idea was to head as far into the National Forest as he could get before dark. Section 54, close to the Rez, was where they were heading. Rodney didn't mind the long drive. Since it was two days before Thanksgiving, he was basically off for the holiday already, so might as well start celebrating. He took another drag on the joint.

He glanced around at the tall evergreens surrounding them. Thick bushes and undergrowth all but hid any breaks in the forest. Very isolated. It was the perfect place to relieve himself before he got back on the road. He rounded the front of the truck and stepped just off the road, unzipped his pants and began writing his name in the dirt. He chuckled again as he held the still lighted joint between his lips.

"What do you think you are doing?"

Rodney jumped and turned toward the deep male voice. A tall thin man with wild, long black hair and a full beard was standing beside a beautiful, blonde teen girl. "Shit! Oh, sorry, sir!" he said as he quickly zipped up his fly and grabbed the joint out of his mouth, cupping his hand around it as he extinguished it between his thumb and finger. "I didn't know anyone was around, or I would have gone over in the bushes."

The man turned to the girl and said, "Go." She moved so fast

Rodney wasn't sure if he had imagined her being there. Must be better weed then he thought. Still, he was sure he had seen her somewhere before, and recently. Where was it?

"You're disgusting," the man said as he took a step toward Rodney.

"Hey, man, don't be like that, I said I was sorry." He backed up as the crazy dude advanced, but then he realized he was stepping in the wet dirt where he had just written his name. He jumped to the side and said, "Shit."

"Your language is deplorable and you expose yourself in front of a young girl. You aren't fit to inhabit your own skin!" The man stepped even closer until he seemed to tower above Rodney, "People like you should not exist on this planet with the rest of us." As he shouted the last words Rodney felt spittle rain over his face.

He wiped at his face with his sleeve and said, "Not cool, dude. You need to chill." The man raised his hand and Rodney felt the full force of a backhand across his face.

The next moment Rodney realized was he was on the ground. His right ear was ringing, and his face felt as if it were on fire. He rubbed the side of his head and gazed up at the man and said, "Jesus, man, why'd you do that?"

"Blasphemer!" Then the crazy dude raised his leg and a huge boot sped toward Rodney's head.

When he opened his eyes again his mouth was filled with the rusty taste of blood, and he could only see out of his left eye. He slowly became aware that he was in the driver's seat of his truck and no longer on the ground. "How did that happen?" was what he intended to say, but it sounded more like a deep gurgle.

The seatbelt was the only thing that kept him upright. It was as if his mind no longer controlled his body. The edge of the cliff moved toward the truck. Rodney tried to lift his hands to the steering wheel, but they felt like lead weights, and they were strapped under the seat belt instead of over it. Huh? He looked through the windshield and the cliff seemed to be moving even faster toward him. "Wait, how can the cliff be moving toward me? Am I tripping?" Another gurgle. He decided the words must only be in his head not on his lips, but why could he feel his lips moving?

He tried to lift his arms again, but nothing seemed to work. His body no longer belonged to him. As the truck sailed off the cliff, Rodney tried to smile, he was flying. He always dreamed of flying. It seemed as if he flew for a long time, then a flip of the truck, and darkness came again.

This time when he regained consciousness he was still partially strapped into his seat belt, but his head was oddly angled, and twisted out of the driver's side window. He not only couldn't move, he also couldn't feel anything below his neck. What an odd sensation. The dark haired man stood high above at the top of the cliff and stared down at him. He seemed so much smaller from this angle. Like an ant, no more like a grasshopper. A tall skinny grasshopper. He couldn't see the girl, but he suddenly remembered where he saw her before, it was on that poster the officer showed him. Same chick, but this girl had looked older. How could that be? Maybe he really was tripping.

Rodney heard a loud wail and since his neck wouldn't move, he turned his eyes toward the sound. The bear was free of the trailer and was limping around the canyon floor. Good, the poor beast isn't trapped like I am.

The animal pulled himself up on two legs and roared loudly at the man on the cliff while he flailed his front paws in the air. Rodney tried to join in and shout "Yeah, take that, shithead!" but it came out as another gurgle.

The bear dropped on all four paws, and yelped as his injured leg hit the ground. He turned toward Rodney and roared again, then charged the truck. As he leapt on the cab and his big paw closed in, Rodney's last thought was, "Holy shit, all I wanted was a pee break and some Rocky Mountain High."

CHAPTER EIGHT
TUESDAY

Rolling her chair back, Maggie rubbed her eyes, then reached into the desk drawer and pulled out a vial of eye drops. Applying the liquid, she blinked several times, then turned to stare out the window.

She couldn't focus on the forest beyond the window, not even the bright red cardinal sitting so regally on a low branch registered. Instead, the images of hundreds of missing girls swirled in her head clouding her vision. Maggie considered herself a well informed and experienced police officer, but the shelter of the reservation and neighboring small town of Noisy Water did not prepare her for what her research revealed on missing children, and the number of young girls who vanished daily. It was astounding. And now it was happening here in her own backyard.

She just knew it had something to do with Felix and his supposed daughter. If real life was like a CSI episode, one of Elsa's favorite shows, she could take a photo of Felix's daughter, which she didn't have, and use some fancy software, again, which she didn't have, and take the girl's age back five years. Snap, bam, boom; bells and whistles would sound and the computer would signal 'positive match.' Problem solved. All within an hour, and allowing time for commercials.

Some happy family would have their child back, and they would find Summer and Shelly safe and ready to be rescued. But this is the real world, and she was faced with some impossible choices. Respect the law, or go with her gut. Evidence, especially enough to obtain a search warrant, was another thing entirely. There just wasn't anything concrete. Not to mention that Maggie had no say in the investigation since it wasn't even within her jurisdiction.

Nothing connected Summer and Shelly's disappearance to Felix. Nothing. Nada. Not a shred of evidence. Only a very slim hunch; the girls looked eerily alike, and Felix was such a nut job.

You can't get a warrant, or drag someone in to be questioned, simply because their elevator doesn't go all the way to the top floor. This isn't a police state and the mountains are full of quirky individualists.

In reality, it was probably some stranger passing through the sleepy mountain town that snatched the girls. Simply a case of wrong place, wrong time. Summer and Shelly were probably taken out of the state almost immediately, and as much as she hated the idea, they were most likely no longer walking among the living.

Maggie shook her head and turned back to her computer. Her hands hovered just above the keyboard for a moment, then she dropped them and gripped the chair arms. "Why am I so sure it's him?" she mumbled as she turned to the window again. Was it because she couldn't stand the bastard? She hoped that it wasn't because of his obvious disdain toward her union with Elsa. But if she were honest, she knew it had to color her reasoning. Like the time she ran into him at the store, and he began spouting bible verse when she said hello. Hellfire and Damnation. Felix fully embraced his right to free speech. No, she shook her head; it was just a gut feeling, and she couldn't act on her gut alone, no matter how much it gnawed at her insides.

Maybe it was only desperation that was pushing her toward Felix.

Another day almost gone, and still no closer to finding them. It was not even her case, but it was consuming all her waking thoughts. Today was filled with silly, minor tribal issues, but as she was writing up summons, or filling out the endless paperwork that followed, those girls in the hands of Felix just kept floating into her head. At this rate, she was not even performing her regular duties properly, much less solving their mysterious disappearance.

Elsa was right when she said Maggie thought she could solve everyone's problems. Usually she tried to talk Maggie down, but this time Elsa was egging her on. Actually, since she knew Jennifer, she was on board even more then Maggie.

Maggie jerked the drawer open and pulled out a bottle of aspirin. After she downed two, she turned toward the computer screen and sat staring at it for a moment before she said, "Damn." She began drumming her fingers on the desk then reached for the mouse and started scrolling through the screens she had just studied. Something in her research was bugging her. But what was it? That nagging feeling was driving her crazy. If she could just figure out what she was missing, maybe everything would fall into place.

There must be a reason she had fixated Felix other than her gut. Slim as the evidence was, he was their best lead—oh hell, he was their only lead, at least as far as she knew. Unfortunately, he was protected not only by his legal rights, but by his self-imposed privacy.

Very few people saw his so-called daughter, and on the rare occasions that they did, the kid didn't interact with them. Maggie saw them only one time, and the kid had stayed in Felix's van while he pumped gas. She remembered making eye contact with the girl and thinking that the child looked a little lost. She could kick herself for not looking into it at the time. That was over a year ago. What if the girl had been in peril all this time and Maggie had done nothing? She couldn't even find someone who knew the girl's name. She thought she heard Felix call her 'Angel,' but that could be just a nickname. It just didn't make sense that they knew so little about the child. With all the missing and exploited children out there they should all be more aware and accountable.

Felix paid for everything with cash; how rare was that? Maggie could not find a single credit card or bank account in his name. His water, electricity, sewer, and heat were all self-contained with generators, wells, and septic tanks. That alone would be suspicious in most areas, but not here. The mountains were full of folks who legitimately wanted to be self-sufficient and off the grid in their rural environment. People here were fiercely private. Maggie respected that, but it also left them open to being the perfect hiding place for someone who was up to something heinous.

If Felix employed workers, they must be undocumented, because there was no paper trail there, either. Maybe she could pursue that with immigration, but their list was long, and this would not be a priority. He could also claim it was a commune with no paid workers. Again, not that unusual in this remote part of New Mexico.

His place was a fortress. The front gate had an electronic panel that required clearance from the main house to enter. The house itself was built sometime back in the 1800's, but when Felix bought it, he had it completely renovated. Rumor had some unusual rooms being built, especially in the gigantic barn, but since he changed carpenters often, there was nothing concrete. Since then, no local workers have been called out to do repairs. Everything seems to be handled in-house.

The place was nestled in a valley and surrounded by deep forest and steep cliffs. From the Reservation side you couldn't see what was going on, even with binoculars. Maggie knew, because she had tried early that morning. The other side was surrounded by National Forest, but it was fenced and posted with no trespassing signs as soon as you hit Felix's property line. The road into the National forest area ran almost adjacent to his land, but the road was surrounded by growth thick enough to completely obscure visibility to Felix's compound.

Just before work, and after her cliff surveillance, Maggie attempted entry at the front gate. She used the excuse of a lost dog, but was refused. The voice on the little box told her they would be happy to search and let her know if anything turned up. Fat chance, especially since it was an imaginary dog.

Maggie thought a moment, then picked up the phone and called Summer's mother, "Jennifer, let's get together again. No, nothing new, I just want to talk. I have some questions I want to ask you two, nothing official, strictly off the record. Just a private, unofficial conversation. Maybe you, or Tyler, can give me some more information that might help." She nodded her head at the phone, "Yes, yes, how about Elsa and I come over there?" She nodded again, "Okay, yes, we are both home from work and we can be there in about an hour. You guys get something to eat. No, no problem. See you soon."

She looked at Elsa who had slipped into their home office when Maggie started her phone conversation. She was gazing at her as she raised one finely trimmed brow.

Maggie smiled, "Want to take a little drive into town?" As usual, the gut had won.

∞

"Felix Alvarez Lea?" Tyler asked as he shoved his chair back from the table, "You have a name?" They were gathered in Jennifer's kitchen. His abrupt movement caused Elsa's wine glasses to slosh over onto the well-worn wood. Elsa grabbed a paper napkin and cornered the dark liquid before it could seep past the surface. Tyler's eyes narrowed and he continued with, "Where do I find him?"

"Please, Tyler. Let's not get ahead of ourselves," Maggie said as she remained perfectly still. She sat ramrod straight and returned his gaze. She said in a low voice, "I only want to know if Summer and Shelly ever came in contact with him. Jennifer, when you were with the girls did you ever run into him? Maybe at the grocery store, or another public place. And if you did, did he take extra notice of the girls?" Maggie sighed and wondered once again if she had already said too much. How did we get here? Oh, yeah, Elsa let Felix's name slip. Maggie knew the wine was a bad idea.

Maggie glanced over Tyler's shoulder. Dinner dishes were stacked by the sink, and from the looks of them, they had not been able to eat much. She looked back at the two expectant faces and could see the obvious strain in them.

"Do you think he has our Summer and Shelly?" Jennifer said as she gripped the table then leaned forward, pinning Maggie to her seat with her red rimmed eyes.

Maggie replied, "We have no evidence of that, Jennifer. I am just trying to consider anyone locally that is even a little suspicious. All I am doing is a little research, nothing more. There is absolutely no reason law enforcement would consider him at this point." She sighed as she said, "And you both know, this isn't my case, or even within the our jurisdiction."

"What brought him under your radar, Maggie?" Tyler asked. His voice was softer this time, and his shoulders a little more relaxed, but she noticed he still held his hands clinched together in his lap.

"Well, part of it is that Elsa noticed his daughter looks enough like Shelly for them to be related, and I can't find any records of his daughter's birth. Also, his intense need for secrecy combined with no personal records before he moved here."

She leaned forward slightly, "Pretty thin, but we have so little to go on. I just want to check out every lead, real or imagined. Again, since it isn't my jurisdiction, I am just looking at this as a friend. I want to make that perfectly clear." She turned back to Jennifer, "Maybe Summer or Shelly mentioned him, or any man, for that matter, making them feel uncomfortable?" Maggie didn't add that just being in the same room with Felix made her uncomfortable. Her Grandma called it 'the Indian sense,' Maggie liked to think it was more of a cop's instinct, but it was probably all just bullshit.

"No, never. I don't think she ever mentioned him, or any man who was inappropriate in Noisy Water. Especially after she and Tyler got together." Jennifer glanced in Tyler's direction then rubbed her hands together as if they were cold, although the house was very warm, "You have to understand that my daughter is very self-sufficient and strong willed; she would never mention something like that to me, anyway, she would simply put the guy in his place. And believe me, she is good at taking care of herself. Is there any other reasons you haven't told us about?"

"Other than him being a total creep, and that he spouts that fanatical religious stuff to anyone who will listen?" Elsa added as she gripped her glass of wine, then took a sip. Maggie turned to look at her partner. Although she didn't change her expression, Elsa dropped her head and mumbled, "Okay, okay, I know." She rolled her eyes, "I'll shut up."

A hint of a smile from Maggie as she turned back to Jennifer, "There are a lot of folks on this mountain who guard their privacy, but not a lot who own a well-guarded compound. No one ever seems to get on Felix's property except Billy Wade Smith, and I don't think he is talking to anyone about what goes on there."

Jennifer turned to Tyler and said, "Billy Wade Smith is famous around here. He has a huge ranch on the other side of town. He's a multimillionaire jetsetter with his own plane. Lots of infamous parties at that gigantic, ostentatious, eye sore he calls home."

"He is supposed to have connections in the upper crust political world and the south of the boarder drug cartel," Elsa chimed in, "I've heard he uses that private air strip to transport drugs." She turned toward Maggie and mumbled, "Sorry, but you know it's true."

Maggie cleared her throat. They were heading down another rabbit hole, "Like I said, let's not get ahead of ourselves. We can't do anything based on just gossip. There is no evidence Billy Wade or Felix have done anything illegal." Maggie spoke in a low even voice, then looked directly at Elsa, "It is still only rumors."

She turned back to Jennifer and Tyler, but before she could speak Elsa said, "Pretty accurate rumors if you ask me."

Maggie cringed then added, "Off the record, I'm going to do some surveillance of his property. It won't be easy, because not only is the front fenced and gated, there are natural boundaries on all the other sides that keep it private. I will also keep digging into his background to see if anything pops. I don't want us to fixate only on Felix, though. I want to check any of the locals who stand out, even though the working theory is a stranger, if they have been abducted."

Jennifer clutched at her throat and Tyler's face darkened. Maggie stood and nodded at Elsa, "The information you gave me will help. At least I know there wasn't any personal contact, that you know about, anyway." Elsa took one last sip of wine and stood with Maggie.

"I assure you the Police Chief is doing everything he can to get your family back to you, and this thing about Felix has nothing to do with him or the Tribal Police; I am acting as a friend on my own personal time. If I find anything concrete, I will get the information to the Noisy Water PD immediately."

Elsa joined in with, "Don't worry, folks, you are in good hands. Maggs is like a pit bull when she gets her teeth into something, believe me I know." She smiled at her partner as they started for the door, but Maggie didn't return the smile.

Tyler had not moved or said a word since his last question. He got up and followed the two women toward the door as he asked, "Would Felix's property be visible by horseback?"

Maggie turned toward him and frowned, "Mr. Reynolds, Tyler, please, don't do anything crazy. Let us handle this." She placed a hand on his arm, "Maybe I shouldn't have come here tonight. It wasn't my intention to get you involved in any way other than an information standpoint. The more information you can give us, the better our search can be."

"I know," he said, and leaned toward her as he continued, "I want you to know that I am really good in the backwoods on a horse, and I know how to keep my head down, and my mouth shut. That is my wife, my daughter, and my unborn child out there, and I can't just sit here on my thumbs and wait. I need to do something."

"Summer is pregnant? Oh, dear," Elsa said.

Maggie sighed, "Just give me a couple of days, okay? Honestly, you wouldn't be able to get close enough to see anything, even on horseback. I have some ideas to pursue on the surveillance end, but I have to move cautiously."

"Okay, but remember what I said, and please understand that nothing will keep me away if there is even a remote possibility my girls are on that man's property."

"I understand," Maggie said as Elsa hugged Jennifer and they went out the front door.

∞

"That was a mistake."

"I don't think so, Maggs" They were in Elsa's little Subaru wagon headed home. The local radio station was playing and the theme was 80's music. Elsa hummed along to a Blondie song as she tapped her fingers to the beat.

"I forgot I'm not talking to you," Maggie gazed straight ahead as she drove.

Elsa glanced at her then reached out and gave her a gentle push on the shoulder, "I'm sorry I let it slip that you had Felix in your sights, but we did the right thing as friends. Besides, the idea was to get information to flow, and we certainly did that. At least they feel like someone is doing something." She cleared her throat then said, "Don't be mad, Maggs."

Maggie smiled at her, "I'm not mad. Really. I'm the one who set this whole thing up; but, I did the wrong thing in the eyes of the law. I never should have revealed so much. I have no evidence, none at all, it's all supposition. What if Tyler goes off halfcocked and has a run in with Felix?"

Elsa frowned, "Would that be such a bad thing?" She snorted, "Maybe he will knock the crap out of him."

Maggie sighed, "Yeah, and what if Tyler gets hurt?" She leaned forward and switched the lights to bright. The moon was just a sliver and it was hard to see. The deer seemed to love crossing the road in the section they were passing through. She pinched the brim of her nose. Her head was really starting to hurt, "I hate to say this aloud, but what if Felix has nothing to do with this, and I just set him up for disaster."

"I didn't think of that. Naaaaa."

"You know how much we both hate baseless rumors and prejudicial hate. I mean, that's something that has screwed with both of our lives at times. Now here I am doing the same thing. I feel like I'm the bully this time."

"Maggs, no way! You didn't do anything like that! Tyler is a big boy, and how he reacts is not your responsibility. Don't beat yourself up, please. It's more my fault, then yours anyway. Like I said, at least you are doing something."

Maggie reached over and gently touched Elsa's hand, "Thank you." The music switched to news and they listened to the day's local incidents.

"Isn't that Sandi Sullivan?" Elsa said.

"I think it is; I heard they pulled her out of retirement when Mike Davis moved to the Roswell station.

"....and the Fish and Game had the black bear that caused all the ruckus in Upper Canyon relocated. He killed the Dawson's dog, and beat the heck out of one of the new dumpsters. Folks, they want us to give you a reminder not to leave your garbage out, to keep your pets in, and doors closed. We have all heard this before, but we get comfortable and do it again. So please listen. Also, let's do a better job with the bear locks on the dumpsters; it doesn't do much good to pay all that money for them if we don't use them. This was a bad summer for bears, and you can expect them in town for at least the rest of the month, so be aware people!"

Elsa and Maggie both laughed and Maggie said, "I hear they did a tag and release close to the Rez. He'll probably claim part of his territory on the Rez, so I hope he doesn't give us any trouble."

"Ummm."

Maggie laughed, "We're almost home."

"Uh huh."

She touched her partner's hand again, "And, Elsa, thanks again."

∞

"What do you think?" Jennifer said as she rinsed the last plate and handed it to Tyler.

He took the plate, dried it and placed it in the cabinet, "Honestly, I want to hunt that Felix character down right now and beat the crap out of him."

"Tyler!" Jennifer filled the carafe with water and poured it into the back of the coffee maker. She poured coffee into the filter, shut the machine and flipped the switch before she turned to Tyler, "I share your anger, I do, and I know I have been a little crazy since, well, since our girls…" Her voice caught, but she took a breath and continued, "Maggie is actually right, you know. As much as I want to march out to that compound and demand entry, we don't have enough to go on yet. We need to let her do her job."

Jennifer being the voice of reason. The world was turning upside down. "I need to do something, Jennifer," he shut the cabinet and turned toward her, "If I don't do something soon, I'm going to put my fist through one of your walls." He rubbed his eyes and said,

"Sorry, but I'm about to go crazy. When I think that it's possible they might be that close, I just want to tear his place down." He pounded his right fist into the palm of his left hand. "I need to do something," he repeated.

"Like I'm not stir crazy? That's my baby and my grandbaby out there, somewhere," she stood with her arms crossed over her chest as she leaned her back against the kitchen counter. The only sound was the drip and hiss of coffee as it flowed through the filter. The smell of roasted coffee beans spread over the room like a dense cloud.

It both soothed and infuriated Tyler. The normalcy seemed so out of place under the circumstances. Why didn't the sky rain fire? With his dark mood, it would seem more rational to have the dormant volcano erupt, than to stand in Jennifer's warm kitchen as they waited to sip coffee. All the comforts of home while his wife and daughter were out there somewhere, possibly lost, or worse, captive of a madman.

Tyler didn't know if he could take any more of it, but he had to be smart and rational. Summer needed him to use his head, not his temper.

He rubbed his face, shook his head, then moved forward and placed a hand on Jennifer's shoulder, "I'm a different man now that Summer and Shelly are in my life. Things are great at school; the kids love me, and actually want to be in my class. That wasn't always the story." He dropped his hand when he felt her shoulder stiffen and he moved over to one of the tall bar stools. He perched on it, and placed his hands on his knees. He stared at her and said, "I was a sorry bastard before I met Summer."

"Tyler!"

"No, I mean it. I don't know how much Summer told you about me, but I was married before Summer to a very wicked woman. She was cute and sexy, but rotten to the core. She did a number on me, and I went into a very dark place when I finally got her out of my life. I aimed that darkness toward everyone I came in contact with. Summer saw right through it, and turned me back into a human being." He smiled for the first time that night, "She is one tough woman."

Jennifer smiled with him, "That she is, even as a little girl she knew her own mind, and once it was made up, nothing stopped her, nothing." She shook her head and her eyes glazed over at some inner memory, "I mean it, absolutely nothing."

Tyler gazed at the older woman. She looked as if she had aged ten years in one day. He suddenly felt very selfish, "Why don't you sit, Jennifer? I'll get the coffee for us."

"Thanks, Tyler. I think I will," she moved to the dining table and slumped in a chair. He filled a mug for each of them, put some sweetener and cream in Jennifer's cup, then he brought them to the table.

"I promise I won't go on a crazy manhunt until we know more, but I won't promise you that I won't check out Felix's compound for myself if we aren't getting some answers, and soon." He sat across from her before he continued, "Most of all, no promises about what I will do to that man if he has our girls."

"I can't ask for more than that, Tyler. Just to be clear, I happen to agree whole heartedly, and will help you get that bastard if it comes to that." Tyler laughed at the sudden animation in her face with her words. Who knew the peacenik had a violent streak when it came to her own?

"Well, okay, good. We have a plan then." He reached across the table and clasped her hand in his. This time she didn't flinch but clasped his back with equal pressure.

CHAPTER NINE
WEDNESDAY

What a glorious crop. Felix Alvarez Lea plucked a green bud from the plant, then rose to his full height. He leaned back and gazed up through the camouflage netting covering the expansive crop. Only clear blue skies above. Extending his arms toward the heavens he opened both palms as he shouted, "Thank you, My Father." He closed his eyes and stood for a moment as he counted his many blessings.

A light tap at his elbow. The electrifying connection he felt with his father was severed. His prayer ruined. His open palms clinched into fists as Felix turned toward the interruption.

Angel-2 stood before him. She held the water bucket in one hand and a silver cup in the other. She raised the cup toward him with a trembling hand. The tremble was from her shame. She knew what she did and that it was evil. He slapped the cup out of her hand. It landed at her feet and rolled over as the water pooled in the dirt. She dropped to her knees to retrieve the cup, but he used his boot to press her wrist into the ground as he said, "Did you not hear me talking to My Father?"

"I am very sorry, Master. It was wicked of me and I should be punished." He gazed at her bowed head and felt his hands relax as the sun danced in the white gold of her hair. He lifted his boot and sighed. The child was weak and could be made the devils pawn so easily. It really wasn't her fault.

She grabbed the cup, rinsed it out then filled it with the cold water. She raised it as an offering as she kept her head bowed. He smiled. To forgive was a virtue. Accepting the cup he drank deeply. When it was drained he said, "Up." She sprang from the ground with the agility of her youth. Ah, he missed the way that felt. But he had not been as privileged as this one. He treated her well—too well sometimes. Not at all like he was treated. Forgiveness had not come so easily to his earth father, nor the numerous foster fathers after him.

Felix handed the empty cup to her as he wiped sweat from his forehead with his kerchief, "Where is Angel-3?"

"She is resting, my beloved," the girl glanced up at him then diverted her clear blue eyes. That bad habit again, will she ever learn not to gaze directly at her deity? Felix shook his head. Pity. Nothing had worked in breaking her of this annoying habit.

Patience. It was almost time for her to go, and he had to admit, but never to the girl, that he would miss this high spirited one. The devil had a strong hold on her and her stubbornness required much training, but she had lasted the longest of any of his Angels, and he still found her a constant challenge. Such an interesting puzzle to be solved.

He reached down and gripped her shoulder. How easily his hand covered it, all the way past her shoulder blade, "Why are you not training her now?" The girl bowed her head even lower and her hair fell away exposing her thin neck. The skin was soft and pale. Felix released her shoulder and touched her neck, then lightly ran his finger down the bones until they reached the rough wool of the collar of her dress. She did not flinch from his touch and that made him smile.

"Master, I showed her how to care for the barn animals, but she was very tired, uh, her journey here left her a little weak. I didn't want to push too hard, at least not yet. You told me I must move slowly with this one, especially after the last time."

He removed his hand from her neck. She was right. They pushed the last one, the unnamed one, much too hard. She hadn't made it to her destiny. Too bad, that one had been gentle, and very beautiful, but too old to train by the time she came to them.

His smile broadened. It was all preordained, anyway. He raised his face heavenward once again and closed his eyes. The answers were here if he just listened. Only he was allowed to see the signs and hear the Great Father's voice. When he first saw Angel-3, she was bathed in a golden light. He knew immediately his father wanted him to have her. She looked so much like Angel-2, but far superior. She had the promise of being even better than any of his previous Angels, or the unnamed ones. She was just the right age and ripe to be trained. She is going to the best of the best. A special gift from his true Father.

He lowered his head, opened his eyes and said, "You're right, take your time." He patted the top of her head then turned and waved his hands over the crop, "Learn from me and tend to her just like I tend to these luscious plants," he said, then laughed suddenly and clapped his hands. She jumped and spilled a little more of the water, it only made him laugh harder. Such a silly creature, "Tonight we will celebrate. This great crop and Angel-3 coming to us; it's a sign from heaven! We will have a feast!"

The girl remained in front of him, motionless with her head dropped nearly to her chest. He placed his hand on her shoulder and squeezed with just the right amount of pressure. This time she flinched, but didn't pull away or look up. She was being such a good girl.

He released his hold and laughed again and said, "Yes, yes. A celebration. We haven't had one in much too long!" He gave her a little shove as he said, "Go, and cook. Prepare all my favorite dishes." He raised his arms to the sky as he spun slowly around in a circle. The sun filtered through the netting and warmed his face. He stopped his circular rotation and stood with his eyes closed as he said, "Oh, it will be a great night. A night to remember!"

He opened his eyes and gazed over his plants. Some of the workers on the other side of the tent had stopped to stare. "Get back to work!" he growled. They dropped their heads in unison and began to hoe between the neatly spaced rows.

Angel-2 whispered, "Should I go now?"

"Yes, yes, go, girl!" he said, then frowned and shouted, "What are you waiting for? Move!"

She scurried out of the tent as he strolled toward the workers.

∞

"Excellent. I am pleased," Felix said as he waved his hands over the dinner table. A delicate Irish linen table cloth covered the long mahogany table. The remains of their celebratory dinner were scattered between two massive candelabras. "You can clear the table after you get me a bottle of Port, make it the dark, tawny one."

Angel-2 jumped up and grabbed Shelly's hand and led her from the table, then out of the dining hall. She returned in a few minutes, but she was alone as she set a bottle of dark port in front of Felix. She began to load a large tray with dirty dishes and the remaining food.

"Why isn't Angel-3 here to help?"

"She's in the kitchen. I have her washing the pots, Master."

Silence filled the room. The girl stood still as she held the heavy tray and their dinner guest, Billy Wade Smith, stared intently at his recently manicured nails, "That's good. I noticed she could hardly keep her eyes open over dinner." Felix squinted at the girl and asked, "She worked hard with you on the dinner?"

"Yes, Master."

"Good, she might as well understand her role right away. Make sure she helps you until the kitchen is spotless and then take her with you to tend to the barn animals. After that she can go to bed. I have decided you should not push her too hard, but regular chores are not too much. Nothing like what I had to do at her age, believe me—now that would break her. And make sure her room is locked for now, but you don't have to tether her. She will understand the consequences soon enough if she breaks the rules. She is your responsibility; you understand that, don't you?"

The girl took a deep breath and nodded her head, "Yes, Master." She stood silent for a moment, but her arms began to tremble with the weight of the tray. She asked, "May I be excused now?"

"Yes, you may." He turned from her and poured a generous portion of the amber liquid into his glass, then Billy's. The girl struggled with the weighted tray as she bowed her head to Felix and to Billy before backing out of the room.

"You have trained her well Felix."

"Yes. She still has some issues, but it doesn't matter now." He sighed deeply before he continued, "Angel-3 will be perfect as soon as she is trained, so Angel-2 will have served her purpose." He passed the glass of port to his guest, "Here, enjoy some of this. It is a superb vintage."

"I will, thank you." Billy pulled two cigars from his jacket, "And here is a little treat for you, Felix."

"Excellent! I wondered if you managed to get any more of these." Felix took his time as he prepared and lighted the cigar, then leaned back in his chair with the cigar in one hand, and the glass of port in the other, "Cuban?"

"Of course," Billy lit his cigar and took a puff.

"Let's go into the game room. I feel like a little pool—how about you, Billy?"

"Sure, why not? A little exercise after that wonderful meal. That girl can sure cook," he put both hands on the table, pushed himself up, and followed Felix from the room.

Felix continued as they walked down the long hallway, "She has great skills in all areas except discipline. She has yet to understand she is a valuable and treasured tool, to be cherished, but only a tool nonetheless."

They entered the game room when Billy said, "Well, she certainly has culinary skills. Is she going to make Thanksgiving Dinner for you on Thursday?"

Felix stopped and turned to him, "We don't celebrate government enforced holidays in this house. Only the Lord's days are revered.

"Can't blame you there, brother. It's all government propaganda anyway. You're right, biblical holidays are the only ones that count," Billy smiled and racked up the billiards, then slid the cue ball toward Felix's end of the table.

Felix tensed and studied him for a moment, then laughed and picked up a pool stick, chalked the end and hit a perfect break, "You surprise me Billy."

"Just share your view on the government. A bunch of greedy bastards that want to break the average man's back." After they both had a couple of successful shots, Billy cleared his throat and took a sip of the port before he said, "Uh, Felix, what are you going to do with Angel-2 when the new one, uh, Angel-3 has been trained?"

Felix paused mid-shot. He rose from the pool table and turned toward Billy, his eyes narrowed to slits, "Why?" he asked.

Billy shrugged, and casually put his right hand in his slacks pocket,

"No disrespect intended, of course. I don't mean to get into your personal business, but you mentioned it as if the girl, uh, Angel-2, won't be needed after she trains the new girl. I just ask because I would be very interested in her, Angel-2, I mean."

Felix felt the familiar heat rise to his head, so he moved to the bar beside the pool table and picked up his glass of port. He took a sip, then took a long drag on his cigar. He stared at the wall as he tried to relax. He felt tension building between his shoulder blades, so he rolled his neck. He knew Billy carried a little derringer in that pocket he so casually stuffed his hand into. What a fool. That pea shooter was a joke, but he didn't want to have to kill Billy, he needed him. "Why?" he repeated.

Billy moved to the other side of the bar, then slid up on one of the stools. Felix turned and looked at him. Even as he struggled to get his girth up on the stool, the man kept his hand in the pocket. Idiot. It was almost comical. Felix set down his port and picked up his pool cue as he gazed at him.

Billy took a deep breath and said, "Well, truthfully, she would be worth a fortune to our friends south of the border. With that hair and her age, wow, she would be worth ten of what I get from my current supplier. Actually, my usual supplier in LA has had some issues with product, lately, so I need some help before I can fill my quota for the cartel." Billy smiled.

"What?" Felix said. He had heard Billy just fine, he just couldn't believe what he had just heard. The heat inside him turned into a fire. Felix did not want to give it full reign. He paused and repeated the thought; I need Billy, before he said in a low voice, "You are not being respectful, Billy. This is my house and my family. You are the only outsider allowed into our inner circle. Don't make me regret that decision."

"Now, Felix," Billy waved his free hand and his smile broadened. A trickle of sweat rolled down the side of his face and became lost in the fat rolls on his neck, "Again, no disrespect intended, please, don't get angry." He leaned forward and said, "Just talking business, that's all, brother. Just business."

Felix gazed at him, "The plants are just business, not my family."

Billy leaned back and pulled his hand out of his pocket. He held both hands palms up before he continued, "Okay, okay, you're right and I apologize. I just wanted to bring it up in case you were interested. You did just say she was a valuable tool, and I thought it would be such a shame to waste a product so valuable, but you are right, it is completely your choice."

"All women are tools, even my Angels. They are to be valued just as you value a fine gun or knife, or even a good hunting dog. I would not want you to ask about those items, either. What's mine is mine."

He turned his back on Billy and tested the weight of his pool cue. Billy stood and said, "Not a problem, my friend, uh, not a problem. I hear you, and I understand. Got it loud and clear. I won't mention the girl again."

Felix tensed, then placed the pool cue in the rack on the wall as he kept his back to Billy, "The plants are going to be the best crop I've had and should be ready in a few weeks. I will let you know when to send me some additional help for harvest."

"Sure, sure," Billy swirled the amber liquid in his glass, then downed it in one swig. He coughed, then after a moment he said, "With all this legalizing crap we may need to look at some other option for our main enterprise, but not today. Today we can still get top dollar on the crop." Felix kept his back to Billy and remained quiet. Billy sighed and said, "Well, it's been a long day, we should call it a night, my friend."

Felix turned around and faced Billy as he smiled and asked, "So soon?"

"Long drive home." Billy set his empty glass on the bar, "We have to do this again real soon." He gazed at Felix, "I will never speak of your family or personal possessions again; this I promise, but, uh, what about the new one, uh, the new girl's mother?"

"What?"

"You know, the new kid, uh, Angel-3's mom? You said they came as a package. By the way, very clever of you to add numbers to their names, much easier to keep them straight." He winked at Felix, but before he could react, Billy asked, "Does she look like her?"

Felix stiffened, "What?"

"The mom, does she look like that cute little blonde?"

Felix's stomach clinched, "No, she doesn't; I don't like where this is headed, Billy." He tensed but stood motionless, "We just established some boundaries and you appear to be breaking them again."

"Well, you haven't made her part of the family yet, and as I said, I will not mention family, but the mother, she is an outsider. She might be worth quite a bit, not as much as the kid, of course, but still, she could bring us a tidy amount, especially if she's pretty. I could sure take her off your hands if you want her out of the way."

Felix leaned toward Billy, the tendons in his arms popping through the black silk shirt he wore. His voice was low and even as he said, "Let's just get this out of the way, Billy. Anyone residing on my compound, that includes my family, my people, and especially my Angels, are off limits. Not that it is your concern, but Angel-3's mother will become one of my workers. If she isn't trainable, she will join the other lost souls on the hillside. No member of my family, or my staff, leaves paradise. Understood?"

Billy held up both of his hands palms up and smiled at him as he said, "Hey, I am sorry. That's the last of it. Never again, my friend." He dropped his hands to his sides, but kept the right one close to his pocket.

Felix didn't return the smile and his eyes bore into Billy's as he continued, "I have been able to remain here this long because I know how to keep my private life private. You are my business partner, and I have also accepted you as a friend and confidant. You are welcome in my home and I have revealed all the aspects of our special lives because you are trusted. I find this conversation offensive. Do not cause me to lose that trust, Billy. I value our relationship."

Billy wiped sweat from his forehead with one of the bar napkins, "I apologize again, Felix. It's obvious I have stepped over the line, here. I wouldn't want to jeopardize our business relationship, or friendship. Please, forget I asked, and I will shut up about the women." He grunted a laugh, "Sometimes I can't help myself when an idea gets planted in my brain. This time I promise, never again. I'm sure the issues my suppliers have right now are temporary. I wanted to give you a chance to expand your business and make a little more profit, that's all." His words seemed to tumble on top of each other and Felix saw sweat rings start to grow around his ample under arms, "Please, please accept my apologies, and as a gesture of friendship, I would like to gift you with that paint pony you admired so much the other day. I'm sure it would make a nice addition to your stable. I'll deliver him personally tomorrow evening. Free, totally gratis."

Felix was silent for a moment. He turned his head toward the ceiling and closed his eyes, then his arms relaxed visibly. You need him.

"Accepted," he moved to the bar and picked up his glass and took a sip, but his smile didn't return. "You know the way out. I'll talk to you tomorrow about the workers for the harvest," he said as he gestured toward the door.

CHAPTER TEN
THURSDAY
THANKSGIVING DAY

Shelly buttoned her jacket to the top button. Stupid clothes, she thought as she followed the blonde teen girl down the rough path. Under the jacket she wore a long, gray wool dress with black tights. The skirt crept up her legs as she walked, so she continually had to tug at it to keep it down. The gray dress and black tights looked like something out of her history book. She liked vintage, but this was ridiculous. She felt like a character in the cast of Les Misérables, and she didn't even like that flick. Totally depressing movie.

Shelly shivered as the wind whipped at her jacket and skirt, "Why do we have to wear these stupid dresses, anyway? Why can't I wear my jeans and sweatshirt?" Her breath formed a small cloud as she said, "This dress is itchy and ugly." She scratched at her neck where wool met skin.

"It's just the way it is, so get used to it," the teen glanced over her shoulder at Shelly. Her expression was soft in the early morning light, even though her voice sounded gruff, "Learn to fight the important battles and let the other stuff go, that's the only way you will survive this." She quickened her step and Shelly had to hurry to keep up with her.

Shelly mumbled, "Is it worth all this bullshit just to survive?" But she matched the older girl's pace in spite of her words. She kicked one of her heavy boots at a rock in the path, then added, "If I had my tennis shoes back, I could move a lot faster."

"You'll be glad for those boots when the snow starts." The older girl snorted, "Actually, you'll be glad you have them when we are shoveling horse crap in a few minutes."

"Why do we have to do that and do all the household chores? It's not fair. I counted close to a dozen workers at that picnic table by the barn yesterday; why can't they do some of this stuff?"

"You sure complain a lot. Fair has nothing to do with life here, so get used to it, princess. We do what we are told. Now listen up, because I am only going to say this once, we don't ask about the field workers, and we especially don't talk to them. You need to work hard at being invisible." She paused and turned to look Shelly in the eye, "Besides, I would rather be in the barn knee deep in horse crap, than in the house close to Felix." The teen pulled her jacket tighter, but not before Shelly noticed purple streaks running down one side of her neck. Shelly couldn't help but stare. It looked like a tattoo of a giant hand. A shrug from the girl at her expression, then she said, "Forget it, don't ask."

Shelly said, "Uh, okay."

The teen turned and tugged at the big wooden door of the barn, so Shelly stepped in and helped her pull it open. They hurried inside and closed the door behind them.

Hay, horses, and wood. Shelly inhaled deeply and smiled. It was almost like the barn at home on Tyler's ranch. Her thoughts drifted to family and the smile left her lips as she asked, "Is my mom really all right?"

"I told you she is; trust me, okay?"

"Why does she have stay locked in that horrible, stinky place, and we get to stay in the house?" Shelly didn't give her time to answer before she put her hands on her hips and said, "When can I see her again?" She moved forward and tugged at the teen's arm, "Look, she is a really strong worker, honest she is, and she could help with the chores."

The older girl turned and said, "Whoa! Hold on. Take a breath, kid." She placed a hand on Shelly's shoulder, "Look, you never should have gone to see her the first time. You have no idea how close you were to getting caught, and what Felix would have done." She paused as fear flashed in her eyes, "I shouldn't have given in and told you where she is, that's on me. But, listen carefully, this is your reality now, and the sooner you get it through your head, the better. You have to obey the rules. Ignore them, and you will not only get yourself dead and buried, you will also sign a death warrant for your mom, and for me."

Shelly gasped and took a step back, almost falling over a bale of hay, "What? What are you talking about? You mean he will kill all of us if I screw up?"

The girl sighed and said, "It is crazy, but so is Felix. He holds me, and even your mom, responsible for your 'sins', his words, not mine. He made it very clear I will answer for your mistakes, no matter how big or small, and it is a given he will kill your mom if you don't work out."

Shelly felt her stomach clinch and bile rose in her throat. Her vision darkened and the older teen moved close, grabbing her arm as she said, "Oh, man, I know how you feel, it's brutal and crazy, and a lot to take in. Sit." The girl helped her to a bale of hay, and said, "Put your head between your knees." She did, and after a moment, her head cleared and the nausea subsided. The teen leaned over her and pushed the hair back from her forehead as she said, "Look, it's really up to your mother if you get to see her again."

Shelly jerked her head away and said, "What does that mean? Of course she wants to see me!"

The girl took both of Shelly's hands into her own and her touch was like sandpaper on Shelly's soft skin. Dark, purple smudges encircled the girl's thin wrists. The bruising was stark against the pale skin poking out of her dark woolen sleeves. Shelly's anger evaporated.

The teen took a breath and said, "Look, you need to forget about your mom for now." Shelly closed her eyes tightly and gave a negative shake of her head. The girl continued with, "I know, that's harsh, I know. It's the hardest thing you will ever do, but it is what your mom would want."

Shelly tried to pull away, but the teen girls hands were like a vise. Her voice rose as she said, "Listen to me, you need to grow up, and fast. You have to prepare yourself for whatever happens. Felix will let your mother out of that cell soon, probably today." Shelly's eyes jerked open and she started to speak, but the girl said, "No, don't get excited, not yet. He'll give your mom a chance to become part of the group, not with us, but with the barn workers. If your mom fights him, well, she will wind up like my mom, but, if she works for him, and obeys his commands, she can live, at least until she is no longer useful. But you cannot, under any circumstance, go near her."

"Why?" She asked, then frowned and said, "Wait, what happened to your mom?"

The teen's eyes moistened, "She was a fighter." Then her eyes moved to her boots, "You know the hill with the white crosses on it behind the cave where your mother is kept?"

"Yes."

"She's there."

Shelly began to tremble, "I'm so sorry." Then her eyes widened and she whispered, "I don't want to lose my mom." She jumped up from the bale of hay, "I have to warn her—I, I have to tell her how much I love her." She gulped back a sob as she said, "I have been such a brat, you don't know, she needs to understand that I didn't really mean it." She gulped at the air as her eyes darted around the room. The older girl placed her hands on Shelly's shoulders and eased her back on the hay.

"If you try to see her, it will only make it worse for her. Felix could decide to get rid of her, just so she won't be a distraction to you. His main focus right now is you, and you need to keep it that way, for your mother's sake. The best thing you can do for her is to keep your head down, follow orders, and obey Felix." She sat beside Shelly, "Look, your mom knows how you feel, she knows you love her. You were just being a typical kid. Mom's know that kind of stuff."

"You don't know how mean I've been."

The girl laughed and said, "You don't know what mean is; unfortunately, you're about to get a crash course in it. I'm serious, you are going to have to forget about being a little kid, and grow up real fast."

"I'm not a little kid," as she fought back tears, it sounded much angrier then she intended.

The girl sighed and said, "I know you're not a little kid, but the fact is that you are much too young to deal with this." She leaned forward, dropped her head and almost whispered, "But you have to do it anyway. That's how I am still alive."

"You have done this a long time, haven't you?" Shelly whispered back.

The girl gazed at Shelly with haunted eyes and said, "Sometimes it seems like forever." She sat up straighter and squared her shoulders as she said, "Look, I sense you are strong and a fighter, but you must trust me, now is not the time to fight, save it for when it will mean something. Listen to me, and you won't suffer as much as I did. Learn the survival techniques I teach you, take advantage of what I have already lived through."

"I'll try…"

"You need to do more then try. Listen and learn."

"Okay."

"I mean it. You have to learn the rules and follow them. I don't think I can stand seeing another girl not make it. You do not make eye contact with Felix and always address him with 'yes, Master,' even if you feel like you will choke on the words. If all you want to do is kick him in the nuts, just bite your tongue and be extra polite, sometimes it keeps him from going off. He will direct most of his anger at me anyway, and that's ok, I know how to handle him. You also need to look out for Jose and Billy." She stood and reached out her hand to Shelly.

"Who is Jose?" Shelly took her hand and stood.

"Don't worry, you'll meet him soon enough. He is Felix's right hand man, and will be in charge of your mom while she is here. He isn't crazy like Felix, but in some ways he is worse, because he is as mean as a snake. He doesn't miss much, and he tells Felix everything." She patted Shelly on the shoulder and said, "One step at a time. Let me handle them, and I'll see if I can get some information to your mom. I know how to slip around both Felix and Jose."

"Oh, that would be great, but please don't put yourself in danger for us." She chewed at her lip then said, "I know mom will be able to handle it if she just knows I'm safe and what to expect. She must be going crazy locked in that stinky hole not knowing what is going on or where I am being kept."

"I'll manage it, just do what I tell you. Now promise me."

"Okay, I promise," she said as she smiled at the girl, "I'll look out for this Jose, but Billy just seemed like a dumb, fat, old guy."

"Don't let his country boy act fool you. He is sharper then he acts, and he can move fast for a 'fat, old guy,' especially with his hands, at least when Felix isn't around. He's a total Perv, but he is afraid of Felix. Just don't be in a room alone with him, and you'll be fine. Jose won't touch you unless Felix tells him to, but that won't happen, so don't worry about him."

In spite of her best efforts Shelly felt tears spill over onto her cheeks, but she didn't divert her gaze, "Thank you for helping us. I will do my best not to let you down. I promise to follow your direction and I'm sorry about all the whining. I know you have been through so much more than me, and I don't want to get my mom or you hurt. It's just that, well, it's a lot to take in."

The teen nodded her head, then turned and grabbed a feed bucket, "I know, believe me, I know, but come on, we're late, and if we don't get these chores done, and Felix's breakfast on the table on time, I will pay for it." She scooped feed into the bucket and headed for the horses.

Shelly closed her eyes for a moment, then took a deep breath as she thought, "Stop crying, you big baby and grow up." She opened her eyes and grabbed her own bucket. Swiping at her tears with her free hand she whispered, "You can do this."

The girls started working silently side by side, but the warm space and hard work did nothing to break the core of ice that had formed in the middle of Shelly's chest.

∞

The scraping noise again, then wood against dirt. Shelly? Summer scooted toward the sound. Light was filtering through the wooden slats in the door, so she eased forward and squinted through the largest gap. She was momentarily blinded, so she blinked several times until her eyes could adjust to the bright light. There was a large silhouette crouching in the doorway. Her vision cleared completely. A man instead of Shelly or the blonde teenage girl was staring at her. She jumped back as he began moving forward.

The door swung open and she was blasted with cool air. She sat back on her heels with her hands clinched by her side, but with a laugh he retreated, then stood just outside the outer door. Summer eased forward through the first door. No command to stop, no dirty, foul smelling rag slapped over her mouth, and the outer door stayed open. This must be how a dog feels coming out of a kennel at the pound for the first time, she thought.

Summer remained poised in the vestibule, her muscles tense. The man still stood just outside in the sunlight watching her intently. He frowned, took a step back and waved his hand toward the opening. Freedom. Just steps away. The cold, clean air, and a strong smell of pine trees washed over her. It was heavenly after the stench of the cave, so she kept moving forward through the outer door. Still on her hands and knees she scooted away from the door and slid up against the rock wall beside it. The man kept his distance.

She sat on the hard ground squinting in the morning light, but tensed as he pushed the door shut and moved directly in front of her. He stood with his hands on his hips and had his head cocked to one side as he studied her. She jumped and almost bolted when he erupted with a deep laugh. It was not an infectious laugh, it was one that sent chills up and down her spine. As creepy as a horror movie, but then, it felt as if she were living in one. She just wished she knew if this movie had a good ending.

He was tall and very thin. Not gym thin, but stay up all night and party thin. Hair. Lots of dark hair, thick and black in the bright sunlight. Wild, wiry curls circled his head and a thick beard covered the lower half of his face. It sprang up from the opening at the collar of his work shirt, too. What she could see of his skin was tan and leathery. Summer guessed he could be anywhere from in his late 30's to early 50's. With all that hair and weathered skin, it was hard to tell.

"Get up," said a deep voice, with no laughter in it this time.

Pushing herself up by using the rock wall, she tested one leg, then the other. Her muscles felt sore and tingly, but she stayed upright, and that was something. She had no idea how long she had been in the cave, but the sunshine hitting her body worked its magic. She stopped shivering and could feel her muscles loosening up.

"You will be treated with respect as long as you are respectful."

She instinctively remained quiet and motionless as he glared at her. He bent to the ground reaching for a chain that was beside his boot, but never took his eyes off of her. As she gazed at the chain Summer's eyes widened with recognition. Shackles. A flashback to some days in the gulf she didn't like to remember. She tensed, but stayed put. There was not enough intel to chance anything, not just yet, anyway. The hairy man knelt in front of her and clamped one of the cuffs to each of her ankles. Iron bracelets sat heavily on the top of her feet and at her heels. Her instinct was to kick him in the face and run, but Shelly's image danced in her head, and that kept her still.

"Good," he said as he stood. It was as if she had passed some sort of test. Noted, she thought. He stared down at her with eyes as black as his hair, "Follow me." He turned and started down a steep gravel path.

Summer shuffled forward, struggling to keep up with him without falling on the winding path. They rounded a corner at the bottom of a small hill and her stomach lurched. White wooden crosses. The hill behind her prison was covered with small, white wooden crosses. She said nothing, asked nothing, she simply shuffled along behind the strange man. The focus she needed to walk in chains helped keep her quiet. They continued until they went over a small rise and a valley opened up in front of them.

Wow.

It was a lush valley surrounded by the mountain on one side and a thick forest on the other. Summer tried to take it all in without breaking her stride. The vista was dominated by a huge barn with an attached corral filled with horses. On the other side of the barn was some kind of camouflage netting stretching over a large field. It looked like a gigantic circus tent. Somehow a circus tent would seem almost normal after everything else that had happened. On the mountain side a rambling adobe house was nestled on a small hill. Stark white with turquoise blue trim, it glistened in the morning sunlight. Terraces surrounded the back of the structure and overlooked the entire spread. The view from those terraces must be amazing. A seemingly idyllic ranch if it weren't manned by the Devil and this wasn't hell.

The man stopped abruptly and waved his arms to indicate the entire area, "This is my empire and it can be your home." He turned and moved forward until he was towering over her petite frame with his boots just touching her feet. "But you will have to earn the right to live in Paradise," he said in a low, almost seductive voice. The small hairs on the back of her neck stood up.

He was toying with her. Summer didn't flinch. She stared back at him with flaccid features as he continued, "I am your Master, and this is the last time you will be allowed to look directly at me. Since I am your Supreme Being, you will bow your head in my presence. Consider this your only warning."

Locking eyes with him for a moment, she shifted her gaze to her feet and said, "Yes, sir." Uh oh. As soon as she spoke she knew her voice had betrayed her. It was much too forceful and without a trace of obedience in it.

She couldn't see the blow coming, but she tensed for it anyway. The side of her head felt the full impact, and as it knocked her to her knees, she could only be grateful it wasn't a fist to her stomach.

Summer kept her eyes to the ground as she spit blood, then she used both hands to push herself up. She stood ramrod straight, but her eyes never left the ground, and she remained silent.

It was very quiet. Neither of them spoke as Summer continued studying her soiled tennis shoes. Absently, she noticed her jeans were caked with dried mud and imagined the rest of her was too. She almost smiled when the thought went through her head that she probably smelled awful. Good, get a nose full, Looney Tunes.

It felt like an eternity before he finally spoke, and when he did, he actually sounded amused, "You are going to be an interesting subject," he said. Then she felt a light pat on her head. Her mind shifted back to the pound dog image. "I think there is a lot going on in there. Only time will tell if that's a good thing, little momma," he said then started to walk away. She glanced up, but then back down when she saw him stop and start to turn toward her as he growled, "Well, come on. We don't have all day. There are plants to tend!"

Summer shuffled along behind him as she screamed inside her head, "Friggin, madman. Oh, Sweet God, how did we wind up in this hell?"

CHAPTER ELEVEN
THURSDAY
THANKSGIVING DAY

The aroma of freshly baked bread and coffee pulled Tyler from a troubled sleep. Sunlight was peeping under the bottom of the window shade and painted a white line across the floor. Realization replaced the yeasty scent, Summer and Shelly were gone.

No miracle call came during the night. He could pretend all he wanted that it was Summer in the kitchen, but the truth was harsh; the aromas that floated around him undoubtedly originated from Jennifer's restless hands.

Shelly wasn't asleep in the next room dreaming of horses, summer vacation, and the latest boy band. Yet the sun had again risen. He cursed softly at the mocking stream of light that slowly started its climb across the floor and up the bedroom wall.

He was in Summer's childhood bedroom; not in her old rod iron bed, but in the large wooden rocker she used to rock Shelly as a baby. The rocking motion must have been soothing enough to let him find sleep, but his jumbled dreams stole his rest.

Tyler unwrapped the quilt curled around his large frame and pushed up from the rocker. He arched his back, winced, then sat again and pulled on his boots. Jake moved to the door, turned, and gazed at him.

"Yeah, yeah—I'm coming," Tyler mumbled, then rubbed the stubble on his chin as he rose and headed to the door. As soon as he opened it Jake rushed out. Tyler smiled at the sound of dog's nails clicking on the wood floors as he scrambled toward the fragrant smells.

In the kitchen, Jennifer was bent over the oven pulling out a tray of freshly baked cinnamon rolls. Jake squatted beside her and lifted his nose to follow her every move.

The butcher block island in the center of the large kitchen was stacked with her night's work. Two loafs of bread, a tray of sugar cookies, and pies, lots of pies. Pumpkin, cherry, apple, and some sort of mixed berry pie. The sink was overflowing with pans and mixing bowls. It looked as if a dozen cooks had been busy throughout the night.

Jennifer set the tray of rolls on the top of the stove and patted her flushed face with a handkerchief, shrugged and said, "Okay—I couldn't sleep." Then she grabbed a bowl and stirred some clear, white icing for the rolls. Her strokes were hard and wild, so some of the goo slopped over the side and dripped onto the floor. Jake sprang forward and licked it clean. Tyler chuckled and said, "You've been busy."

Jennifer didn't speak at first. She kept up her wild stirring while staring at the bowl she was about to break with a wooden spoon. She finally turned and said, "Today is Thanksgiving, so I want to be ready when the girl's come home." Her voice sounded high and manic. Silver hair was pulled loosely on top of her head in a crooked ponytail and flour rested in several places around her face and clothes. Red swollen eyes with brown craters below each of them gazed at him as she said, "Summer refused to learn to cook or bake, but that doesn't mean she isn't crazy about baked goods. Both my girls have a sweet tooth."

Tyler couldn't remember a time when this formidable woman seemed frail, but he was afraid she was about to shatter at any moment. He moved forward, took the bowl from her hands, and without saying a word, he engulfed her in a hug. He held her until the struggle against him turned into submission, then longer as she sobbed into his shoulder.

When she stopped and pulled away, she wiped her eyes with her apron, picked up the bowl, and continued as if nothing had happened. But this time she stood a little straighter, and her stroke was normal. They would get through this together. Not a union Tyler had ever imagined would happen.

Jennifer said, "I couldn't get inspired to paint or sculpt, but baking felt right." She looked up at Tyler as a tear leaked out of her right eye, "I baked all of Shelly's favorites."

Frowning he said, "Jennifer…"

But before he could continue, she jumped in with, "I know, I know. There is no indication they will be here today, but they will be coming home, and when they do, I will have Thanksgiving waiting for them!" She turned away and mumbled, "Even if I have to freeze it."

"Coffee?" Tyler asked.

Jennifer nodded toward the corner on the other side of the kitchen, "Made a fresh pot just a few minutes ago, help yourself."

Grabbing a mug, Tyler poured himself a cup. After a long sip he headed toward the kitchen door with the mug still in his hand, "I'm going to take Jake for his morning walk, then I'll sample one of those rolls." He gave her a half smile as he held the door open for the dog. Jake hesitated as he sniffed at the fragrant air, but then dropped his head and he scooted out the door. The sunshine and walking with Tyler had won.

"You might consider a shower and shave when you get back,"

Jennifer said as she spread icing on the golden rolls.

Tyler chuckled as he stepped out into the morning light. He was worried about Jennifer, but hadn't considered his own appearance. He had slept in his clothes and hadn't cleaned up since he had arrived in Noisy Water. He could probably grab a sign and bucket and collect big bucks on a street corner right now.

Jake started for the woods behind the house, but when Tyler whistled, the dog stopped in his tracks and cocked his head toward him. Tyler nodded toward the road in front of the house. Switching directions, the dog headed down the steep drive at a brisk pace. Tyler followed and soon they were on the mountain road in front of the house. It was paved as it cut through dense forest land, but there were no sidewalks, and the shoulders were narrow, although no cars were traveling the road this early on Thanksgiving morning.

The air felt crisp, but the sun was warm and bright. Just the same, Tyler wished he had taken the time to throw on a jacket. Shivering, he increased his pace. Keeping up with Jake kept him moving fast anyway. The thick pine trees bordering both sides of the road blocked his view of the neighbors, but there were a lot of dirt roads branching off of the main road. Most had signs posting the owner's last name, or the name of the house or ranch. Hacienda de Caballo was the sign that drew his attention. A horse ranch. Just what he needed.

As soon as he spotted it, he gave Jake another whistle, then turned and started down the dirt road. There was no gate or 'keep out' sign, so that was good. Tyler watched Jake as he moved steadily in front of him, turning occasionally to make sure the distance between them wasn't too far. It still amazed him how many whistles the dog knew and obeyed. Jake was one smart pooch. Tyler had the ribbons to prove he was the best cow dog in three counties.

As they rounded the corner at the end of the lane, the trees opened up to a large meadow. It was a nice ranch. The stable was in front of, and larger than, the main house. Right away he noticed several beautiful animals in the attached fenced pasture. He paused and watched. They pranced around the grassy field as they tossed their tails and heads high. Tyler loved watching the horses as they played in the cool morning air, but he was on a mission, so he headed for the main house.

As he moved closer to the house, he called, "Hello" to the man who stood on the expansive front porch. The older man looked about eighty, but stood straight and gazed at Tyler with piercing blue eyes.

"Morning." He nodded at Tyler, then pointed to the empty cup still in his hand, "Refill?"

"Sure," Tyler walked up the steps and stuck out his right hand, "Tyler Reynolds, Jennifer's son-in-law." Jake sat in the yard a few feet from the men. The dog cocked his head back and forth as he listened to every word. When he sensed no animosity, he flopped on the grass with his head on his front paws.

The older man said, "Yep—that's what I figured. Seen you in town with Summer once." Tyler tried not to wince when he heard Summer's name. He smiled and handed the man his cup. "I'm Wilbur Reston. Sorry about your troubles—the wife and I planned on coming over later to see if we can do anything," he shook his head, "Damn shame. Jennifer and Summer are good people, and that little Shelly, well, she is very special. Damn shame." He started toward the door with Tyler's cup in hand, "Black?"

Tyler smiled and nodded, "That would be great. Thanks."

"Sit, make yourself comfortable and I'll be right back," he nodded at the rockers on the porch, then headed inside.

Tyler gazed at the big rockers but didn't trust himself not to fall asleep, so he chose instead to sit on the steps while he waited. He gazed up at the cloudless sky and noticed a hawk circling above them. The large, dark creature seemed to zero in on the side of the barn farthest from the pasture. Tyler squinted and saw some movement in the tall grass. The hawk suddenly swooped down, but the movement in the grass turned into a flash of gray and white. The hawk flew away without his breakfast after the rabbit dove down a hole close to a clump of trees beside the barn. Jake had raised his head to watch the drama, and although he quivered, he kept his position in the yard and resisted the urge to join in the chase. Tyler said, "Good boy." Jake gave him a dog smile and thump of his stubby tail.

Reston reappeared and handed Tyler a steaming cup of coffee, then sat beside him on the top step.

"That's a mighty fine dog you got there."

"Yes, he is great with my cattle."

"Where's your spread?"

"Texas, just outside Idalou, South of Lubbock."

"Flat land there."

"Very, I have some good pasture land for the stock, though, and a nice creek runs through it."

"Sounds beautiful. Wife's gone to church, but I can get you something to eat if you're hungry."

"No, thanks. Better save my appetite. Jennifer's been baking."

"Yeah. I never ate better then when my wife was worried about our boy when he was off to college. Seems to help, and I sure don't mind the baked goods," he winked at Tyler as he patted his small round bump above his belt buckle. The man's eyes were almost lost in a sea of wrinkled and freckled skin, but they twinkled and still held wonder.

Tyler smiled and replied, "There is something I would like to ask you—do you rent your horses and gear?"

"Nope, but I would sure let you use one." Wilbur took a loud, toothless sip of the hot brew then nodded his head toward the pasture, "The big bay is great in the woods, but the smaller one is the fastest horse I own. Need some help with your search?"

"No—just the horse and gear. The bay would be great. Might be gone a while, though."

"Not a problem. Whatever you need. All I ask is treat 'em right, but I can see that by the way you are with your dog." He took another loud sip, "Plus, you're Jennifer's kin—that's good enough for me." He lifted his head to gaze at the sky as he said, "Got plenty of camping gear too—gets mighty cold out there at night, and snow will start any day now." He gazed at Tyler then continued, "Folks round here help each other. That's just the way it is. Prolly the same in your parts, I recon."

Tyler smiled and felt his shoulders relax for the first time in days. "It is, and thanks, Wilber," as he stuck his hand out and they shook on it. Jennifer had her baking, now he had something he could do, "I'll let you know when."

CHAPTER TWELVE THURSDAY THANKSGIVING DAY

Summer rose from her squatting position and stretched. She tilted her face toward the sky, closed her eyes and breathed deeply. The work was exhausting, but it felt wonderful to be out of the cave. The fresh air and sunshine were like balm to her wounds. She placed her hands on her hips as she glanced over her shoulder, and then dropped back into a squat. The creep was at it again, and it wasn't the first time since she started work this morning. She jerked more weeds from the loose soil and stuffed them into the burlap sack tied around her waist as she felt Jose's eyes on her back. Even half way across the field she was his main focus. He hadn't said much to her, but his eyes spoke volumes.

Weeding the weed. That's just great. She smirked at the thought, but couldn't quite muster the energy to laugh. God, she was tired, bone tired, and the day was barely half over. Her time in the cave took its toll, and at the rate they were pushing the workers, it would be hard to regain her strength. It didn't help that she hadn't eaten much, and what she did eat seemed to come right back up.

As if on cue Jose blew a whistle and the workers stopped what they were doing to head to a long picnic table at the edge of the field. Summer followed, but the shackles chaffed with every step, so she was the last one in line. Just as well.

It was a silent walk. No one else was tethered, but they all walked wordlessly with their heads down. It felt like some stupid zombie horror movie. Except it wasn't a movie. It was all too real. She shuffled along behind the group. She was just one more stupid zombie, and right now there was nothing she could do about it.

Jose stood at the end of the table, and as she caught up with the group, he gestured for her to sit. She felt her skin burn under his gaze as she slid in beside a small woman with deeply wrinkled brown skin. The old woman's face was slack and she stared at Jose as if he held the answers of the Universe.

Jose turned as a young woman approached from the barn with a small covered cart. She uncovered the cart and took a stack of plates and utensils from the bottom and handed them to the workers sitting at the head of the table. As they passed them down, she placed a big bowl of beans and rice in the center of the table along with a dish of steaming tortillas.

The girl had dark hair and her skin was the color of honey. She wore a plain wool dress, dark stockings, and work boots instead of the pajama like pants and top the field workers wore. Maybe there were separate workers for the kitchen and house. Maybe she knew where Shelly was being kept. Summer felt her pulse speed up, but she tried to stay as expressionless as the old woman sitting beside her.

Jose seemed fascinated with the girl's heaving, generous chest as she lifted the heavy dishes onto the table. Summer smiled; a new home for those burning eyes. She heard a youthful giggle and turned to see the old woman sitting next to her give him a broad, toothless grin. The young girl and her fragrant dishes must be the highlight of the day. After time in the cave, simply breathing fresh air was the highlight for Summer's day.

After everyone had plates and spoons they all sat very still. Jose nodded at each of them one by one, and with each nod, the worker would load their plate. The old lady was the first to get a nod, and Summer was the last. She could tell Jose was enjoying his power in this tiny fiefdom. It didn't matter. She rubbed the small bump of discontent in her tummy and wondered if she would be able to keep the heavy food down. Just the aromas drifting from the old woman's plate was making her stomach turn over. She had not been very successful with the bowl of, well, whatever it was they gave her this morning, staying down.

Summer was dressed in the same ill-fitting loose pajama like outfit, and sturdy brown boots the workers wore. The hairy Master had taken her from the cave to Jose, then turned and left without a word. Jose had led her inside the barn, handed her the rough cotton pants and top along with a bar of soap and ratty towel. "Go," he had said, pointing to the communal bathroom in the center of the barn.

The shower would have felt great, even with the tepid water, if she hadn't done it under the watchful eye of Jose. He stood just beyond the cinder block wall that was supposed to give her some privacy, but she felt his eyes on her each time she turned her back to the opening. She couldn't wait to get out of the water and into the baggy outfit. Being filthy meant being protected. Showering the smell of the cave down the drain was like holding an empty pepper spray bottle.

Summer played with her spoon as the others wolfed down their food. She finally dug into her plate of beans and rice and ventured a bite, but gagged before she could swallow. Unfortunately, the tortillas were gone by the time she was allowed to get a serving and they had looked delicious. She didn't want to think about how the workers had earned their place in Jose's line of nods, but she hoped to stay at the bottom of the list. She had no desire to gain favor with Jose. Even if being at the bottom meant never getting the most desirable dishes, or not getting food at all.

She touched her tummy bump again. She needed food. With a sigh she nibbled at the rice. Much to her surprise, this time the food tasted wonderful, and she didn't feel a bit of nausea. Maybe she was finally getting a little past the morning sickness phase, or maybe her body was just desperate for nourishment, either way, she was adjusting.

This pregnancy was completely different than with Shelly. No morning sickness the first time, but this little one had her barfing since day one. Maybe it was a boy. She smiled as she pictured Tyler's face. Oh, God, please let us get through this and be a family again, please!

She felt movement and noticed each worker leaving the table after they ate. They weren't heading back to work, though. Some stretched and walked out of the tent, a couple went for a smoke, and the old woman sat on the ground by the barn. It wasn't long before Summer could hear her snores as she napped in a sitting position.

Summer froze. She felt someone behind her, and then strong hands gripped each of her shoulders. A low guttural whisper warmed her ear. "You have thirty minutes of free time but stay where I can see you," Jose said. A light squeeze and he was gone. Her stomach churned and her skin felt hot where his hands had rested. It was all she could do to stay still and not rub her ear where it still felt wet from his breath. She eased her head around and gazed over her shoulder. He was several yards away as he sauntered across the yard, then he stopped to light a cigarette and draw deeply on it. His eyes narrowed as he spotted the young serving girl. He glided toward her with a smile that looked more like a grimace and offered her a cigarette. She giggled and shook her head, but placed one hand on his arm as she gazed up at him.

Yuck!

Summer studied the group of workers as they milled around the dining area. She was the only one restrained by shackles. She wasn't about to ask anyone questions, especially since she had no idea who to trust, or what they had been told about her. The fact that they were tending illegal crops was enough to make her assume the worst. Of course, she was doing the same thing, so they could be just like her. She simply had not gained enough information to start nosing around yet.

She rose from the table and shuffled away from the others. As she edged toward the netting she strained to see through it to the yard and house beyond. She turned to see what Jose was doing. He was leaning in toward the serving girl and she saw him lightly touch her neck and trace his finger down toward the front opening of her dress. Summer shivered, and then moved a little closer to the tent edge.

No one was in the outside yard, and she didn't have a clear view of the house, so she gazed back at the barn. The thing was massive. She had gotten a quick tour this morning after her shower. It held separate quarters for men and women, communal areas, animal stalls, a feed storage room, a tact room, and an enormous room to dry the pot. Jose had given her basic instructions of where she was allowed, what was expected of her, and where she was not to venture under any circumstance. There were rules, lots of rules, and she wasn't ready to openly break any just yet, at least not until she knew where Shelly was being kept.

Movement on the other side of the barn caught her eye. Three figures were leading a paint pony toward the attached corral. Summer stopped breathing. It was two men and a blonde girl. Her breath escaped in a whoosh. The girl was too tall to be Shelly. It must be the teen girl who snatched her child away from her.

The center of the group was the tall hairy man. The Master. He towered above the other guy, some short, fat man, who smiled a lot. The egomaniac who thought he was God would hardly look at the little man, then suddenly, he turned and patted shorty on the shoulder and laughed so hard, Summer could hear it all the way across the field. After they put the pony in the corral, they all turned and began to walk up the path toward the main house. The two men ambled along side by side and the girl followed a few feet behind them.

Summer shook her head and shifted her position, straining to see the house nestled up on the hill. The group continued up the path and disappeared through the back door. Shelly had to be there. A chill went up Summer's spine. Her baby girl was in a house with that nut job who called himself Master. Her hands moved into fists and she leaned into the netting.

Jim Jones and so many others since him, all using God's name to commit whatever atrocity their crazy brains told them to do. What is it with these maniacal freaks? Just the thought that he might touch her child made her want to kill him with her bare hands. She could picture it in her head vividly. She forced her breathing to slow and unclenched her fists. Shelly seemed sincere when she said they hadn't hurt her, so Summer held onto that, but the blonde teen girl looked beaten down. It wasn't the first time Summer saw that look. She saw a lot of women and girls with the same look when she was in the Middle East, and again, right here in the States, when she volunteered at the battered women's shelter.

How had this happened? Normal one day, insanity the next. "Damn!" she said in a low voice as she looped her fingers through the netting. She needed to find Shelly and get them out of this hell hole.

"Back to work."

Summer jumped as the words yanked her back to her reality. She slowly turned around and Jose was right behind her. He moved a step closer as he said, "Don't even think about it, little momacita." He lightly touched the gun holstered at his side, "Things around here can be hard, or they can be easy." He eyed her up and down, "Do what you're told and life will be a lot easier."

She nodded, dropped her head and started shuffling toward the plants. She jumped again when Jose blew his whistle and everyone else headed back to work.

Summer moved to her spot, squatted, and dug with a new energy. She glanced up and caught Jose's eyes on her again. This time she welcomed it. Maybe she could gain enough trust to have her shackles taken off by being docile. She needed those shackles gone.

She paused, sat back on her heals and pushed her hair back. Being docile would also make her vulnerable. She frowned and renewed her digging. A cost she would have to pay for mobility. As she dug around a vine, she hit something hard, so she brushed the dirt away. A rock. The frown turned into a smile. It was nice and round on one side and sharp looking on the other. Perfect. It was small enough for a pocket and big enough to do damage. After another glance at Jose, she slipped it into her pocket in one fluid movement. Another glance and she knew she was home free. Sleep would come to her tonight after all. A nice rock under her pillow would make all the difference.

Summer began humming as she moved down her row taking a small, unexpected pleasure in digging in the loose soil. She kept an eye on Jose as she worked. Him, she could handle, but the crazy one, the Master, now he was a different story. He was unpredictable, and that made him dangerous. It was a challenge, but one she would win. There was simply too much at stake and the alternative unthinkable.

∞

Shelly cocked her head to one side and listened, nope, nothing, so she went back to her book. At least her room felt safe and away from the crazies, but it was just so boring. Not that there was anything to do in the rest of the house besides work. God, she hated to admit that, even to herself. The thought made her blush with guilt. There was so much more going on here than her boredom. But, she was existing in such a different world, and it was hard for her to shift her thinking to the new reality.

There was no TV, and worse, no electronic toys or games. She wasn't allowed near the internet, if they even had internet in this crazy place. It was a good thing she liked books, but the ones in her room were ancient and dumb. She sighed, put the book down, and stared at the wall. The purple painted wall was the only alternative since there wasn't even a window in the tiny space.

The bedroom wasn't much more than a small closet. The bedspread on the small twin bed was bright pink and a princess script with a painted tiara was arched across the white headboard. What kind of crazy shit was that? It looked more like a toddler's room than a teen's room. The rest of the furniture consisted of a small desk, chair, and chest of drawers filled with girl's underwear, socks, and frilly gowns. Worn stuffed animals sat in a jumbled pile on the floor. She had tossed them there in a rage last night when she had heard the lock on the door click. This was some crazy shit.

The girl they called Angel-2 had left her here and was the one who locked her in. Shelly picked up the teddy bear on the top of the stack and stared into its one good eye. The other eye was just a couple of dangling threads. She hugged the ratty bear to her chest and sighed. She shouldn't have had her temper tantrum. It could have set the nut job in charge off on the girl. He was completely bat shit crazy.

Shelly couldn't stay mad at the teen girl for the locked door. Poor girl. Now, her life was a real nightmare. Shelly was determined not to end up like her. To survive was one thing, but to live like this for the rest of your life, no way.

The stack of tattered books came from the teen girl. God only knew where she got them, but Shelly hid them under her mattress just like she was told. They were children's books, and each was worn and looked like they had been read a lot, but as stupid as they were, at least they eased the boredom and quieted her fearful thoughts.

Shelly jumped and turned her head toward the door as she heard footsteps, then the doorknob turned. She stuck the book under her pillow. The door opened and the teen girl paused in the threshold as she signaled with one hand for her to come while she held a finger to her lips for silence with the other.

Shelly followed the older girl down the long hallway to the kitchen. The room smelled delicious. A blend of onions and garlic with a whiff of something light and sweet—cookies, maybe it was sugar cookies. Without a word, the teen tied an apron around Shelly's waist and handed her a small paring knife and bowl of potatoes to peel. As soon as Shelly started on the potatoes, the older girl went to a large glob of dough that rested on the stainless steel island. She sprinkled some flour, and then expertly kneaded the dough.

They worked in silence for a few minutes. The kitchen was pleasantly warm, and Shelly was actually grateful to have something to do with her hands, even if it was work. She found herself smiling. Then the door burst open and the Master strode into the room wrapped in a cloak of cold air that surged into the space.

"It smells good in here, girls!" He barked. Shelly held her breath as he moved to the teen girl, placed both of his hands on her shoulders and leaned forward to gaze at her work. "Fresh bread. Yum," he spoke softly as the girl stiffened, but continued to knead the bread. Shelly stared as his fingers gripped her shoulders tight enough for the material of her dress to bunch up, then he pulled back and gave her a light pat before saying, "Good work, good work!" Next he turned toward Shelly, "Little one—yes, yes, you too! Now don't feel slighted." He smiled and approached. Shelly cringed and moved toward the wall with the knife gripped by her side. She could see the older teen shake her head behind him with a look of panic on her face. Shelly froze, but it was too late. His face darkened and his arm tensed as he towered over her, but before he could do anything, the older girl darted between them as she wiped her hands on her apron.

"Master, did you want some wine with your dinner tonight?" She bowed her head, but stood squarely between them as she said, "Uh, I have worked with Angel-3 on wine selections, and she has done quite well. If you like, she can get a nice red from the cellar? Uh, since its beef tonight, a nice hardy red would be good, right Angel-3?"

Shelly nodded her head, but couldn't find her voice, or seem to move. He stared at her a moment longer, then turned his attention to the older teen. His hand shot out in a lightning strike. The girl went down, but scrambled back up, and then returned to the dough without a word. He turned toward Shelly and she felt her legs go weak. This time he grinned as he said, "That is good news! Yes, little princess, go pick out two bottles of red wine because we have a guest for dinner tonight. Now scoot, show me what you learned," his voice was soft and singsong, like when you spoke to a very young child. She glanced at the older girl's back, but jumped when he shouted, "Now!" So she tossed the potato and knife she was holding into the potato bowl and rushed to the cellar door. She bounded down the stairs without a backwards glance.

When she reached the bottom step, she risked a looked over her shoulder, but he had not followed her down. Her breath came in short pants, so she paused until it returned to normal, then she flicked on the light switch, and headed to the back of the cellar for the wine shelves.

Shelly hated the basement when the older girl had shown it to her, but right now it felt like a sanctuary. The crazy man didn't seem to have any of the boundaries other adults had. She held no experiences in her memory that could help her with how she dealt with any of this, so for the first time in her life she felt completely clueless.

A solitary tear ran down her cheek. She didn't know which was worse, to see the older girl take a blow for her, or imagine how it would feel when it was her turn, because she knew that time would come.

Stupid bully. Stupid asshole bully.

She turned and glared toward the staircase. It was empty. "I hate you, you stupid asshole!" she said through clinched teeth. It was low enough that she knew it wouldn't be heard, but it still made her feel better.

Florescent lights did little to brighten the dark corners of the basement and it smelled like a damp sponge. The wine bottles were dusty with cobwebs that laced around the top corners of the rack. Shelly grabbed a step stool and scrambled up to pull out the two bottles that the teen girl had pointed out to her before. "These are for red meat, the middle ones for chicken, and the bottom ones for fish. Stop fidgeting and listen, kid—this can make the difference in a pat on the head or a fist to your face. No errors or attitude." The words had shocked Shelly enough to make her words stick, and now she understood, but the older girl had gotten the blow she should have received.

Why would she readily take a blow so obviously meant for Shelly? She didn't understand the sacrifice, or why she would risk herself for a complete stranger, but Shelly vowed she would find a way to repay her.

As she trudged back to the stairs, a child's red suitcase caught her eye. It was tucked up under some blankets behind the staircase, but she could see its bright color as it poked out from the drab olive green wool.

Another glance up the stairs, then she turned back to stare at the case. It had a dark red plastic handle and was covered in little white flowers and butterflies. She placed the wine bottles on the bottom step as the case drew her in. She tugged it out, and flipped it open. Inside it was full of the most beautiful drawings she had ever seen. Most were pencil sketches, but at the bottom were some glorious watercolors. Vivid blues, greens and reds. The scenes were of other worlds. Gorgeous landscapes with beautiful skies and exotic plants. Fairies and angels paraded through the fantasy lands, and several had a golden haired child with a raven haired mother. As Shelly gazed at the drawings and paintings they made her feel free.

"What's taking you so long?" the man shouted from the top of the stairs.

Shelly jumped and slammed the case closed, then shoved it back under the blankets. "Got them. I'm coming," she called as she grabbed the bottles and raced up the stairs two at a time.

CHAPTER THIRTEEN THURSDAY THANKSGIVING DAY

The bell above the door chimed as Maggie entered the mini-mart. She paused, then headed to the counter just to the left of the front door. She glanced up at the camera above the counter but dismissed it—everyone knew it didn't work.

"Hi" the girl said as she gazed at Maggie, "Hey, you're that two spirit cop, aren't you?"

Maggie frowned at the tribal reference to her being gay. The girl had the reputation of saying the first thing that popped into her head, and today, she hoped it would continue. She needed to hear anything this girl thought about the abduction. Even trivial, random thoughts might help.

This girl was simply a product of her generation; these kids said what they thought. Maggie wasn't sure if that made things better or worse. Maggie wasn't bullied in school, but she spent most of her youth being ignored. Since she liked being left alone, she didn't feel scarred by the accepted behavior of her generation. However, the unspoken word could be very loud at times. If she lived at the time of the ancients, it would have been very different, they had actually revered two spirit people. Come to think of it, Maggie didn't think she would like that either. Too much attention either way.

"Have we met?" Maggie asked the girl.

"No, but I had Miss Elsa in school."

"Oh." Then she shifted the conversation away from herself, "I'm surprised you are open today." Although she knew the skinflint owner would have some poor soul manning the store, holiday or not.

"Yeah, whatever, owner thinks we will make extra bucks, but you are the first person to come in," she said as she gazed toward the plate glass window at the empty parking lot.

Maggie laid a copy of the wedding photo of Summer, Tyler and Shelly on the counter and pointed to the picture, "I understand you saw these two in the store?"

The girl seemed to perk up as she picked up the photo, "Yeah." She put it back on the counter and scratched her head as she gazed at the images, "After this guy talked to me about them, the head cop came by and asked me some questions, but he didn't act like he believed me." Her dark hair was braided and she had a streak of purple running down one side. She frowned at Maggie as she continued, "I told him I wasn't making it up. He just nodded and smiled, and I could tell, he thought I was full of it." She leaned back in her chair and said, "He didn't even think it would make TV, or even the news." A frown, then she brightened as she said, "Are the tribal cops handling it now?"

"We are all doing what we can," Maggie evaded her question, then pulled out a small notebook and pen, "I have a few questions for you if that's all right?"

"Sure, fire away," the girl smiled, then crossed her hands on the counter, and gazed at Maggie.

"Mr. Reynolds's stated that you said they looked happy, or at ease when they were here. They didn't seem concerned or stressed?"

"Yeah, I mean, no, that's right." She leaned toward Maggie and gazed at the holstered gun at her side, "Hey, you know how to use that thing? Ever shot anybody?"

Maggie continued as if she had not been interrupted, "Was anyone else around that morning?"

The girl leaned back and was quiet a moment, "Well, let's see, it was a quiet morning. Actually, the mom and kid were the first out-of-towners in the store in days; you know we don't get many tourists this time of year." She frowned, "I guess I can't call them tourists since the lady grew up here, right? But, like, I didn't know that when they were here."

Maggie edged forward slightly and asked, "How about locals? Any locals in that morning, or just after they left?"

The girl was quiet again and gazed out the storefront window for a moment, then her head snapped around and she said, "Oh, yeah—that weird dude, you know, the hairy one who lives on that compound—uh, Felix something? The one that talks like some kind of religious nut?" She snorted and said, "For a church freak he sure buys a lot of booze. He was here right before them, bought some beer and several bottles of wine."

Maggie felt her pulse quicken. She leaned closer and asked, "Felix Alvarez Lea?"

"Yeah, yeah, that's right, that's his name."

"Was he alone?"

"Yeah."

"Did he use a credit card or write a check?"

"No, he always pays in cash. Has big wads of it. I always wondered why he carries around so much dough." She grinned and added, "And where he gets it?" a wink, "He always smells a little like weed." She held up a hand and said, "not that I would know firsthand what weed smells like. Uh, just what I noticed on some of the stoner kids." She gazed at her hands, then moved them to her lap.

"What kind of vehicle was he driving?"

"That van of his—the old one that looks real Hippy—straight out of the olden days. It even has the curtains in the windows so you can't see in the back." She snapped her fingers and said, "Oh, yeah—like one of those ancient Cheech and Chong movies. Hilarious! Did you see the one where the dude turned into a lizard? I laughed my butt off, and I was like, totally straight. Woops, you know what I mean, not high. Ah, not that I do that kind of thing, officer."

"Did he leave going north? Just like the Reynolds?

Pause, then she said, "Oh, you mean the lady and kid? Well, yeah—now that you mention it, he did; came and went right before they came in, he probably passed them in the parking lot." Her eyes widened, "Hey, do you think he had something to do with their disappearance? Like, OMG! You're kidding?" She slapped the counter, "Whoa—sketchy!"

"I didn't say that—we just need to check all possibilities. It could only mean he was a witness to what happened to them." Maggie picked up the photo and frowned, "But we would like to ask him if he saw anything." She took a step back, but asked, "Uh, what do you mean 'sketchy'?"

"You know—creepy, scary, skin-crawling moment. Totally horror movie stuff."

Maggie smiled and said, "Okay, I get it. It's just that we want to interview anyone who might have seen something." She handed her card to the girl, "This is where you can reach me if you think of anything more, especially if you think of someone else who was around that morning."

The girl took the card and nodded her head as she said, "Sure, sure. Absolutely."

"Okay, then—thanks for your help."

Maggie turned to leave and the girl said, "Hey, tell Miss Elsa that Cocheta Chato says 'hey'—she was my fav teacher."

Maggie looked back at the girl for a moment, "Okay. And don't forget to call if you think of anything." Then she headed for the cruiser as she shook her head. That girl was a trip. Teens—Maggie didn't 'get' them when she was one, she sure didn't understand them now.

∞

Heading north toward town, Maggie stayed 20 miles under the posted speed limit. As she drove she strained to see both sides of the road, but nothing looked out of place. There was no break in the thick cedar and pine trees to indicate a car had left the road.

When she reached the outskirts of Noisy Water, she made a U-turn, then made the same slow trek back to the mini-mart. Still nothing.

In the parking lot she turned the cruiser around, and again, headed toward town. This time she only concentrated on the road to her right. It bordered the forest, then made a steep climb up the side of the mountain.

When she was about half way back to town, she spotted a slight depression in the weeds on the shoulder. She stopped the cruiser, got out and approached the area as she zipped her jacket against the cold.

The area was about the right size for Felix's van. She squatted and gazed at what looked like tire track indentions in the soft dirt under the weeds. Worn tire tread. There was something dark that stained the greenery in the center of the area. She reached for one of the stained blades and plucked it, then brought it to her nose. Oil.

Maggie stood. No break in the trees and it was an incline just beyond the tree line, not a drop off. She gazed all around the area and spotted what looked like tire marks just beyond the indention. They made a sharp turn back onto the highway. She walked along the shoulder as her feet crunched on the gravel between the road and weeds.

When she reached the marks, she stopped and gazed across the road. A stack of tree limbs and debris. It wasn't noticeable when she drove the road, but really stuck out from this perspective. She looked up at the trees above the debris—new growth, green branches. The old wood should not have been there, it was staged.

She moved across the two lane highway and kicked at the branches with her boot. Underneath were deep indentions of tire tracks.

Maggie pulled on her gloves and pulled the limbs and tossed them aside until the area was partially cleared. Now she could see obvious indentions. More debris was stacked to cover a narrow break between the trees, a break large enough for a car to squeeze through.

This side of the highway had a steep drop off just beyond the tree line. Maggie examined the trees on either side of the break and they both had fresh gouges in the bark. A car could have wedged through.

She walked through the trees toward the drop off until she reached the cliff edge. The incline was sharp and then opened up to a valley covered in thick brown brush. The blue top of a car shimmered in the sunlight, just breaking through the deep brush. She felt her pulse quicken as she looked around for a safe route down the hill. She finally spotted an area that looked manageable.

Maggie pulled out her phone and hit the Chief's number. As he picked up she spurted, "its Maggie Littlejohn. We've caught a break."

As soon as Chief Anderson said he had help on the way, Maggie headed for the route she spotted and started down. It was tricky, and she slipped a couple of times on the dirt and pine needles that covered the narrow path, but each time she managed to right herself before she fell down the hill. Then at last, she was at the bottom, and thigh high in tumbleweeds and thick brush.

On the valley floor, she made her way through the brush until she reached the car, all the time being grateful for her thick pants and rugged boots. Her reward was the blue Toyota from the BOLO.

She pushed aside a big tumbleweed and gazed through the driver's window. The car was empty except for a multitude of stuffed animals and bedding strewn all over the interior. No visible blood or bodies. She looked around the exterior area. No sign of disturbance or tracks leading away from the vehicle. She opened the driver's door and popped the trunk, then she edged around the car and held her breath as she opened the truck. Luggage, but again, no blood or bodies. She sighed and gazed around the car. With this much undisturbed debris surrounding the car, it could only mean one thing; it did not have anyone in it as it plummeted over the edge of the cliff.

Maggie gazed up the hill as the sound of sirens drifted down, then got louder, and finally, flashing red lights beyond the tree tops. The police chief appeared at the top of the cliff. She waved at him then shouted, "I'm coming up." She rushed through the weeds to get to the steep climb. Whatever happened to Summer and Shelly was on the road up above. She needed to fill him in and have them secure the area before it all got trampled. She smiled. Now we have a crime scene.

CHAPTER FOURTEEN THURSDAY THANKSGIVING DAY

"What do you mean you can't get a search warrant for Felix's compound?" Jennifer said.

Chief Anderson and Tyler stood across from her in the kitchen. Jennifer had not offered the Chief a seat or coffee, and with the latest news, Tyler suspected that she wasn't going to offer him anything but the door.

"I know we have the car, but there was no sign of the girls, and nothing to indicate Felix had been there. The brush wasn't disturbed around the crash site, and there were no footprints leading away from it. No sign of blood in the car, either." Jennifer gasped and clutched the counter, but nodded her head and waved her hand for him to continue, so he said, "Uh, sorry folks. So it looks like they must have exited the car before it went over the cliff. Unfortunately, we have no evidence that connects Felix, or anyone else to their disappearance — nothing except a rather unreliable witness who put him at the mini-mart around the same time as Summer and Shelly—that's just not enough to get a warrant." He glanced over her shoulder at the mounds of baked goods that lined the counters, then said, "We are working on it, though. Forensics is analyzing the tire tracks and some oil drippings to at least tie them to the same make as Felix's van, but we don't have the facility to do the work here, so the state is analyzing it."

"Ralph…" Jennifer started, but the Chief interrupted her with a raised hand.

"Now, hold on, Jennifer, I want you to know we are working as fast as we can, but at least we can treat it as an abduction, now."

She crossed her arms over her chest and dropped her head as she said, "For God's sake, Ralph, of course it's an abduction." She raised her head, moved even closer to him, and poked her finger in his chest, "They could be prisoners with that awful, crazy man—or worse." Her voice choked as she continued with, "You have to do something, someone has to do something."

Chief Anderson turned and gazed at Tyler, but Tyler stared back and remained silent, so the Chief sighed, turned back to Jennifer and said, "I know how upset you are, but we are doing everything we can, really."

He moved her hand away from his chest but held onto it as he continued, "I went to the compound, but Felix wouldn't let me in. He did agree to come to the office in the morning for an interview." He sighed again and said, "Don't look at me like that, I am not the enemy here. I am trying to treat him like a witness in order to get him to cooperate. If I work it right, I might get him to let me head out there and have a look-see, but I have nothing to compel him to let us on his private property—nothing! I have to be patient so we don't lose his cooperation, which is about all we have right now. Even if I could reach a friendly judge on Thanksgiving Day, he wouldn't issue a warrant with a case this thin. All I can do right now is ask Felix if he saw anything on the highway the day they disappeared, but that might get him talking enough to revel something."

She pulled her hand free and moved against the breakfast bar. He eyed a bar stool beside her, but Jennifer pushed it under the counter and glared at him.

Tyler rose from the kitchen table, and said, "Thank you, Chief for keeping us in the loop."

Chief Anderson swallowed hard and said, "I'm sorry I don't have more for you right now, but please understand, we will do everything we can to get them back…."His voice trailed off.

Jennifer nodded and walked out of the kitchen toward the front door. She opened it and said, "Thank you, Ralph."

The Chief hesitated, then moved down the hall and joined her at the door as he said, "Jennifer, please." His eyes pleaded.

She held up a hand and shook her head, "I understand. I don't have to like it, but I understand." She took a deep breath and stood straight, as she continued with, "Keep us informed if anything new develops, and please thank Maggie for all her help." She looked him in the eyes, "I know it isn't her jurisdiction, as you have made abundantly clear, but she has given us our only serious lead."

"Awww, Jennifer." He sighed, then walked through the open door. He paused on the porch and turned to them and said, "If there is anything I can do to bring those two back—short of breaking the law—I will. And, please, Tyler let us handle this. Don't take the law into your own hands, that will only make things worse. I don't want to have to lock you up instead of Felix, or whoever else is responsible."

Tyler had moved in behind Jennifer. He placed a hand on her shoulder and said, "Duly noted, Chief."

Jennifer nodded, then pushed the door shut and locked it.

∞

Tyler turned as Jennifer knocked on his open bedroom door. "Come in," he said. Jake sat on the floor by the bed watching his every move. Packing meant action and the dog had not had any serious exercise for days.

"Do you need anything?" she didn't ask him why he had clothes and equipment laid out on the bed beside a large saddlebag.

"If you have some jerky, and maybe some bread?"

"I'll pack up a small bag of food supplies—some dog food for Jake?"

"He can eat what I do."

"Okay, I think I have everything you will need." She turned to go, but paused in the doorway and said, "You can check the shed if you need flashlights or camping gear."

He looked up at her and said, "Thanks, I will. Your neighbor has a good horse he is loaning me." He sat on the edge of the bed and said, "You know I won't be back until I've covered every inch of his land. If they are there, I'll find them."

"I know." She walked across the room and kissed him on the forehead as she whispered, "Bring our girls home."

"I will." Jake barked and his stubby tail quivered, he was ready for action.

CHAPTER FIFTEEN
THURSDAY
THANKSGIVING DAY

Footsteps? The teen girl known as Angel-2 froze, but could no longer hear anything. She peeked through the open door and gazed down the empty hallway. Just nerves. She sighed and eased the door shut, then slid behind the desk and opened the laptop. It was an old computer and the cooling fan seemed to echo in the home office like thunder. She stared at the door and gripped at her dust cloth and bottle of furniture polish. When Felix didn't rush in, she set them aside and returned to the computer. Felix would know cleaning the desk was a ruse, but at least it would give her something to say before he hit her.

Bastard.

The startup finished and she tapped the mouse on internet explorer. Felix's browser history wouldn't lie to her and he didn't know enough about technology to clear his tracks. The history trail showed her where his evil mind took him, and sometimes enabled her to stay one step ahead. This time he had looked at maps, climate, and banking information for Mexico, and South America. Not good. He had also researched several drug cartels. Did this mean he planned a move? Or just a new business partner?

She knew something was up, but she didn't know exactly what. If it was a move, and it was looking more like one all the time, she would bet that she, and the kid's mom, were not going to be part of the grand plan, at least not a living part of it. His crumbling relationship with Billy was probably at the crux of it, and it could also be the heat was being turned up with his latest acquisition. The new kid and her mom didn't look like the throwaways she and her mom had been. It was likely they would be missed, and their disappearance was hitting the news. Felix never could resist once he set eyes on a girl he liked, no matter what the cost.

Something was about to happen, she could feel it. Felix was crazy and unpredictable, but lately she sensed he was also restless. And he looked at her differently. It was with something like pity, and that was not an emotion she saw in him often. Only when someone, or something, was about to die.

She was tired. Bone tired. But she was still determined. The new kid would not experience the living hell she had, or wind up on the hill like the others. Not this time. This time she would take action. She was older now. She let evil have its way until now—just to survive—but no more, it wasn't worth what she had to pay with little bits of her soul.

A noise from the back of the house made her jump. That was real, not just nerves. She hit the power key, slammed the laptop shut, and slipped out of the office. When she was half way down the hall she stopped, then turned and ran back to the office to retrieve her cleaning supplies. She had to be more careful. That would have been a major issue and she couldn't afford Felix looking too closely at her activities right now. She had gained his trust and she needed to keep it if this was going to work.

Once she reached the safety of the kitchen, she stowed the supplies, scribbled a quick note and shoved it into her pocket. The kid was safely stashed in her room for now, so she grabbed her jacket and eased out the back door, first checking inside and out for activity before she made her exit.

It was still early, but the sun had already begun to drop behind the mountain. Pink streaks pierced the sky. Day turned to night fast in the valley. It was as if a giant light switch abruptly turned off the day each evening. She smiled because darkness was her friend right now.

The field workers were headed to the barn for dinner. She could see their silhouettes as they trudged in single file toward the side entrance of the barn. Just like a bunch of cows or sheep. She couldn't see the kid's mom, but hoped she was still with them. She kept to the path until she was nearly within hearing distance, then moved around to the back of the barn as she hugged the shadows.

At the back of the barn she peeped through the rear doors. There was a padlock on them, and she didn't have a key, but the gap as she tugged at one of the doors allowed her to peek through. The lights in the hallway made it easy for her to see inside, but she was relatively hidden in the dusk.

The workers were headed to their quarters. They each broke off the main hall and headed into the dormitories and the wash room. She knew they would be allowed a few minutes to wash before they would miss their dinner. A large picnic table was set up in a central room for the workers at night and in severe weather. She needed to make this work before they got to the dining area. There were fewer eyes to detect her here.

She got lucky, a few minutes was all she needed. She spotted the kid's mom and whistled softly. The woman's head jerked up. As soon as they made eye contact, the woman glanced over her shoulder and stretched, then ambled over and leaned against the wall by the barn door.

The teen smiled and nodded. Maybe this one was smart enough to survive. This could actually work. Slim chance in hell, but a chance.

She whispered through the crack between the large doors, "Your kids okay." Then slipped the note through the crack as the woman's hand grabbed and pocketed it, "Don't let anyone see that—get rid of it as soon as you read it."

∞

Summer turned slightly to respond, but the girl was gone. She glanced around the hallway, but she was alone, so she unfolded the note, read it, then slipped it into her mouth and chewed until she was able to swallow without choking.

The note said Shelly wasn't allowed anywhere near the workers, so this girl was her only contact with her daughter. The girl was obviously under the madman's thumb, so her first instinct was to not trust her. Maybe this was some kind of test. It was such a crazy place it was possible, and her suspicion was on high alert. But what choice did she have? She was desperate for any news of Shelly, and if this girl was to be believed, she would protect her daughter, so she had to cling to that.

The note had also said Shelly was safe and the girl was "training her." That statement sent chills down her spine. What kind of training? Summer suspected her sweet daughter was being groomed to become another slave for the crazy guy in charge. He was probably some kind of Jim Jones knock off, but she would not let herself go there.

The teen could not have survived this hell hole without being able to read situations and adjust. So, did that mean she really had Shelly's best interest at heart, or her own? Somehow Summer had to get her child out of here. She could not bear the thought of what would follow if Shelly became a slave to that man.

The teen also hinted in the note that she had a plan, but she would need help. Summer had no problem with that, and the sooner the better, but could she trust the girl? Summer felt like she had to at least keep quiet about the contact long enough to learn more. Plus, she felt a small tingle of hope in her chest for the first time since she woke up in the cave.

"You gonna eat?" Jose growled at her.

Summer jumped. Where the hell did he come from? "Oh, I'm coming." She must have been so deep in thought she hadn't heard him approach. Damn man had a way of doing that, though.

She moved away from the doors and shuffled to the table in the indoor communal area. She kept her head down and sat where she was told.

As she sat at the table staring at the goop they were plopping into each workers plate, she decided she was all in. She would put her trust in the teen and together they would get Shelly to safety. They had to get out of this place, and she would clutch any straw that was offered. That was the way it was. All or nothing. The choice was made.

She leaned over her plate and smelled the mixture. Not too bad. She took a bite and thought it must be some kind of stew. As she ate, she thought that the first thing on her list was to find a way to get the shackles off. You can't run with your legs bound together. She glanced up and Jose's gaze rested on her chest. Okay, she could use that. She reached into her pocket and felt the rough surface of the rock. But, if he didn't free her soon, she would try the rock on the shackles.

CHAPTER SIXTEEN THURSDAY THANKSGIVING DAY

Maggie gazed at her hands and closed them into fists. She clinched her jaw and sweat popped out on her forehead, so she pulled a rubber ball from the desk drawer and squeezed it as she turned to stare out of the substation window. Breathe in, one, two, three, four, exhale out, one, two, three, four. Her ear still felt warm from pushing the phone against it as the clipped words popped out of the ear piece and assaulted ear drum. Her boss never raised his voice, he didn't have to, he had the ability to make simple words spring out like daggers.

A squirrel scampered out of the underbrush and jumped onto the base of a gnarly ancient pine tree. There he froze and turned his tiny eyes toward the glass, then he jumped from his perch and disappeared in a flutter of leaves and pine needles.

Maggie chuckled. Her anger must be strong if it permeated the glass and hit the hapless squirrel in a wave. She pulled out her cell phone and called Elsa, but now she wore a smile.

"Hey"

"Hey, yourself"

"I'm just about to leave school. I had to grade some papers and make some lesson plans. What time are you getting home?"

Maggie frowned and said, "I just got a new case." She closed her eyes, took a breath and continued, "I have to stake out the casino parking lot, all night if necessary."

"What?"

"Apparently, someone has been vandalizing after hours and they need a babysitter—seems to be my specialty lately."

"What about Summer and Shelly? Don't they know you have your hands full?"

"It was made abundantly clear that it is not our case." Maggie sighed and said, "That's why I am on babysitting duty."

"What?" Elsa echoed her first question.

"It's never been our case, Elsa. It's not our jurisdiction and they aren't particularly happy that I stuck my nose in it."

"You're kidding me."

"No, I'm totally serious. It was implied that my services would better serve the tribe if I dealt with actual tribal problems on the Rez."

"Maggs, Jennifer said that you are Summer and Shelly's only real hope. The Noisy Water PD is getting nowhere fast." A pause, then a little breathless, "You're the one who found the car—what will become of that?"

"They turned it over to State forensics, but it doesn't look like they have found anything to connect with Felix."

"Yeah, and Ralph will get all the credit, and still not be able to do anything with it."

"I don't care who gets credit, I just want them found, and while they are still alive."

"I know, I know—they just don't realize there is nobody better then you at this. They need to let you keep investigating."

Maggie smiled and relaxed her shoulders. She said, "Don't worry. It doesn't mean I'll stop, it just has to be on my own time." She sighed and leaned back, "Elsa, we have to be discreet about this."

"I'm discreet."

Maggie laughed and leaned forward as she gazed out the window. The squirrel was back and had a cheek full of nuts as he dove under a pile of leaves. Maggie said, "Right, of course you are, but discreet also means you can't talk to anyone about this. Seriously, you can't."

"I won't."

"Good. But about tonight, I will most likely be gone all night. We can't have the vandals scaring the tourists away, now can we?"

"Oh, good grief! You know not that many tourists hang out at the casino this time of year. There are a lot more locals then out-of-towners, and no amount of graffiti will keep them from the slots and tables."

"I know, but it still has to be done."

"Baby, I'm sorry. Can I bring you something?"

"No, I'll grab a sandwich from the snack bar. Oh, don't forget, the cell reception is spotty out there, so I may not be able to check in before bed time."

"You shouldn't have gone in after you found the car, they should have given you the rest of the day off."

Maggie snorted, "Like that would happen—a reward for misbehavior?"

"How could they feel that way with the results you got? Oh, that's just ridiculous, they should be proud of you. I certainly am!"

"It's okay. I can take the heat. Even if it means I'm stuck with babysitting duty." Maggie lowered her voice slightly, "And, thanks, I love you too."

"Do you really think you will you be gone all night?"

"Probably, unless the little creeps come out early and I can take care of this and get home."

"Okay. Love you."

"And you."

∞

The teen ran around the barn, but kept to the shadows. Dusk had turned to dark, but she didn't use her flashlight. She crossed the yard at a slower pace as she watched for rocks and rough patches. It was cold and it felt like it was going to snow. She pulled her jacket close, and quickened her step as she risked a fall on the uneven ground.

She needed to get back to the house before she was missed. It was almost time to serve dinner, and it would be unthinkable for her to be late. She smiled. Mission accomplished. She could tell the kid's mom was a fighter, but she was smart, and would bide her time. They might be able to actually survive and get out of this hell hole.

As she reached the fork in the path that lead to the cemetery or house, she risked a moment to pause and gaze toward the white crosses at the bottom of the hill. They reflected the light from the moon and seemed to hover above the dark earth. "I love you, mom," she whispered, then turned and headed in the other direction toward the hacienda.

Her mom was not much older than her when she had her, but she had loved her new baby girl fiercely. She had also had a weakness for drugs, booze and men. When the last of her creeps turned his attention toward her child, she instructed him with a baseball bat not to mess with her daughter. Her mom forgave her own bruises, but not her daughter's. They left him in a bloody bed, and she didn't even know if the jerk was alive or dead. Really didn't care, either.

They lived in the car for a while on the streets of Albuquerque, then Felix appeared. He was full of praise and sympathy for her mother, and offered them a place to stay 'with his family.' Her mom fell hard. She lapped up his words and attention like a kitten at a milk bowl. It was a sealed deal when he asked if she wanted to 'toke one up' and then drink a toast with a good bottle of wine.

They abandoned their car and traveled with him all the way to Noisy Water and Felix's compound. As soon as they got out of the car, her mom was dragged off to the cave cell and she was christened Angel-2.

Four long years with Felix did nothing to dim the memory of her mother, or the day she died. It had been a clear, sunny morning. The air was crisp and cool; it was about this time of year. She had been eleven years old and held Angel-1's hand like a baby as Felix let her mother out of the cell. Her mother fought him like a wild beast. When she bloodied his face and arms with her nails, he turned her over to Jose. As the man held her mother, Felix put a bullet into her head. The blood looked dark, almost black instead of red as it pooled at their feet. Then Angel-1 led her away and they buried her mother on the hill. She knew which white cross was hers because she saw the fresh mound of dirt the next day as they went to feed the stock.

Her mother was never spoken of again. It wasn't long before Angel-1 was buried next to her mother. She suspected now that it was a relief for the girl who was gentle and kind.

On the day her mother was executed, she decided two very important things. One, she wanted to survive, and two, she would do whatever it took to see Felix suffer for what he did. But now her priorities had shifted. She was tired of simply surviving. Existing wasn't life, and revenge wasn't a reason to exist. She wanted to live, not to exist, but more than anything, Felix had to be stopped, not made to pay.

At the kitchen door, she was jolted back to the present as an arm flashed out of the shadows and shoved her against the wall. She hit the wall with enough force to knock the air out of her lungs. Her first thought was Felix, and she had been caught, but a protruding belly pressed against her, and the stale smell whiskey and cigar smoke assaulted her.

Billy.

Damn.

He must have seen her leave, and waited for her in the dark like the sneaky predator she knew him to be.

"Billy, leave me alone—you've been drinking."

"Now, now, little girl, I know you're used to this."

She felt his hand reach around to the small of her back and pull her even closer, "Felix won't like this, and you really don't want to piss him off."

"I can handle Felix, if you can handle me."

She tried to shift position, but the man was massive, "You're drunk. Come on, Billy. Don't do this, you aren't thinking straight."

"Felix thinks I'm on my way home." He bent and nuzzled her neck before he whispered, "He had some business, so I was excused from dinner. You have a pretty new pony in the barn. I know you like ponies." He nibbled at her ear lobe as he mumbled, "I can do a lot for you. I can take you places you've never even dreamed of, now wouldn't you like to get off this ranch? You could live a life of luxury. We can slip away right now, my truck is just up the hill. Felix will simply think you finally split."

As he attempted a wet kiss she bit down hard on his lip.

"Shit!" he screamed, "You little whore!" The blow from Billy's big fist drove her to the brink of unconsciousness and she crumpled to the ground. Her ears rang and her vision was blurred. His words seemed to come from a long way off as he said, "Don't you know what he has in store for you? You will be worm bate on the hill. I was trying to save you, bitch."

"What are you doing, Billy?" Felix's voice, but he seemed so far away.

She gazed up at them through a haze and she heard Billy say, "She friggin bit me, man! I'll teach her some manners." He screamed as he turned back and kicked her in the stomach.

She moaned and curled into a tight ball as darkness edged in on her vision, but she could hear a strange repetitive noise. Smack, squish, smack, squish.

She struggled and finally opened her eyes. A dark sky and intense pain in her head and abdomen. It was beginning to snow. Her eyes began to focus as the fat, white blobs hit her face. Her vision cleared and Billy's inert body was on the ground beside her and what was left of his head lay in a dark puddle in the dirt. Felix stood beside him and as her head moved up his body she saw a bloody brick in his hand. She scooted away, then managed to stand on shaky legs.

"What happened? Wh, wh, what did you do?"

"Go into the house and clean yourself up. You are a mess. I am going to see Billy out, then head into town to pick up some supplies," he said in a strange voice.

She stood frozen to the spot, "See him out?" She looked at Billy's mutilated head then back at Felix.

He smiled and said in a low, soft voice, "Go now. I'm not angry with you, and you won't be punished. Now, get to bed and I will join you shortly."

She hurried into the house to do as she was told. But as she ran she couldn't help but wonder if the blow to her head had finally sent her over the edge. That, or Felix was more bonkers then she ever imagined.

CHAPTER SEVENTEEN THURSDAY THANKSGIVING DAY

Elsa picked up a package of fresh spinach and tossed it into the basket. She turned toward the meat section as she glanced at her watch and sighed. She picked up a package of steaks and gazed at the bright red meat before she put them back and headed to the pasta isle. Some pasta with sauté spinach, mushrooms and garlic would make the house smell wonderful, and with the chill in the air she was craving comfort food. If Maggs made it home before bed time, she would have something delicious waiting for her, if not, it would keep until tomorrow night. A nice red wine and some good pasta would make getting home early more special for her partner and a nice solace for her if she spent the evening alone.

After she picked up the rest of the ingredients she remembered they needed light bulbs, so she turned to the hardware section. As she rounded the corner she stopped short. Felix Alvarez Lea was standing at the other end of the isle. She almost gasped and ran. What were the chances?

He was taller then she remembered. And hairier. He had a hand held grocery basket, and as she watched, he placed a roll of duct tape into it. She edged closer while pretending to study the labels of the light bulb packages. He glanced up, and she froze, but he turned his concentration back to the shelf. It was as if he didn't recognize her.

Odd. Very odd.

She edged even closer and gazed at the other items in his basket. Black plastic garbage bags. Extra-large size. She felt a chill. Oh, come on! This is just too much.

Elsa picked up the nearest light bulb package and noticed her hand was shaking. She began reading the disclaimer, but the words were a blur as she felt the pulse pound in her temples. She put the package in her basket and studied his clothes as she turned to pick up another package. Something was on his shirt. Dark burgundy stains. It looked like it could be rust, paint, or possibly blood? Crazy images popped in her mind and she had to shake her head slightly to clear them.

She said, "Late night shopping?" Then laughed, but her voice sounded high and brittle. The next words she said were rushed, "Me, too, never enough time in the day—guess that's why they stay open late, even on Thanksgiving."

He turned and studied her, but said nothing.

She quickly said, "Hi. I'm Elsa. My partner is Maggie Littlejohn. I think we met at the casino a couple of times?" She stuck out her hand, but Felix didn't return the gesture, so she dropped hers back at her side.

"I don't think so," he said, then walked away.

What? As soon as he was gone Elsa pulled out her phone and called Maggie. It went straight to voice mail. Damn. She put her hand over her mouth and waited for the beep, then spoke in a whisper, "Maggs, I'm at the grocery store. Guess who is here? Felix! Guess what he's buying? Duct tape and giant plastic garbage bags. I am not kidding. This is crazy! It's not just that, he has what looks like rust or paint stains on his shirt." She dropped her voice even more, "I swear I didn't imagine it. I don't think it's really rust stains, Maggs—I think its blood! What should I do?" She ended the call and headed down the aisle toward the checkout stand while straining to see where Felix had gone.

When she got to the front of the store he was in the ten items or less aisle, and he already had his cash out. She slid in behind him. He grabbed his bag and walked toward the door. He was out of the store before the clerk said, "Hi Miss Elsa. How are you?"

She turned to gaze out the front window. It was dark, but the lights in the parking lot reviled Felix as he was getting in his van. "Uh, fine," she glanced at the checkout girl who was a former student, "Uh, Britney, I'm kind of in a hurry, I want to meet Maggie in a few." She smiled.

"Sure, sure, I'll get you out of here mucho pronto! Besides, you need to get home before it starts sticking."

"What?"

"The snow—it's really coming down. You better head home quick, Miss Elsa."

She looked out the windows again. It was snowing and she could just see Felix's tail lights as he headed for the exit, "Oh, yeah, boy are you right, I better get going."

The girl finished and handed her a receipt, "Be careful out there."

"Thanks, you too." She grabbed her bags and got to her car just in time to see the van as it pulled out on the main road. She jumped into her car, started it up, and followed.

Elsa hesitated only a moment at the highway. She glanced at her phone, then turned her car away from the route that would take her home and toward the van's tail lights. "I got this, Maggs," she muttered as she turned the windshield wipers on high to keep the snow from accumulating. She hunched forward, focused only on the duel red dots ahead of her.

∞

Summer shuffled into the women's bunk room and headed for her assigned cot. The room was long and narrow with at least a dozen beds, but not all were occupied. Each bed had floor to ceiling curtains that surrounded it, but privacy was impossible.

She entered her cubicle and closed the curtain. The sounds of the women around her drifted through the thin cloth, but at least she felt the illusion of being alone.

A small utility table by the bed held a battery operated lamp, wash bowl and pitcher for water. The bowl contained a bar of soap and worn hand towel. She was too tired to get water for the pitcher, so she fell on the bed fully clothed, dirt and all. This was not a new experience for Summer. She spent many nights in the Middle Eastern desert the same way. Only it was desert dust that joined her on her cot, not field dirt. She turned on her side and closed her eyes, then flipped on her back and sighed. American dirt was just as gritty as foreign sand. Maybe it was worth the trip to the community bathroom.

"Sit up."

Her eyes flew open and she bolted upright. Jose. Her hand absently went to the pocket with the rock. He stood just inside her cubical and the curtain was closed behind him. She had not heard him enter and the cubicle suddenly felt very isolated.

"Put your feet on the floor, but stay seated."

She did what he told her to do and was suddenly wide awake as she watched him reach to his side and pull a set of keys from his belt. An elastic band kept the large bunch of keys still attached as they rattled in his hand. He reached for her shackles and she allowed herself a small smile when he wasn't looking.

After he removed the chains he rubbed her ankles with rough hands. "The iron can really do real damage to the skin," he said as he gazed slowly up her legs and body until his eyes rested on her face, "You are lucky you have behaved so well. You have earned a little more freedom." He squeezed her ankles and said, "No damage here, your skin is still soft—soft like velvet." His hand felt hot where it rested on her leg and his voice sounded course and oily.

She swallowed hard and held her legs still. "Thank you," she said as she shoved her hand deep into her pocket and squeezed the rock.

"Does that feel better?"

"Yes," she tried to focus her eyes down and to the side as he stood. He replaced the key bob and then slid his hand to his waist and started to unbuckle his belt. Her eyes darted to his face and he gazed down at her unsmiling as small beads of sweat popped up on his forehead.

Summer froze, shit, she thought as she gripped the rock tighter. Then a voice called from beyond the curtain, "Jose, I'm ready," a sing song voice that sounded like the girl who served their meal earlier in the day.

Jose froze and glanced over his shoulder, then back at Summer. "Another time, chica," he said as he bent, picked up the shackles, and slipped out through a crack in the curtains. The material swayed a moment after he was gone, then fell back into place.

Summer scooted up on the bed and moved her knees to her chin. She had a strong desire to rub her ankles where the shackles had rested, but she didn't want to touch where his touch had lingered. She shivered, jumped from the cot and grabbed the pitcher, before she headed for the community bathroom. A good scrubbing was in the cards after all.

As she left her cubicle, she could hear guttural sounds and moans from behind the curtain just across from hers. It must be where the kitchen girl slept. Great. Sleep would not come this night after all.

She glanced around the curtained hall. Plenty of empty cots, maybe she would 'accidently' slip into the wrong one on her return. She might get the shackles put back on, but at least she would be a little harder to find in the dark.

CHAPTER EIGHTEEN THURSDAY THANKSGIVING DAY

Elsa slowed the car to a crawl as she strained to see through the onslaught of white flakes. Felix's taillights had not been visible since the last turn, and the road was now a solid white. The wipers sounded loud and one of them squeaked each time it made its arc across the windshield. "Where are you?" she whispered.

She pulled to a stop and checked her dash, but the wipers were set at the highest speed. Still, the road ahead was barely visible. "This was a very bad idea. Colossal. Of all the bad ideas you've had, and you have had plenty, this is right up there. It could be the worst, ever in a lifetime of bad ideas," she shook her head and started to edge toward the side of the road to attempt a U-turn.

Just as she started her slow turn she glimpsed something ahead on the side of the road. She leaned forward, but couldn't see it clearly, so she rolled the window down and stuck her head out of the car. Was it the van? No lights or exhaust coming from it. It just looked like a big, dark bump at the side of the road. She eased her car forward and turned on her high beams. It was the van. The rear door was open, but it was too dark, and too far for her to see inside. It was parked on the shoulder and it appeared to be deserted.

"What tha?" she mumbled as she pulled farther onto the shoulder and eased forward. It was Felix's van, all right, but where was Felix?

As she got closer, she turned off her headlights and put the driver's window back up, but she kept the engine running, it was a frigid night and the snow was still falling. If he was in there, he would have seen the lights, but maybe he thought she passed him or turned around. Maybe the van broke down and he got out to walk to town. There was another possibility. Maybe he had spotted her and knew she had been following him. She glanced around, but only darkness surrounded her.

She eased the Subaru forward a little closer without turning on her lights, then put it in park again. As much as she strained, she still could not see into the van.

"Don't be stupid, Elsa," she said aloud as she picked up her cell phone. She hit Maggie's number, but still no answer, so she turned it off and put it back on the seat by her purse.

She gazed out of the front windshield once more. If he abandoned the van, Summer or Shelly could be restrained in the back. She glanced at her cell phone. Maybe she should call the Noisy Water police. She peered back at the open door, then released her seat belt. She should at least take a peek so she would know what she was reporting. She started to reach for the door handle, but stopped and pulled her hand back as she said, "Don't be so friggin stupid!" She grabbed her phone and punched in a text to Maggie: Don't be mad. Followed Felix. No sign of him but I think the girls could be in the van. I am calling the NWPD.

Pop! The driver's window exploded and tiny crystals rained over her. Elsa instinctively covered her eyes as she turned and dove to the side. She landed face down on the passenger seat, but felt a sting in the left side of her face from the glass. She started a text, but shoved her phone under the passenger seat as she heard the driver's door open and felt someone grab her legs. She tried to kick, but was dragged across the gear shift as she reached out to grab at something, anything. Her hands found the gear shift, but a mighty tug, and she was out of the car. A rush of cold air before she hit the pavement with a loud thump.

She blindly kicked until one of her boots slipped free of his grasp, so she kicked harder, and felt contact again and again until a sudden release. I'm free! She thought as she scrambled and crawled on the wet pavement trying to gain her balance and push herself up, but she felt a boot hard in her side. She gasped for air and curled into the fetal position.

She lay like that for a moment as she tried to catch her breath, but then she felt a foul smelling rag go over her mouth and nose and Felix's voice whisper, "Yes, I know who you are—you are an abomination to the Almighty."

She clawed at the hand and rag, but her breathing deepened and the world got fuzzy. She felt her hands twitch as they froze in place, then she watched the snow as big, wet flakes floated down and the world went black.

∞

Tyler zipped his jacket to the top and pulled the wool neck scarf up over his chin. The flurry of white was getting thicker, and there was a small hill of snow between his jeans crotch and the saddle horn. Jake's black and gray coat was almost solid white. He pulled up on the reins and glanced around. Jake paused, looked over his shoulder at him, and then shook the white blanket from his back. In moments it was white again.

Tyler shielded his eyes with his hand and scanned the surrounding area. There. An outcropping of trees was thick enough to keep a small area from gathering snow. It looked like a good place to shelter the horse and set up a camp.

"Sorry, Jake," he said. He should have done this an hour ago, but desire overruled logic.

He rode over and dismounted. Jake shook the new snow off his back again and headed under the trees where he plopped down and watched Tyler work. The dog looked happy, and Tyler could almost swear he was smiling, "Like this rugged stuff, don't ya?" The dog answered with a low bark and tail wag. "Damn, fool dog," he said with a smile.

He tethered the horse and removed his gear, then ran a brush over the animal's back. Satisfied, he covered the horse's back with a blanket before he moved on to the camp. He erected a simple lean-to, then he used a limb to clear away what snow had drifted in before he rolled out a blanket. He spread his sleeping bag on top of the blanket, then tugged off his boots and crawled inside fully clothed. He gave a sharp whistle. Jake jumped up and ran over, but Tyler said, "Hold on." The dog shook the snow off, then joined him in the sleeping bag. He was damp but still felt like a warm hot water bottle tucked up against his side.

Tyler set a LED lantern by their head and flicked it on, then pulled his pack close and reached in for some beef jerky, bread and water. Jake's head popped up and he started his food pant. "Yeah, all right," Tyler said as he held his palm out. Jake grabbed a beef jerky, then settled down while he lay chomping on the grizzled treat.

Tyler thought about a fire as he chewed, but they were a little too close to the compound, and the damp wood would smoke. Since they had made such good time, he hated to stop, but the gray day had turned into a black night, and snow covered the trail. It would make travel both slow, and treacherous. He couldn't chance a lame horse, or Jake hurt, or even worse, to stumble into a compound guard and set off an alert. He did not want them to see him coming. There would be no rescue if he were captured, killed, or even sent to jail for trespassing.

Tyler carefully unfolded his map and studied it under the lamp light. If his calculations were correct, they were on a ridge just above the valley compound. If he was lucky, the morning light would reveal the best way to get into the grounds without being noticed. They might even need to go the rest of the way on foot. He had made the right decision. As hard as it was to wait, he needed to scout before barging into the grounds.

He put the food away, then placed his pack behind him to use as a pillow. After he shook another blanket out over the sleeping bag, he turned off the lamp then wrapped the wool scarf around his head with just his eyes exposed. He slipped deeper inside the sleeping bag and zipped it up, leaving only enough room for Jake's nose and his head to be out of the bag. Their mutual body heat would help during the cold night.

Morning wouldn't come soon enough for him, but he would be patient. He could be a patient man when he needed to be. But come morning, nothing would keep him from searching every inch of that place. He would not leave until he was satisfied his girls weren't there, and had never been there. If he found any trace of them, Felix Alvarez Lea was his. Forget the law. So he settled back and soon Jake was snoring softly by his side. Morning would come soon enough.

CHAPTER NINETEEN THURSDAY THANKSGIVING DAY

Felix paused at the edge of the cemetery, dropped the rope, and picked up his shovel. He gazed at the snow covered hill. The little crosses were barely visible against the white backdrop. So many faces floated above each one. So many failures to reach perfection. Failures, but not evil like his burden tonight, "Hello All. I'm sorry to bring you someone so unworthy to rest with you."

He raised the flashlight and scanned the hill, then scraped away a spot of snow with the toe of his boot. He stabbed at the bare spot with the shovels sharp edge. The vibration radiated up his arm; It felt like hitting concrete.

He raised up and muttered, "No digging tonight, nope, nadda, no." He looked at the shovel in his hand and said, "I don't need this." He dropped the shovel and threw his hands in the air as he shouted, "My Father has shown his wisdom once again. You will not have this pond scum sharing your eternal home."

Felix picked up the rope attached to the sled and tugged until he was able to drag it along the snow covered path. The large mound wrapped in black plastic and bound with duct tape was all that remained of Billy, but the man was still giving him trouble, even in this lifeless form.

As he rounded the corner of the cave prison, he paused and smiled at the muffled cries drifting through the wooden door. The Abomination, "I know you are anxious, but you must wait for my attention. Contemplate your sins as you remain in purgatory. Your sins will be forgiven if you can make it through the purification. Be patient, you're time will come."

Mountains to the right, and forest to the left. A vision of trees and a snow covered mound flashed through his head. His Father was speaking to him again, "Forest it will be." So he moved in that direction.

When Felix reached the edge of the forest, he stopped, pulled out a knife, and bent to cut the duct tape that attached the body to the sled. He shoved the bundle with his boot and watched as it rolled down a slight incline until it came to rest against a tree. It landed face up, with Billy's big belly straining at the black plastic wrap, "You were a glutton, idolater, and fornicator. You will not rest in peace."

The snow began to cover the black plastic. Soon it would be invisible to the eye, but the animals would find the scent of rotting flesh intoxicating. That was fine with him, and all this empty meat bag deserved. Another abomination. His Father was pleased such an unworthy being was no longer breathing. He spit on the top of the mound, grabbed the sled rope, and headed for the hacienda.

Two weeks. That was all the time he had needed to get the crop in and make some more arrangements for his new life. A rebirth. It was a good plan, but he needed two more weeks, and unfortunately it was two weeks he no longer had. He would not question why it all fell apart. He was sure there was a reason his Father sent this sign to him.

He stopped and looked up at the dark night sky. A flurry of snow filled the air. The flakes swirled and twinkled like a million tiny stars.

"I am sorry, Father. I had a weak moment. I will not doubt you again. This is right. It is time. Your will, not mine," Felix smiled and laughed. His Father's voice was getting louder every day.

The crop was not to be.

The time was now.

It would be glorious.

∞

FRIDAY MORNING

Maggie pulled into the parking lot as the sun was coming up. She turned off the cruiser and gazed at the pink streaks in the sky. A blanket of snow covered the ground and clung to the pine trees. It was a peaceful setting until a loud burp followed by deep giggles erupted from the back seat. Maggie closed her eyes and counted to ten, then got out of the car. She held open the back door of the cruiser and said, "Get out."

Two hulking teen boys exited and walked unsteadily toward the building. She shut the car door and sighed, the truck reeked of booze and puke. It would take a lot of scrubbing to get their night of revelry out of her vehicle.

Stupid punk kids.

She followed the boys to the door, then led them into the building, and the holding cell. The stench clung to them like a cloud. They stood swaying as they waited for her to take off their cuffs. Once freed, they entered the cell without a word, and each claimed a corner. She could hear their collective snores before she was two feet from the cell.

They knew the drill. Being picked up for intoxication was not a new situation for them, but the charge of vandalism was, and their parents were going to be pissed when they saw the hefty fine. Maybe they would get community service since it was their first time. Maggie wished she could assign the punishment. It would be to clean her cruiser and the holding cell until they no longer stank of drunken teens.

She yawned and headed over to her message box. Several calls from her contact in the FBI. She found an empty desk and picked up the phone. Before she dialed, she glanced at the time, and decided it was too early to call, so she checked her e-mail. Pay dirt—the agent had sent her a message with an attachment. The reference line said Felix Alvarez.

She scanned the e-mail. It looked like Felix Alvarez had resided in El Paso in 1976 before he moved to Noisy Water. He was in the system because he was a counselor at a group home for kids. This Felix matched the general physical description she had put out, but hold on—there was a problem, this Felix died in a fire in 1976. What? This just keeps getting better and better. Maggie opened the attachment file.

The picture was of a young man with the same build and dark hair, but this man had a kind face and blue eyes. Maggie frowned—obviously not our Felix, but with almost the same name? Similar physical description? Almost the same age? Maggie frowned deeper; she didn't believe in coincidences.

She slumped forward and squinted as she scrolled through the rest of the information. This Felix was only twenty when a fire at the group home killed him. The fire not only took his life, but killed five of the residents.

He was an intern at the home while he was getting his degree in social work. The fire was of suspicious origin, but they couldn't pin down an arson case.

Maggie sat up a little straighter and used the computer's search engine to see if she could find more information. A newspaper article from the same year popped out at her and a chill went up her spine.

It was about a scandal at the group home. Only weeks before the fire one of the older boys was accused of molesting a twelve year old girl. Unfortunately, the girl was killed in the fire along with the others, so nothing came of the charges. The name of the boy was withheld since he was a minor.

Maggie glanced at the clock, then shrugged and called the El Paso Police. She got a sleepy desk sergeant on the line who passed her on to a detective. It took some time, but after she explained that they possibly had a dead man walking, and drew on some favors owed, he gave her the name of the 'boy' who would be in his early 50's now. His name was Kimo Huang Wong Lee. The detective refused to release the file, but finally relented to reading some of the information to her. The boy was of Hawaiian and Chinese decent and came from a particularly abusive family. The detective paused, then said, "Whoa, get this, his mother was burned to death by his father when he was a toddler, and the kid was a witness."

The rest of the details were equally gruesome. The father was a member of the Chinese mafia and the mom a Hawaiian prostitute. The kid was shuffled through several foster homes and then put into this group home. "He hasn't showed up in the system since then," the detective said, then paused.

Yeah, because he took the dead guy's name and landed right here in our lap.

Maggie thanked him and asked if he would fax her a photo of the kid. He reluctantly agreed, but said, "We never had this conversation."

When she pulled the paper out of the fax she smiled and said, "Hello, Felix."

Maggie faxed the photo to Chief Anderson along with a note and pertinent sections of the e-mail, then she called him and filled him in on the rest of her research. They agreed to meet in an hour.

As the morning shift started filing in the door, Maggie finished her paperwork and handed it off to them. They could deal with the snoring boys.

When Maggie pulled into her driveway, she parked the cruiser, then left the windows down as she headed up the drive. A hot shower was all she could think about.

At the house she paused and stared at the empty carport for a moment. It didn't register in her tired brain, but something felt wrong. Wait. It was much too early for Elsa to be headed to school. Did she tell me she had an early day? She frowned, then moved on past the empty slot.

The snow covered the weeds and muffled the early morning sounds. She stopped abruptly and turned to gaze at the driveway. There were no tire tracks. If Elsa left early, there would be tracks. She must have gotten home without her car. What happened to her car?

As Maggie headed to the door, all she could hear was her boots crunching on the fresh snow. The snow had begun early the night before, so even if someone dropped Elsa off there would be tracks. Her steps quickened.

Odd. Very odd.

The house felt empty and cold. She walked over and checked the thermostat. It was still set low, as if no one had been home. She called out, anyway, "Elsa? Got some news you won't believe." No answer. She headed straight for the bedroom.

The bed was still neatly made. It looked just like it did yesterday when she left for work. The window was cracked open and snow had drifted in onto the floor. She moved over and shut the window, then got a towel to mop up the rapidly melting snow. As she stood, her head spun around the room to look for signs of Elsa's presence, then she went to the closet and jerked open the door. She let out a breath she didn't realize she held when she saw all of Elsa's things hanging neatly on her side of the wardrobe. The smile she had allowed herself turned into a grimace. Where is she?

Maggie moved back into the living room, unsure of what to do next when she heard her phone chirp. She looked at it, the battery had died. She plugged it into the charger and when it came to life she checked the readout.

She grabbed the phone and checked the readout. A voice mail, four missed calls, and a text message from Elsa.

Maggie paled, then sat heavily on a barstool as she listened to Elsa's excited voice giving the description of the contents of Felix's basket. Her stomach contracted. She read the text message, checked the time of the call, pulled the phone from the socket, and ran for the cruiser while she punched in the police department's emergency number.

∞

A slight swerve of her rear tires made Maggie ease her foot off the accelerator, but in a moment, she increased the pressure again. Her pounding heart simply would not let her slow down.

Where is she? Please, please don't let this happen. Not Elsa, please not Elsa.

Maggie scanned the highway and shoulders, as she searched for the Subaru, or even the seedy van—anything—but there wasn't a single other vehicle on the snowy road. Then she saw something. She took her foot off the accelerator and tapped the brakes. The cruiser started into a skid, so she lifted her foot off the brake and let it right itself before she braked again, but a little easier this time. The cruiser slowed, then when she felt control return, she pulled it off the road and onto the shoulder. She swiped at her eyes as she stared straight ahead through the windshield.

Elsa's car. It was covered in snow. There was no exhaust smoke. The driver's door hung open and had a broken window. A pipe was laying on the ground in the middle of shattered window glass.

Maggie took a deep breath, then banged the steering wheel with both hands. She swiped at her tears and got out of the cruiser and walked closer. There was a disturbance in the snow from Elsa's car to an empty spot ahead of the car.

Struggle and drag marks?

No, no, no—

My fault, all my fault.

Her hand hovered over her weapon as she moved forward. It felt as if she were in a dream as she walked the distance to the abandoned vehicle. Her footfalls echoed in the deathly quiet of the snow covered road.

She approached on the passenger side of the car first and peered into both the front and back seat. Broken glass was scattered over the front seats and floor and the keys still dangled from the ignition. Elsa's purse was spilled onto the passenger side floor, and groceries filled the back seat.

Maggie moved around to the driver's side and popped the trunk. She moved to the rear of the car and hesitated only a moment before opening it.

Empty—Thank God!

Maggie turned in a circle and scanned the frozen landscape. No movement and no body size bumps in the snow. She swallowed hard and moved to where she could view the open driver's door and broken window.

The depressions in the snow did look like a struggle. Her eyes followed what appeared to be drag marks moving away from the struggle to a set of tire tracks in front of the Subaru. The tire tracks went from the shoulder, back onto the highway, and then disappeared in the distance on the road. They were headed in the same direction of Felix's compound.

Elsa—Gone—

Maggie walked back to the Subaru and climbed into it on the driver's side. Forensics could wait, she only wanted Elsa. She gazed at the empty passenger seat, then the purse contents scattered on the floor. No cell phone. She leaned gingerly over the seat and lifted Elsa's purse from the floor. She riffled through it, but her search still didn't produce the phone. She sat a moment then pulled out her own phone and tried calling it. A muffled ring and vibration came from the passenger side of the car. Maggie leaned over and felt under the seat until her hand located the vibrating phone. She pulled it up and keyed in Elsa's password. An unfinished text message appeared. It held a single word: Felix

Maggie leaned back in the seat as tears ran down her cheeks. The vision of Elsa on the ground struggling, then being subdued and dragged to Felix's van moved through her mind. Then she pictured her own cell phone left at home and Elsa's excited messages. My fault. Maggie gagged then bolted from the car. She found herself behind the cruiser retching in the ditch. She stood and wiped her mouth with the back of her hand. Her hands shook and her legs felt weak, but she took a deep breath, returned to the cruiser and sat heavily in the driver's seat, before she pulled out her cell phone.

She got his voice mail, so she cleared her throat and said, "Ralph, it's me, Maggie. I need you to come to mile marker 52. It's Elsa. Ralph, she's been taken. I won't be here when you get here, but you will find all the evidence you need. It's Felix. This time we know. Elsa left a text with his name on it before she was taken. I'll leave her phone on the driver's seat. I'm going in the back way and you better come in the front way as soon as you get this message."

CHAPTER TWENTY
FRIDAY

The bed was empty. Ahhh, no Felix. She closed her eyes and smiled, then bolted upright. No Felix. Oh, God—Billy? She gasped and jumped from the bed.

As her feet hit the floor she winced and almost doubled over from the pain. The teen shuffled into the bathroom and lifted her t-shirt. Huge bruises covered her from her hip to underarm. She grabbed a couple of Tylenol's from the medicine cabinet, downed them, then lifted her arms and eased off the t-shirt.

She splashed water on her face and leaned in close to the mirror and examined the black eye and swollen jaw. Billy. God, he had to be dead. His head looked like mush. She leaned over the sink and dry heaved, then splashed water over her face once more, and brushed her teeth.

Blue eyes streaked with red peered back at her from the flat mirror surface. "You can do this," she said, then threw on her dress and boots before she left the sanctuary of the empty bedroom. She didn't bother with makeup for the eye. It was too big to cover it anyway.

The sun was just peeping under the blinds, so she tiptoed into the hallway and made her way toward the kitchen. The house was quiet, but as she neared Felix's office, she heard muffled voices. In spite of the tremble in her legs, she plastered herself by the office door and strained to hear the conversation.

"Yes I know, Jose, but it looks like I am in need of a new partner. Billy just isn't working out."

Felix.

"Oh?"

"No, that relationship is over."

The teen rolled her eyes and clamped her hand over her mouth. Yeah, right. It's over since you took a brick to his head. She heard steps in the room and pressed her body even tighter against the wall. She held her breath for a moment, but when she heard a chair slide, she allowed herself to breathe again.

"Sit, Jose."

"Si, señor."

"How long have you been with me?"

"Seven years, señor ."

"And you have served me loyally during that time, Jose."

"Gracias, señor ."

"No, I thank you! Because of this, I have decided to give you a chance to become a larger part of my operation." A pause. "How would you like to become my, well, let's say junior partner?"

"I would be honored, Señor Lea."

"Good! Now, with the promotion you will have new responsibilities. Do you think you can handle some very special jobs, Jose?"

Right—Like he did when he held my mother as you put a bullet in her head?

"Si, absolutely, Señor Lea."

"Okay. We are going to shift some things, mainly our place of operations. I was thinking of South America, but since a big problem was just eliminated, I can now consider Mexico. What would you think about going to Mexico, Jose?"

She knew it! Felix's web browser never lied.

"Si, señor, Mexico was my home."

"Excellent!" Another pause. "You can return like a conquering hero—an El Jefe." Felix paused to take a breath before continuing with, "We will have to clean things up here first, Jose, are you up to the task?"

" Si, señor."

"Okay, listen to me carefully. Here is what we are going to do. I will take care of my family, and you will take care of the workers and the crop. I know this is the best crop we have ever had, but unfortunately we don't have the time or the manpower to harvest it."

"Señor?"

"I know, it sickens me to do this Jose, but the last thing you will need to do is burn the crop and the barn. You will have to do a good job of it—just like we practiced. Use the gas tanks to spread the accelerant, then torch everything."

"Si, señor."

"Pity I can't help you with that, I would like to see it done, but I have other obligations." Another pause and she thought she heard a deep sigh, but couldn't be sure which man made the sound. Then Felix's voice sounded again, "You will also need to take care of the workers, and that will come first, you know, before the fire." Silence, then, "I ask you again, Jose, are you up to it?"

The teen bit her tongue and moved her hand over her mouth. The monster was casually talking about mass murder as if it were nothing.

"Uh, si, señor." She heard Jose clear his throat, then he said, "But, Señor Lea, some of the workers are very well trained and could help us. They are also from Mexico, and would be happy to go with us."

"Jose, I will give you a little latitude because I just told you were promoted, but that doesn't mean you can offer suggestions. Is that understood?"

"Si, Señor Lea."

"I just want you to follow orders, is that clear?"

"Si, señor."

"Good. That was part of Billy's problem. He couldn't seem to stop that annoying habit." A pause, then she heard him continue with, "Now, where was I, oh, yes—you know where I keep the special stuff?"

"The cyanide?"

The teen took a quick breath but stayed in her position against the wall.

"We don't need to mention specifics, but, yes. You know how I showed you to measure it?"

"Si, señor."

"Use the orange juice, they won't taste it in the juice."

"All of them?"

"Of course."

"Si, señor."

"Jose, I know this is sudden, but it has to be done now. It is ordained."

She placed her hands on her knees and sucked air into her lungs. Oh, God, Oh, God, Oh, God.

"Now? This morning?"

"That's what I said. Right now."

"Si, señor."

"I trust you, Jose. You continue to earn my trust and good things will happen. You will be rewarded." A pause. "Now, you also know what happens when I no longer trust someone."

No shit.

"Si, Señor Lea. I will not let you down."

"Good!"

She jumped when she heard a clap, then a pause before Felix said, "I will gather my family here in the house and as soon as that's done, you take care of the workers and the crop."

She started to ease away from the wall when she heard Jose say, "What about the new lady?"

"The one I gave you for the fields?"

"Si, señor.

"She goes with the rest."

"Si, señor."

"Oh, and there is a new resident in the cave, but I will deal with her personally."

The teen pulled away from the wall and didn't stop moving until she entered the kitchen. Once there, she stood and stared at the coffee pot for a few minutes as she tried to still her wild thoughts and racing heart. What to do? It was all happening so fast. After years of waiting and surviving. All those people were going to die today.

She reached for the carafe, but her hand shook like she was a weak, very old woman. She stared at her hand. It was as if it belonged to someone else. She closed her eyes and tears streamed down her cheeks. What to do? What to do?

She tightened her grip on the carafe and filled it with water before she started the coffee brew cycle. As the comforting smell of coffee spread through the kitchen she gazed out the window at the barn.

My God, he gave the order to kill all those workers and the kid's mom. He only sounded sad about the stupid plants. What a madman. He was even crazier then she had imagined.

She glanced over her shoulder to make sure she was still alone, then pulled out a notepad and scribbled furiously. Satisfied, she shoved the note into her pocket, then looked out the window again. It was time to feed the animals, so she had an excuse to go to the barn.

She might not be able to save the workers, but she could give the kid's mom a heads up, and maybe even save herself and the kid. The hell with it.

She had pushed her luck for survival much too long. She knew this day would come from the moment she saw her mother die. She had dreamed of the day she would grow the stones enough to escape. Now that the day was here and she was terrified. Terrified and exhilarated.

It didn't matter. She would be the first one of his 'family' to wind up on the hill or a bunch of ashes in this house. Just maybe she could do some good before that happened. It was time to get the hell out, or die trying. She grabbed her coat and headed out the door without waking the kid.

∞

The sky went from black to gray. Tyler took a deep breath and exhaled a puff of smoke. It was very cold, but the snow had stopped. He lay motionless and listened, but the surrounding woods remained silent with the exception of a whiney and foot stomp from his restless horse.

Jake wiggled out of the sleeping bag, stretched, then stood at the edge of the lean-to as he gazed at the white landscape. Everything was white and frozen. The dog turned and looked at Tyler still wrapped in the sleeping bag, then scampered out into the white stuff. He sniffed and scooped up bits of snow with his black nose as he bounced through the drifts. Finally, he paused, lifted a leg and created some yellow snow.

Tyler chuckled, stretched and unzipped the sleeping bag. As soon as he stood, he felt the full impact of the frigid air. Winter had come early in the mountains. The skiers would be happy, but it might slow his plans for the day. He reached for his boots and jammed his feet into the cold shells. Tyler couldn't risk a fire, so he stomped in a circle and waved his arms in a circular motion. Jake returned to watch his gyrations, so he stopped and reached for his pack and the beef jerky. "The breakfast of champions," he said as he tossed Jake a piece then bit down on his strand of the foul smelling nourishment. As he munched, he took down the lean-to and packed up the camp.

The sun climbed in the gray sky and visibility was good, so he headed to the cliff edge and scanned the valley below. In the clear morning light he could see Felix's property in the distance, so he peered through his binoculars and studied the valley. He immediately spotted movement. It looked like farm workers, but not like any he had seen before. They all wore odd, loose fitted gray outfits, coarse brown coats, and combat boots. Like some kind of weird uniform or prison garb. He couldn't tell them apart. Hell, it was even hard to tell if they were men or women, except some had longer hair, and that didn't really mean anything gender-wise. Summer's bouncy, auburn ponytail, or Shelly's golden locks were not among them. He sighed. Did that make him feel relieved or disappointed? He honestly didn't know.

He needed to get closer. He turned the binoculars to examine the rugged terrain of the sides of the cliff, and tried to pick the best route to the valley below. Once he was satisfied it could be done, although it meant he would have to back track a little, he hurried to finish with the camp site.

When Tyler mounted his horse and whistled for Jake, the sound pierced the quiet morning. The snow both muffled and magnified sound. He would need to be careful when they reached the valley not to attract attention. He kept the horse reined in at a slow walk and Jake close by.

When they reached the valley floor there was a wider trail, almost like a snow covered one lane road. Tyler paused, but shrugged and followed it toward the compound.

When they were close to the ranch, Tyler stopped and dismounted. A fence and gate cut across the road, but it looked simple to climb, and there was a gap by the fence post that Jake could easily squeeze through. He gazed up at the surrounding trees and down at the fence posts. No visible cameras. He assumed the rugged terrain provided enough privacy for Felix's paranoia without a lot of fence maintenance. There were several 'No Trespassing' signs posted on it, though. It was obvious Felix didn't want anyone getting too close. He must be hiding something. Whatever it was, Tyler would soon find out.

Once the horse was tied to a sturdy limb that was just out of sight from the road, Tyler pulled his rifle from the saddle and approached the gate. Jake's head whipped in his direction. He nodded at the gap in the fence and the dog scooted through, then Tyler climbed over and landed in the snow with a soft thud.

Jake stared at him, so he held his hand flat and pushed downward toward his boot. The dog moved in tight to Tyler's side and kept pace with him as they edged forward. He loved to watch Jake work like this with the cattle, every muscle tense and rippling, but this time there was much more at stake than spooking a few cows.

When they were within sight of the barn Tyler stopped and used the binoculars to search the area. They were in an outcropping of trees, but once they left its protective cover, they would be out in the open.

Jake stopped with him, but held his head high as he sniffed at the air and whined. Tyler glanced at him then gave him a nod. The dog moved forward in a crouched motion and circled a snow covered mound. He sniffed at it, then sat and turned his gaze to Tyler as he emitted a whimper from deep in his throat. A chill ran down Tyler's spine.

Tyler moved toward the mound and brushed part of the snow off with his boot. Under the thin layer of snow, black plastic stood out against the stark white. He dropped to his knees and placed his rifle on the ground and his stomach plummeted. As he swept snow from the mound with both hands, a shape began to emerge. He swallowed hard and moved to what appeared to be the head area and swept it free of snow. The shape appeared too large to be either Summer or Shelly, but he still felt bile rise in his throat and his eyes stung.

A warning growl as Jake gazed behind him tore his attention from the plastic covered face. Tyler grabbed his rifle and spun around, but then lowered it immediately. Maggie Littlejohn eased forward with a raised a finger to her lips. He murmured to Jake, "It's okay, boy."

The dog quieted and Maggie moved in to gaze at the body, then whispered, "What are you doing here?"

Tyler shrugged, then whispered back, "Same as you, I recon."

They both turned to the body. The head was wrapped in plastic and secured with duct tape. Maggie frowned and dropped down beside Tyler as she pulled out a large hunting knife and deftly cut the wrappings from the head.

One side of a man's head was bashed in and covered with frozen blood and gook. The skin looked like blue marble. Tyler gagged, and he heard Maggie blow out a deep breath as she touched Tyler's shoulder and pointed behind them toward the trees. They rose in unison and headed for the shelter of the forest.

As soon as they were out of sight of the barn, she said in a low voice, "That's Billy Wade Smith, or at least it was."

"Did you see his head? Talk about over kill."

Maggie leaned in close and said, "Elsa is missing."

"What?"

"I was gone over night on a case at the Rez and couldn't get my cell messages. Long story, not important. This morning I got my messages from the night before and she said she was at the grocery store when she ran into Felix." Maggie's eyes narrowed as she said, "I found her car this morning. It was abandoned on the highway. Broken window and signs of a struggle. Her cell phone had an unfinished text to me that had a single word: Felix."

"Oh, Maggie, I am so sorry, but now we know." Tyler turned his gaze toward the compound and said, "They might all be there."

Maggie touched his arm and he brought his attention back to her as she murmured, "That's not all, I found evidence that Felix is most likely living under a false identity and was a suspect in some very serious previous crimes back in the late 70's and early 80's. Possible molestation of a younger child, and even murder and arson."

Tyler's hands became fists as he said through grinding teeth, "Does the Chief know?"

"I didn't wait for him at the scene, but I left him a phone message that I was on my way here. There has to be enough for Chief Anderson to get a search warrant and put together a raid. As soon as he has it, I'm sure he will come in through the front gate."

"You mean this madman has gotten away with crap since he was a kid and remained free to spread his evil?" He tensed as he growled, "Free to take our girls."

"I suspect he reinvented himself with the identity of the man he probably killed, but there is no proof of that, at least not yet." She shook her head and continued as she gazed toward the compound and said, "It doesn't matter now. I'm not waiting any longer." She looked back at Tyler and her eyes were hard black circles.

Tyler stood straight and gripped his rifle as he said, "Me either. How do you want to do this?"

"I know you are a civilian, and I shouldn't allow you to be involved, but right now, I'm just a civilian also, and we both have missing loved ones who are in immediate danger."

"We're on the same page then."

"Why don't you check the barn and I'll check the house." She pointed at his rifle, "I assume you know how to use that?"

"Yep."

She handed him a two way radio and showed him the talk button before she said, "Then do it, but stay safe and make some noise if you need me."

"Sounds like a plan."

They bumped gloved hands and started up the valley side by side.

CHAPTER TWENTY-ONE
FRIDAY

Summer almost missed the low whistle. She was deep in thought, but she paused and looked up as she listened. The second whistle was a little louder and more distinct. It came from the stable area. The area was strictly off limits for the workers, but as she turned toward the sound, she spotted the teen girl in one of the stalls. As soon as the girl caught Summer's eye, she tossed a wadded piece of paper over the top of the stall and it rolled to a stop at Summer's foot. When she looked up, the girl was gone and she was alone in the hallway. She scooped up the paper and kept walking.

Just before she got to the outside door, Summer pretended to bend and tie the lace on one of her boots. As she knelt on one knee, she unfolded the note, and read the scribbled words.

Don't drink the orange juice at breakfast it's poisoned! I think their plan is to clean house and take only your kid to Mexico. I heard them talking about killing everyone and it's happening today! I'm going to take her and make a run for it if I can. I'll do my best to keep her safe. We'll head east into the forest. If you can get away, follow us. We'll wait for you at a gorge on the other side of the forest as long as we can, then we'll cross it and head into the Reservation land. Good luck.

Summer's hand shook as she stuffed the paper into her boot. She would keep this one until she had time to read it again. It was too crazy to be believed. Why would they kill all the workers? They had to have someone bring in the huge crop. She shook her head and rose. Some workers passed as they gave her curious glances. She lowered her head and followed them to the outside communal picnic table.

It was freezing cold and the ground was blanketed with snow, but there they were; huddled around the picnic table. No one questioned why they were outside when there was a place to eat in doors. At least an awning and the netting kept the table clear of snow, but what kind of madness had them outside in the frigid weather for a breakfast picnic?

She noticed some of the other workers glance at each other and then at Jose. There—one of them shrugged his shoulders at another. So this was different. Nothing about this place was sane, but this seemed very out of place, even for here. Summer felt her body break out in a sweat in spite of the cold. But poison? She edged into her place at the end of the bench next to the toothless old woman, then lowered her head and stared at her hands.

A plop of oatmeal appeared in the bowl in front of her, so she looked up. The same young serving girl doled it out from a steaming pot. As she worked, the girl repeatedly glanced at Jose, but he ignored her. When her serving bowl was empty, the girl stopped and glared directly at Summer, then turned and swished back to the barn.

Summer's mouth fell open. The girl was actually jealous of that creep. She almost burst out laughing, but stifled it. This was not a good time to draw attention to herself with nervous laughter. She sobered as another thought popped into her head. Could the oatmeal be poisoned? The note said orange juice, but there was no orange juice.

Summer had not been able to see the teenage girl's face clearly in the dim light of the barn, but it appeared to be badly bruised and swollen. What had happened? She tensed. Had Shelly been hurt? She couldn't contain a low moan and the toothless woman turned to glare at her.

Jose's voice switched the attention from her as he said in a booming voice, "A treat this morning, my people. The Master is pleased with the crop, so he has provided fresh orange juice to celebrate!"

Oh, God.

Should she shout a warning and get shot in the process? She glanced at Jose's hand as it rested on the gun at his side. A large caliber weapon. She was certain he could take her down before she got the words out. But she couldn't just sit there and do nothing.

Summer felt a chill run up her spine and she gagged. She managed to turn the gag into a cough, then join the others in the cheer that rang out. Her ears rang and time slowed.

The serving girl returned and handed Jose a large pitcher of orange juice. She turned and scurried back toward the barn as Jose began to pour generous portions into each glass. As he poured he said, "Drink up! Enjoy!" The cheerful words challenged his grim demeanor. She watched in horror as the workers began to gulp the juice.

Summer wanted to shout at all of them to stop, but she sat frozen in her seat, unable to speak. She stared at the glass in front of her unsure what to do next. Make a run for it? She knew she wouldn't get far. A bullet from Jose's gun would find her back before she reached the yard. Her baby would never get to have its first cry.

The fat man who sat across from her drained his glass and eyed hers. She shook her head at him, but he grabbed her full glass and shoved his empty one in front of her. She glanced at Jose, but he was busy at the other end of the table.

The fat man emptied the second glass, slammed it down on the table, and grinned at her. She stared at him as his smile vanished and he grabbed his stomach, then he lurched from the table. The sight delivered a momentary quiver of guilt, but she rubbed the small bump in her tummy and it was gone.

All of the workers began the same horrific pantomime. Some dropped hard to the ground, while others began retching before they fell down. Summer's morning sickness hit in full force. She didn't have to pretend as she held her abdomen and joined the others as they retched and moaned.

She stumbled away from the table and found a place in the snow close to the barn. She lay down and covered her face with one arm. As she shivered with cold and fear, she peeked out from under her arm to look for Jose, but instead she saw the serving girl. She carried a small knapsack and was dressed for travel.

The girl dropped her knapsack when she saw the horrific scene around the table and tried to throw her arms around Jose. He pushed her away and shouted something in Spanish at her as he pointed toward the main house. Summer got a full view of the girl's face—sheer terror. She recoiled from Jose, grabbed the knapsack, and headed for the back of the tent at a dead run.

Jose moved among the crumpled workers as he checked a couple for pulses. Summer gripped the rock still in her pocket, but he stopped and stood very still as he stared at the bodies strewn around the table. It was quiet except for an occasional moan. The workers all appeared to be either dead or dying.

Jose made the sign of the cross, then he headed over to the old woman who was sprawled close to the table. She was on her back and her face was turned toward Summer. Her eyes were wide open, but without sight. He felt the woman's wrist, then stood and mumbled, "Soy lo siento mujer vieja." He bent and covered her face with a napkin. From Summer's small understanding of Spanish, she knew he must have respected this old woman, but not enough to save her life.

Jose turned and headed toward the barn. Summer kept her place and tried not to move, although every fiber of her being told her to run. Not yet. Moments later he returned with a large metal tank attached to his back. He moved past the bodies and through the field of plants where he started to spray the plants.

The smell was strong. Gas. It burned at Summer's nose and teased at her delicate tummy, but there was nothing left in her to expel.

When Jose reached the farthest end of the row, Summer scooted on hands and knees out of the tent and toward the barn. As soon as she rounded the corner, she stood and ran to the cover of the outside corrals.

As she ran, her head darted back and forth. Where were the girls? Had they made it out? Oh, God, please let them be safe.

Nothing moved in the yard, so she continued until she was around the corner and at the back of the barn. There she hesitated. Behind the barn was a large flat pasture filled with snow and bordered by forest. The note had said head east, but should she check the house first? Had they already left, or were they restrained in the house?

She scanned the horizon as she strained to see any movement. There! Two small figures. They were at the very back of the pasture and were headed into the thick forest.

She was about to follow, but sensed movement, so she plastered herself against the barn wall. The corral fence gave her some cover, but if whoever it was looked in her direction, she would be easy to spot. It was only a shadow at first, but then she could see him clearly. Felix.

He paused, knelt, and examined the prints in the snow. He stood and stared across the pasture, his focus solely on his prey. Summer wanted to burst forward and tackle him, but a reality check made her stop. She needed something better than the rock in her pocket, especially if he called to Jose. Felix headed across the pasture.

Summer started to follow, hesitated, then headed back around the barn and slipped inside. Once inside the barn, she whirled around in a circle as she scanned the walls and horse stalls. There were some farm tools attached to the wall by the horse stalls. She scanned the tools, but most were harmless. Think, Summer—think! The only one she could find of any weight was a pitch fork. It was the one the girl used that morning to clean the stall. It had probably been only an hour ago, but it seemed like a lifetime.

"This will have to do," she said as she grabbed it and ran from the barn. No sign of the girls and Felix was already at the edge of the woods, so she ran after them as she held the pitch fork in both hands.

∞

Shelly glanced over her shoulder as they ran. She wasn't sure who she searched for more, her mother or Felix? Every time she slowed her step, the older girl would yank her forward, and each time she slipped on the snow, the girl pulled her even harder.

"Ouch! Hey, slow down," she said.

"We can't."

"Please, I don't want to leave my mom."

"You don't have a choice." The teen paused at the forest edge, then jumped over a downed limb, and pulled Shelly into the dense grove of trees.

"Why can't we find her and bring her with us?"

"She is going to meet us."

"What? You talked to her?"

"Sort of."

"What does that mean?"

The older girl stopped in the grove and turned toward the compound. She gazed over Shelly's head. Both girls were out of breath and Shelly could feel her heart pound. She looked in the same direction as the teen. The barn was barely visible through the trees, but a shadow moved around the barn, bent to the ground, then rose and came in their direction.

"Hey, is that my mom?"

The older girl squinted, gasped, and then turned back toward the center of the forest. She grabbed Shelly's hand even tighter and said, "Run!"

CHAPTER TWENTY-TWO
FRIDAY

Small white crosses dotted the snow covered hillside. Not an unusual sight on a ranch of this age, but this graveyard sent chills up Maggie's spine. She moved closer and examined the crosses. Each one was painted a brilliant white and had a single date etched on it in black. No names or date of birth, and the dates were all within the last fifteen years. This was a cemetery that honored death, not the life before death had visited.

As she studied the crosses, she heard something. She cocked her head and listened—there it was again—a low voice. She couldn't make out words, just the muted sound.

She turned in a complete circle. No one was around, but the sound continued. It was muffled, like it came through a wall, or from the ground. She looked at the snowy ground, shook her head, and then gazed up the hill. Where?

Maggie frowned, then felt her body tighten, and she broke out in a sweat. The graves? She rushed through the graveyard as she checked each cross for today's date. "Is someone there?" she shouted, then she stopped her movement. She stood very still as she closed her eyes and took a deep breath, then her eyes flew open. It was coming from somewhere to her left and it was a voice. She eased toward the sound; it was weak, but she could almost make out the words. It was coming from behind the cemetery, so she raised her rifle higher and followed the path around the hill beyond the graveyard. The muted voice turned into a banging sound, and it got louder as she moved forward. A moment of silence, then the banging turned into another muffled cry.

When she rounded the corner of the hill, there was a disturbance in the snow. She looked beyond it and saw a small padlocked door recessed into the hill. She bent and examined the lock, but it was too strong to kick or knock loose. She could try to shoot it, but that would alert everyone at the house and barn, and it probably only worked in the movies. Then the stench hit her. It was the smell of something rotting, but it was combined with something slightly sweet, Lilacs? Oh, God.

Maggie dropped to her knees. "Elsa?" she called through the door. The pounding stopped. She called out again, "Elsa, is that you?"

Muffled reply, "Maggs?"

Maggie pressed against the door, "Oh, my God, Elsa?"

"I'm here—I'm here! I knew you would come!"

Maggie yanked at the lock and shook the door. She stopped and said, "Are you all right?"

"Yes, sort of. I need out of here; right now, Maggs! I can't breathe in here."

"Hang on, I'm here." Maggie leaned back and examined the door hinges and lock again before she said, "I have to get something to open this lock—I'll be right back."

"Noooooo. Don't leave me! It's pitch black in here and it smells awful!"

"I have to, Baby. I won't be gone long, but I have to get something to get this lock off. I promise I won't be long."

"No!"

Maggie rose and ran toward the barn with her rifle gripped at her side and her finger on the trigger. "Damn you, Felix. You are a dead man," she said through clinched teeth.

∞

Tyler paused by the outside corral of the big barn. He held his rifle tight to his side, but no one was around. None of the workers were in the yard, although he saw them milling around earlier through the binoculars. He gazed up at the main house, no movement there, either. Strange. Where were they? Some kind of mid-morning siesta?

He gazed at the path to the main house but didn't see Maggie. She should be there by now. She took the left fork in the trail at the mouth of the valley property, but she had plenty of time to check it out and get to the main house. Still, no sign of her either.

Tyler turned his attention toward the barn. The doors were closed, but there were a couple of horses that paced in the outside corrals. Fresh hay was spread for them, but they ignored it, and they seemed agitated. He reached through the fence to a small paint pony, but the animal skidded sideways. The pony flung his nose in the air as his nostrils flared and his eyes were wild. "Easy boy," Tyler said softly.

Jake was by his side, but moved over to sniff some tracks by the corral, then he ran in a couple of tight circles before he sat in front of Tyler and quivered all over.

"What is it?" The dog chortled deep in his throat and gazed at the side of the barn and pasture beyond where the tracks led. "Later,

Jake. First we have to check inside the barn."

Tyler stayed close to the corrals as he moved to the barn door. He turned and Jake was still rooted to the same spot. "Jake," he said in a terse whisper, "leave it!" The dog rose and joined him, but his head and tail were down.

Tyler eased the barn door open and peeked inside. Very quiet. Tyler's rifle lead the way into the dim barn. The only light came from a dusty window high above the barn door.

As he entered he was greeted with the familiar sounds and smells of livestock, but there were no human sounds. He gave the stalls a cursory check, then moved on until he reached a long hallway.

"Ahhhhh—this must be where the humans hang out," Tyler whispered as the floor switched from dirt to wood planks. Jake glanced up at him and gave a low, guttural "Oooph" in response.

They were now in a long, wide hallway. It was well lit with a string of fluorescent lights. The sides were lined with a number of closed doors and there was a big double door at the end that faced them.

He moved along the hall and opened each door, but the dormitories, communal bathroom, and what looked like a dining area, were all empty and the whole place felt deserted.

"What the hell kind of barn is this?" Tyler mumbled as he gazed into one of the dorm rooms. He shut the door and moved on, conscious of the sound his boots made on the hardwood floor. It didn't seem to make any difference. No one appeared to check out the noise.

At the end of the hallway was the most intriguing door of all. It wasn't a double door after all, but one massive steel door that hung in a metal frame. There was a padlock, but it was unlocked, so he removed it and pushed the door open.

He entered a vast room. Tyler gazed around in amazement. Heat lamps were spaced along rows of multi-pronged iron hooks that hung from the high ceiling, they trailed almost to the dirt floor. Dried, dead vines twisted around a few of them, and smoke machines lined the floor. These weren't like any farm implements Tyler had seen before. What was the room used for? Tobacco?

Jake sniffed at the air, then whined and headed for the door. He sat and continued to whine low in his throat, but didn't leave the room without Tyler.

"What is wrong with you, Jake?" Not much spooked that dog. Tyler had seen him take on a 3,000 pound bull and dance through a horse's legs without hesitation, but today he seemed nervous as a filly about to give birth. "It's okay, Jake. Let's get out of this crazy place and find our girls. They sure aren't here."

Jake scurried in front of him as they backtracked down the hallway toward the front of the barn. The hall was still quiet, but once they reached the horses in the inside stalls, all hell was breaking loose. The animals kicked at the gates of their stalls and the walls, and a big bay reared when Tyler walked by him. "Easy, easy," Tyler called.

Jake reached the outside door long before Tyler and began to scratch at the door and ground as if he could dig through it.

"What is going on with these animals?" Tyler said, but as he got closer to Jake, the smell hit him. Fire. He pushed the barn door open and Jake rushed out as smoke rushed in. The dog stood poised to run, but held his ground and barked at the smoke. "Jake, be still." But he continued to bark in the direction the smoke.

Tyler followed Jake's line of sight and saw flames shooting up toward the sky as a thick cloud of smoke engulfed the side of the barn. The fire was coming from the giant tent made of netting. He wasn't sure how the tent was used, but it could contain horses, or worse, the workers.

Tyler ran in that direction, and as he rounded the corner of the barn, time seemed to slow down. The first thing he noticed was a man who stood watching the fire as it ate long rows of plants and lapped at the netting. The smoke filled air had a strong sweet smell mixed with gas fumes that made Tyler's stomach churn.

About a foot from where the man stood was a picnic table. Scattered around the table were bodies. Lots of bodies. A couple of people still sat at the table with their upper bodies sprawled across the top. There were both men and women all dressed in the same odd uniforms. The workers he saw from the cliff. Obviously dead. All dead.

"No!" Tyler shouted.

As soon the words were out of his mouth, the man turned and surged at him. Tyler went for his rifle, but before he could raise it, the man swung a metal tank at Tyler's head. Tyler ducked, but the bottom of the tank caught his shoulder and sent him sailing.

On the ground, he struggled to rise as the man advanced with a gun pointed toward him. Tyler reached blindly for his rifle, but it was just out of reach, then he saw a blur of fur rocket through the air and land squarely on the man's chest. Tyler made it off the ground, grabbed his rifle, and moved toward them, but Jake was a flurry of movement as blood flew from the man's neck. The gun in the man's right hand fired wildly until Tyler managed to step on his wrist.

"Hold, Jake!" He said.

The dog backed off immediately, but remained poised, just inches from the guy's throat. The man grabbed at the wound on his neck and struggled to speak. His eyes bulged and his shirt was drenched in blood.

Tyler stood above him and examined the wound. The bleeding had slowed to a trickle. The bites were ragged and nasty, but not too deep. Jake chose to stop the man, not kill him.

"Keep that dog away from me!" The man finally managed to whisper, "Es un perro del Diablo!"

Tyler laughed. Fluent in Spanish, thanks to his childhood best friend, he understood every word, "He's not a devil dog or he would have your throat in his mouth, and you would be dead." Tyler turned to Jake, "Watch him." Then he took his foot off the man's wrist and picked up his gun and tucked it in his belt.

The fire had picked up momentum and moved toward the bodies at an alarming rate. It seemed to gobble up everything in its path. Tyler headed to the bodies and checked each one. They were mostly male. No Summer or Shelly. "Thank you, God," he whispered.

He headed back to the man and pointed his rifle at his head.

"Where are my wife and child?"

"No, please, who do you mean? I don't know your familia."

He pushed the rifle closer, "NOW—where are they? I know you work for that crazy man, Felix, and I know he took them."

"Please, señor. I do not know who you mean."

Tyler pulled the rifle back slightly and said, "Maybe I will let Jake here have you." He turned toward the dog, "You'd like that wouldn't you boy?" Jake thumped his tail.

"No, no, please. Uh, do you mean the blonde girl and the new woman? The little brunette? I did nothing to them. The girl was with the master and his daughter, they stay in the main house. I have no contact with them."

"What about the woman?"

"I don't know, I don't know!" he said but turned his head toward the netting closest to the barn.

Tyler moved over and looked at the spot. There was a slight depression in the snow and a place where someone had gotten sick.

Tracks lead from the spot to the barn. Small feet—just like Summer's.

He moved back to the man still prone on the ground and raised his rifle again and said, "Where are they now?"

"I do not know."

Tyler nodded toward Jake but didn't take his eyes off the man, "He won't take long to tear your throat out, but you won't die right away, because I will call him off and have him take his time —now, again—where?"

"Señor, I swear, I don't know. I was supposed to take care of this—just the workers only, and burn everything, then meet the master in Mexico. He said he would take care of his family. The brown-headed woman was there—where you looked, but now she is gone."

"His family? My family! They are my family!" Tyler shouted at him.

"I didn't hurt the child. I wouldn't, I promise."

"But you would kill your own people." Tyler gazed at the carnage, "How could you do that? These workers were probably just trying to make a living and survive a rotten life, and you killed them all? And for what? Some insane man's orders?" The man started to cry and pray in Spanish.

Tyler stepped back and gazed at the side of the barn with the corrals. He needed to let the horses out before the fire got worse. And the bodies—what should he do about these bodies? Then he remembered the tracks. There were more tracks by the outside corrals. Jake was very excited about those tracks. Maybe Summer had made it out. Maybe, just maybe. He gazed up at the sky and whispered, "Please."

CHAPTER TWENTY-THREE FRIDAY

"Ouch!" Shelly said as she tripped on a branch hidden by the snow. There was just enough of the white stuff to disguise the tangled roots and rocks, but not enough to cushion them.

"Come on, we're almost there," the older teen said.

Shelly glanced up. Sunlight. They both quickened their pace toward the bright arch at the end of the forest path. As they broke free of the trees, a flat field of snow stretched out in front of them. They stood for a moment and caught their breath. The forest was brutal, but it offered cover, and the open field promised total exposure.

"Where do we go now?"

"There," the older teen pointed to a cliff edge on the other side of the field.

Another dense forest beckoned on the other side of the field and gorge, but Shelly couldn't see a bridge, or another way to cross the chasm. "That's a cliff, and it looks like a ravine, but how do we get to the other side? I've never done rock climbing if that's what you're thinking."

"Come on, I'll show you." The teen girl grabbed Shelly's hand and pulled her forward, "Come on! We have to go, Felix is probably right behind us. Please, you have to trust me."

Shelly grimaced and pulled her hand free, but kept pace with the older girl and said, "What makes you so sure he'll follow us? He doesn't know where we are."

"I saw him at the barn just as we entered the forest. He'll know where we're going because he's the one who showed me this place. Don't underestimate him. He won't give up, because he never gives up. Believe me, I know what I'm talking about. The man is completely obsessed when he gets focused on someone. Right now that someone is you. So come on—we don't have time to waste."

"Me?" Shelly shivered, but let the older girl lead her straight for what appeared to be a dead end. The teen had protected and guided her, and she took a blow from Felix for her, so she had to place her trust in her now. "Why me?" she mumbled, but the older girl didn't acknowledge the question.

As they reached the other side of the field, the teen slowed, then stopped at the edge of the cliff. They both peered over the side and Shelly gasped at the steep drop into the gulch below.

Jagged, snow covered rocks gave way to a thin ribbon of a mountain stream. At the bottom of the gulch, a mangled truck with an attached trailer lay on its side across the stream. The metal of the trailer was twisted, and the truck was bashed in on its side. It must have sailed off the cliff and rolled several times to end up where it rested. The wreck was covered in snow, but Shelly could still see that the driver's window was broken, and what appeared to be blood on the jagged glass and driver's door. There was a lot of blood but no body.

"Wonder what happened?" Shelly said.

"You don't want to know." The girl shook her head and looked at Shelly as she continued, "More of Felix's handiwork."

"What?"

"Never mind, it's a long story and we don't have time for it now, so let's put all our energy in getting out of here safely, okay?"

"Uh, okay."

A rope was tethered to an iron hook just below the cliff's edge. Shelly followed it visually as it stretched across the chasm to a hook on the other side. Small rope ladders hung on both sides from the cliff edge to a few feet below where the rope was anchored. Shelly gulped in air, "We're crossing on that?"

"Yep," the teen girl said, then put her hand on Shelly's shoulder, "I know it's scary, but not as scary as Felix."

Shelly managed a shaky laugh and said, "You're right about that, but still, is this the only way? Isn't there somewhere farther down the canyon that's an easier crossing?"

"Look, kid, it's the fastest way to get away from Felix. If we can get across and cut the rope behind us, it will take him longer to catch up. You want to live to see your mom again?"

"Of course," she sighed, then placed her hands on her hips and said, "Wait. Won't that cut my mom off too?"

The older girl rubbed her hand over her face, "Maybe, but maybe your mom went the other way to get help, and will be waiting for us with the police on the other side. Besides, she would want you to be safe and this is what we have to do right now to stay alive." The girl sat and looked up at Shelly, "We need to keep going as fast as possible." She looked down at the rope, then turned back to Shelly and grinned, "Come on, it will be fun—like a zip line. Tourists pay big bucks for stuff like this."

Shelly examined the rope. It had a handle hanging from the end that was attached to a pulley and tethered to the hook. Very crude, but it might work, "I don't like leaving without my mom, but you've protected me and I do trust you." She gazed at the rope and shifted her weight from one foot to another, "I can't say it looks like fun, or a real zip line, but I'll do what you tell me."

The girl frowned, "That's good, but trust your own instincts, and right now, they should be screaming for you to get as far from Felix as possible."

Shelly smiled for the first time in what felt like days, "Okay, you're right, let's do this."

"That's the spirit," the older girl said. She sat on the cliff edge with her legs dangling. She reached down and pulled up the rope handles and shoved her wrists through the two loops and gripped the tops, then turned to Shelly and said, "Let's go together. Our combined weight is less than when I saw Felix cross it, and it will be faster."

Shelly blew out a breath and blurted, "Yes, that sounds good. Together." She dropped to the ground just behind the older girl and wrapped her legs around her waist and her arms tightly around her neck, plastering herself close into the teen's back. She felt the older girl inch forward and she could feel the dampness from the snow seeping through her dress. Just as they reached the edge, she heard Felix's voice from a distance as he shouted, "Stop! Don't you dare!"

Shelly glanced over her shoulder and saw Felix running towards them from the woods. "Go!" she yelled as the teen shoved hard with her legs. They fell freely until the rope went taunt and then they began to fly across the chasm. She flattened her head against the older girl's back, not daring to look down or back.

The wind roared and blocked out all other sound. Shelly tried to raise her head and stare straight ahead, but her eyes began to water and her vision blurred. She didn't dare loosen her grip to wipe her eyes. She heard the teen moan and she glanced up; the rope loop was cutting deeply into her hands and wrists, but she held tight.

The cliff wall appeared to race at them at a tremendous speed. Shelly gasped and braced herself for impact, but just as they were about to slam into the wall, the teen pushed her legs out in front of them with her feet raised. The collision almost knocked Shelly loose, but she managed to hold on as she heard a yelp from the teen girl.

"See if you can climb up," the girl said through clenched teeth.

Shelly glanced down at the sheer drop and froze, then she took a deep breath and reached a shaky hand toward the rope ladder. She managed to grab it on her second attempt, then somehow pulled herself over the teen and scrambled up. At the top, she turned and lay as flat as she could on the cliff as she tried to catch her breath.

From her perch, she could see Felix on the other side. He was at the cliff edge and was screaming at them. She gasped as he pulled out a gun and pointed it toward them. "No!" Shelly shouted.

The older girl had her feet and one hand on the ladder, but still struggled to get her other hand free. It was hopelessly tangled in the handle. Shelly reached down to help her as a bullet thudded into the side of the cliff about a foot from them.

"Hurry!" Shelly screamed.

The girl pulled out a pocket knife and cut the loop holding her wrist, then scrambled up and over the side of the cliff as another bullet hit right beside her.

A barrage of bullets flew through the air. It sounded like hard rain as they hit the snow and dirt all around them. The girls scooted across the snow on their bellies and took refuge behind a large rock a few feet from the edge. The bullets stopped for a moment as Felix screamed something unintelligible, and then another onslaught began.

Shelly trembled, terrified of the sounds, but even more afraid to hear it stop. Silence could mean he was crossing the ravine. "We have to go," she whispered.

"Don't worry, if he hit us at this distance it would just be dumb luck. Felix is a terrible shot." The teen grimaced, "He needs to be at close range to do his worst." The older girl turned and scanned the woods behind them, then looked back at Shelly as she said, "We are going to get out of this."

"He is really pissed."

"Yeah, he is, and when Felix gets mad bad things happen, so let's get the hell out of here." The teen crouched and prepared to run, then said, "Wait." She pulled out the knife, "I can't believe I almost forgot." She started to crawl around the edge of the rock toward the cliff.

"No, don't try it, please."

The girl put a single finger to her lips, then said, "We have no choice." She turned and crawled away until she disappeared around the rock.

Silence. Oh, God, Oh God. Shelly cowered against the rock with her eyes glued on the forest escape route. The silence was broken by another barrage of bullets and insane screams from Felix. Shelly squeezed her eyes closed and mumbled, "Please, please…".

Silence again, then a rustle. She felt the weight of the teen as she flopped beside her. Shelly's eyes flew open and she grabbed the girl in a fierce hug. The teen lightly patted her back, but Shelly felt her flinch, so she pulled away. The girl's hands were bloody and bruised from the ropes. "Are you okay?"

"This is nothing. Believe me, I have had much worse."

Shelly gazed at the girl's swollen and bruised eye and could only imagine her other injuries, "I'm so sorry."

The girl smiled at Shelly, "Don't be sorry, I couldn't be happier. The rope is cut and asshole is on the other side." She grinned and said, "I am away from that beast and there is no going back." Her expression hardened, "Ever." Felix's wild laughter floated from the other side of the gulch, "That man is completely insane." She put the knife back in her pocket.

Shelly shook her head and said, "You are amazing. I could never be so brave."

"Not brave—just a survivor," she gazed at the forest again, "By the way, my name is Ashley. Ashley Thompson."

Shelly said, "Glad I met you, Ashley."

"Me too, Shelly." The girl got in a crouched position and looked ready to spring toward the forest, "It's too quiet—I think he must be reloading—this is a good time for us to make a break." She looked at Shelly, "Keep your head down and zigzag."

With that she jumped up and ran toward the woods. Shelly sprinted forward and followed her lead. They reached the woods just as the sun was beginning to lower behind the mountain to the west.

∞

Maggie ran toward the barn but stopped just short of the main doors. Her attention was drawn to a dark cloud of smoke and flames that billowed from the side of the barn. She glanced at the door again, then walked toward the smoke, and as she got closer, she saw the field shrouded in netting was engulfed in flames. With her rifle held high, she slipped through the netting and rounded the corner.

"Dho!" She mumbled in her native tongue.

Bodies were scattered in the snow and around a picnic table in pools of blood and vomit. A fire burned though a bunch of marijuana plants and was headed straight for them. The smell was overwhelming and Maggie's gag reflex kicked in as she gulped at the air. Tyler stood poised above an injured man lying on the ground and had his rifle shoved in the guy's face.

"What the hell happened here?"

Tyler turned toward her and said, "Summer, Shelly and Elsa aren't here, did you find them at the house?" His voice was an angry shout.

Maggie dropped her rifle barrel toward the ground and held up a palm as she said, "Haven't gotten there yet. I found Elsa, but she is alone. She is locked in some kind of underground dungeon, and I have to get something to break the lock." She took a step toward Tyler, "Uh, it might be a good idea to lower your weapon, Tyler—it might go off." She noticed his finger was moving up and down on the trigger.

Tyler pointed at the man on the ground with his rifle and said in a lowered voice, "That's Felix's partner. He has been 'cleaning up' and was supposed to meet Felix in Mexico." Tyler reached out and nudged the man with his boot, "Right?' The man nodded. "You got keys to that dungeon Officer Littlejohn is referring to?"

"Si," he said and turned slightly so they could see the key chain attached to his belt.

Maggie moved in closer, "Okay, good work Tyler, now please, step back and lower your weapon."

He moved back a step and pointed his rifle toward the ground but kept his hand close to the trigger. Maggie moved toward the man on the ground and snatched the keys. She took a quick look at his neck wound. Nasty. It still oozed blood but didn't look fatal. She stood straight and met Tyler's eyes, "Did he tell you where the others are?"

"Claims he doesn't know. He was supposed to meet them in Mexico but was given orders to kill all the workers." Tyler closed his eyes a moment then looked at her again, "I checked and Summer and Shelly aren't with the bodies and the barn is empty. I think Felix has Shelly and some other girl, but he is being vague about Summer. She may have been with the workers when they drank the poison he said he gave them." Tyler's jaw tightened and she could see the vein in his temple bulge.

"Look, I have to get Elsa, so you check the house, they may be there."

"I'll give it a quick check, but I think they're gone." He glanced back over his shoulder toward the house, "It looks empty and I saw some tracks by the barn that Jake alerted on. They lead around the side toward the field and forest."

"Okay, but we still have to check the house. It's possible Felix left them there and, uh, they can't respond. I really have to free Elsa now, she's trapped and may be hurt, or I would go to the house with you. Do you think you can manage it?"

Tyler nodded, "I'm okay, just worried and angry."

"I don't blame you, I feel the same. I would like to put my boot through this guy's neck, but we can't—understand? We just can't. Besides, we may need him for information later. As soon as I free Elsa I'll come help you with the house and then we can check out the tracks."

"You're right—I know, you're right." He frowned and gazed at the man on the ground and said, "What about this Bozo?"

"Take him to the house with you," Maggie pulled out some handcuffs, "Cuff him to something solid and the police can take care of him when they get here."

"Did you call them?"

"My phone isn't getting reception out here, but they should be here soon, anyway. Even without a warrant someone will have spotted the fire and called it in." She glanced at the man's neck, "He can wait."

"Okay. I need to let the horses out of the barn in case the fire gets to it. If the girls aren't in the house we'll meet back at the barn."

"Be careful, Tyler. Felix may be holed up there, too."

"Damn, I hope so!" Tyler pulled Jose up by the arm, "Come on, fellah. It's your lucky day. I was tempted to turn you into dog food, but I don't want Jake to get a stomach ache from eating something so bad."

Maggie chuckled, he was all right and had his temper under control. She turned and sprinted for the graveyard as Tyler headed for the barn holding the limping man by one arm as Jake followed close behind.

CHAPTER TWENTY-FOUR FRIDAY

Police Chief Ralph Anderson glanced at Jennifer. She was perched on the edge of the seat in his police SUV as he raced down the highway. Her hands were braced on the dashboard as she gazed through the front window. His attention went back to the highway as the mile markers whizzed past them.

"Jennifer, sit back, if something happens you're gonna get an air bag in your face.," he had to shout for her to hear him over the siren, "You shouldn't be riding up front, oh, hell, you shouldn't even be in the car."

She glared at him, but scooted back and checked her seat belt as she said, "Then watch how you drive if you are so worried, Ralph. If you drive properly, there won't be a problem."

"Want me to slow down?"

"No!" she shouted.

He chuckled and leaned forward as he strained to see the exit for

Felix's compound. His eyes weren't what they used to be and he knew he drove too fast, but something about Jennifer Mae Warrenton made him act like a young fool. "You're something else, you know," he mumbled as he stared straight ahead.

She glanced at him, "What do you mean?"

"Never met another woman like you, Jennifer, and I don't think I ever will."

"I asked what you meant, Ralph, not for you to repeat yourself in different words."

He laughed aloud and said, "You just proved my point."

She waved her hand in the air as if she swatted at a fly, "That's just nonsense."

"I don't mean anything by it—just talking. I don't want you to spoil that pretty face of yours if I hit a slick spot."

Her head snapped in his direction, "Good, God, Ralph! Are you flirting with me at a time like this?"

He chuckled and stole a glance at her before he continued his vigil, "First time in a long time I have you as a captive audience."

She rolled her eyes then gazed back at the highway, "Highly inappropriate, but that's not unusual behavior for such a backwoods, redneck like yourself." But he noticed a slight twitch at the side of her mouth.

He laughed again, louder, then sobered as he spotted the sign for Felix's property. "Hold on," he said as he tapped the brakes and flipped on his turn signal to alert the two squad cars that followed them.

He turned into the drive and sped down the gravel road for about a mile before they came to a locked gate. He pulled up close to the gate and parked the car.

He opened his radio and spoke to his officers, "Wait while I check in." He got out of the SUV and approached the gate. It was metal mesh and attached to steel posts with an electronic lock. A 'No Trespassing' sign with bold letters hung above the intercom. He rang the bell and waited. Nothing. He rang it again, and said, "This is the Chief, please open the gate. I need to speak with Felix Alvarez Lea, and it's important." No response.

He turned and gazed at his truck and the two squad cars, then held up his palm in a 'hold on' gesture before he turned back to the gate. He examined the hinges as well as the lock, then he returned to the truck and climbed into the driver's seat.

"You aren't going to let that stupid sign stop us, are you?" Jennifer said.

"Nope." He got on the radio, "Back up a bit, McWilliams and Barker." He watched the officers reverse until they were out of his way, then he backed his truck up a few feet.

"Ralph, you can't give up." Her voice rose as she said, "Please—don't give up now."

He simply said, "Hold on." Then gunned the SUV and raced toward the gate. The impact burst the lock and the gate flew open and banged against the steel post with a loud clang. His heart raced and his palms were moist.

Damn that felt good.

"Well," was all Jennifer managed to say.

He turned and looked at her, "I think you kinda like that redneck behavior now?"

She didn't say anything, but this time a real smile pulled at the side of her lips. He thought, very generous lips, too, then, damn—keep your mind on the job.

He turned off his siren and concentrated. The road was tricky with dips and sharp turns, so he had to slow his speed. The day went quiet as the officers behind them followed suit and turned off their sirens.

A glance in the rear view mirror confirmed they were still tight on his bumper—actually, a little too tight. He would need to have a word with them later about defensive driving. He understood they were a little excited since this was a lot of action for such a sleepy town. He was a little excited too, well, maybe a lot excited.

They rounded a corner and the white adobe ranch house came into view. All three vehicles skidded to a stop in the snow covered driveway.

Jennifer bolted from the truck before he could stop her. He followed as he yelled, "Jennifer, wait—damn!" He caught her by the arm, "I let you come along, but you can't go in there. Get back in the truck until we check things out."

She started to say something, but stared into his eyes and stopped, then turned and stomped back to the SUV.

He watched until she was seated in the truck, then he turned away from her glare and gestured for the three officers from the other two cruisers to follow him. He eased up the front steps with a hand on his side arm, then gave a 'go ahead' nod to one of his officers who rang the bell. Again, no response.

Ralph pushed past him and used his meaty fist to knock hard on the door. "Police!" he shouted, still, no one answered. Strange. With their noisy entry onto the property, he expected a loud reception.

He pulled his gun from the holster and weapons came out in unison as his officers stood poised beside him. He nodded at one of them and pointed to the side of the house. As soon as he disappeared around the corner, he called out, "This is the Police, open up."

Still no answer, so he leaned back and kicked the door, but it didn't budge. He tried not to show it, but it hurt like hell, and he limped slightly as he moved away. He glanced over his shoulder, yeah, she saw it. Damn.

Windows lined the deep front porch, so he headed toward one and broke the glass with his gun butt, then moved it around the frame until he cleared most of the shards. Still no response from the house. It had to be deserted. Or it was a trap.

He nodded at the smaller of the two remaining officers, his only female, and truthfully, the best of the lot. He whispered, "Alyssa, go on in and unlock the door. Be careful, it could be a trap." She was also the only officer he usually called by a first name. Guess he was a bit of a redneck. She climbed through the window and had the front door unlocked and open in moments.

Ralph frowned at the broad grin plastered across her face as she held the door open and gave the other officer a smug look. "Keep your weapon up and your attention in the house!" he said in a fierce whisper. She went into a ready stance, then moved inside.

Ralph nodded for the other officer to enter, then started to follow, but he sensed movement behind him. Jennifer. He turned and said, "No way—you stay where you are!"

"Good grief!" she said, then, "All right, all right!" She went back to the SUV and leaned against it.

They moved through empty rooms filled with exquisite furnishings. It was like something out of a fancy magazine or museum. Elaborate tapestries, paintings, and artwork everywhere. A lot of money had gone into this place.

They cleared the back rooms first. No people, no family photographs, hardly any personal possessions, but the same elaborate furniture and art throughout.

It was the tiny bedroom at the end of the hall and the master suite that gave him chills and made his blood pressure soar. He could only shake his head at the dead bolt on the outside of the smaller bedroom's door, bars on the windows, and leg shackles carelessly thrown on the floor of the master suite along with scratch marks on the door.

Static from his shoulder radio, then, "Chief?"

Ralph answered his radio, "Yes."

"I am at the kitchen door. No one has come out, but I can see some movement down by the barn, and it looks like some kind of field cover is on fire, maybe the barn as well. There is a ton of smoke so I can't make it out completely."

"Okay, we're headed that way—hold your position, Mac." The 'Mac' was for McWilliams. He smiled with realization. Maybe Jennifer was right about him. Redneck chauvinist.

He turned to the officer beside him and said, "Alyssa, go to the squad car and call Sharen. She said she would man dispatch until we were through here. Tell her to alert the Fire Department. Tell them we have a fire, and it's close to the National Forest line, so they better let the Forest Service know. Also notify the Tribal Police, the Rez might be in danger, too." He turned to them both and said, "I bet they are on the run and tried to burn some evidence before they left. Oh, and Alyssa, check on Jennifer while you're out there. Brandon, you stay with me."

They retraced their steps and Alyssa left through the front door as they cleared an opposite wing off the living room. More of the same expensive furnishings but no people. Glad Felix didn't burn the house before he left. What a waste that would have been. The seizure on this property was going to be a boom for the taxpayers. Probably going to be a battle on which department made the seizure.

Just off the living area they found the kitchen and a surprise. An injured man handcuffed to an oak post. He held a bloody towel to his neck. Ralph recognized him as Felix's number one man, Jose.

"What tha hell happened to you?" Ralph asked.

"Dog of the loco cowboy tried to kill me. I need a doctor and I got rights. You gotta get me a doctor. He threatened to kill me and then left me here, and that Indian police woman didn't stop him."

"Damn. Looks like that hurts," Chief Anderson said. A glance at the cuffs—Tyler and Maggie, he smiled, then got on his radio and said, "Alyssa, tell Sharon to call for a bus too, then get back in here, we need you." He headed for the kitchen door to let his other officer in.

"Anything new?" Chief Anderson asked.

"Not around the house, but the fire is worse, and I think I could see someone down by the barn. Oh, and the horses are out of the corrals and running all over the place."

"Okay, probably good they are out—come in, Mac. I got a babysitting job for you." He moved aside and motioned to Jose, "We have an injured prisoner. Don't take your eyes off him and don't take off his cuffs." He gazed out the kitchen window at the billows of smoke, "When Alyssa gets back, one of you check out the basement, but stay in constant radio contact."

"Okay, Chief."

Ralph checked his gun, then started for the door, "Brandon, you're with me. Stay alert, we need to clear the barn." He stopped again, turned and said, "Oh, don't let Jennifer come out there—I 'spect she will be in here at any minute. Keep her here." He shook his head, "Damn woman has a mind of her own, and that's for sure."

∞

Maggie fumbled with the keys but none seemed to fit the padlock, "Crap." She pulled off her gloves and went through them faster.

Click. At last.

"I'm here, Elsa," she pulled open the outer door but froze when only silence greeted her. "Elsa?" she scooted forward on her knees and tried more of the keys on the inner lock until she found one that worked. As the door scraped open a putrid stench rose from the cell. "Oh, God—Elsa?" Maggie covered her mouth and nose, stuck her head inside the darkened room, and used her flashlight to scan the space. Her partner crouched against the back wall. She didn't move or make a sound.

"It's okay, Baby. I'm here, now," Maggie's voice was low and gentle.

Mud from her golden hair down to her snow boots. When Elsa lifted her head and gazed at Maggie, there were dark bruises across the left side of her face. "You left me," a single tear cleared a path through the dirt on her cheek, "I thought you weren't going to come back."

Maggie's jaw clenched but her voice remained calm as she said, "I am so sorry, there was a situation at the barn, but I came back as quick as I could. Now let's get you out of here." She held out her hand. Elsa crawled forward and passed her without touching her. Maggie followed her out of the cave and they both stood in the sunlight as they stared at each other for a moment. Elsa burst into tears, which soon turned into racking sobs. Maggie grabbed her and held her tight until the sobs subsided and turned into hiccups. They both laughed and Elsa pulled back and punched her on the arm, "You took too damn long."

Mud now covered both of them, and the smell was awful. Maggie took her hand and led her toward the barn. As they passed the graveyard, Elsa glazed at the white crosses and she said, "Oh, God. It was dark when he brought me here and I was barely conscious. I couldn't see much—kind of glad now."

"I am so sorry. I didn't get your messages until this morning. Uh, and I have to be honest, it wasn't the poor reception at the casino, the battery on my phone died."

"Geeze, Maggs. How many times do I have to remind you to plug your phone in?"

"I know, I know. I'm so sorry."

"All you have to do is plug it in at night before you go to bed."

Maggie decided not to mention that she wasn't home in bed last night. No reason to fan the flames. Elsa stumbled and Maggie tightened her grip, "Are you all right?"

"Yeah. He didn't really hurt me—not much, anyway," she reached up to her cheek before she continued with, "I was in the car trying to text you when he surprised me and broke the window. I fought him and he hit me, then I think he drugged me—stuck a rag in my face, and everything went black. When I woke up he was carrying me. I fought enough to get free, but he slugged me again. I wasn't out, but I couldn't fight, so he pulled me along the ground by my arms the rest of the way—like I was a sack of potatoes or something. The snow wasn't too bad, but that gravel by the house hurt like hell."

Maggie felt her face grow hot. She said, "Haven't found him, or Summer and Shelly, but there is a whole lot of bodies by the barn." She glanced up at Elsa, "I think he had Jose kill off all the workers, and you were probably next on the list."

"I knew you would come—I wasn't worried."

A smile tugged at Maggie's mouth, "You did, huh?"

"Never doubted it," she said, then frowned and sniffed, "I was just pissed you left me in that crap hole after you found me."

Maggie knew better then to argue at this point, "Sorry, Baby."

"You should be," she punched Maggie's arm again, lighter this time and Maggie knew she was going to be all right.

CHAPTER TWENTY-FIVE FRIDAY

The prints were deep and free of new snow. Interesting patterns and groupings. Tyler gazed up at the sun, but the air temperature felt cold enough to hold the prints, at least for a while, even under full sun. Jake sniffed at the smallest footprints and started to whine.

"Tyler." He jumped and turned at the sound of Maggie's voice. Maggie was right behind him and she held Elsa by one arm. Elsa leaned heavily into Maggie's support, her face was badly bruised, and they were both covered in mud. The smell that floated around them set off his gag reflex, but he suppressed it, although Jake whined even more, and backed away from the women. Elsa had only been in Felix's hands one day. Tyler's stomach lurched as he thought of Summer and Shelly nearly gone for a week.

"Are you all right?" he asked.

Elsa nodded,. "Looks worse than it is."

Maggie gazed at the tracks Tyler studied, then across the field toward the woods, "Are those the tracks you mentioned?"

"Yeah."

Elsa disengaged herself from Maggie and limped to the corral where she lowered herself to the ground and leaned against the fence. "I'm okay, Maggs. Do your thing," she smiled.

Maggie bent to study the impressions in the snow, "Several different groupings."

"Yeah, I think the smaller ones went first, then the larger heavy ones, probably Felix, then these." He pointed to the last grouping, "These look like Summer's size, and it looks like she took off at a run."

"I agree." Maggie rose and they locked eyes, "Should be easy to follow, especially with your cow dog." She glanced at Jake and asked, "Is he good at tracking?"

"The best in several counties."

Maggie nodded and shifted her gaze to the empty corral, "That's good, because the horses might destroy some of the tracks as they run around the pasture."

"That was my thought, and if it snows again, it will get more difficult. I'm ready to get going now." He glanced at Elsa, but spoke to Maggie, "I feel like time is important here, but will you be okay if I head out first? Can you manage?"

Maggie frowned and said, "We're fine, but I don't like the idea of you out there alone." They both looked at Elsa.

"What? I told you I'm fine, but from both of your faces I don't think I want to look in a mirror, at least not until I shower."

Maggie laughed then turned back to Tyler, "I need to get her medical attention."

Voices drifted down from the house. Tyler and Maggie turned

toward the sound and raised their rifles, but it was only Chief Anderson and Officer Brandon. They were too far away to hear what they said, but the Chief held up a hand. They lowered their weapons and waved back.

Maggie looked at Tyler as she moved towards Elsa and said, "He will have a lot of questions." She gazed at them as they descended the path, then turned and locked eyes with Tyler, "You go, I've got this. They can help round up the horses and control the fire while I get Elsa help."

"You sure?"

"Yeah," she bent and helped Elsa stand, "I'll get Elsa settled, get the police up to speed, and then get search and rescue to help." She waved her hand toward the field, "Hurry! If you wait, Ralph won't let you go alone, and with the body count and fire, it will be hours before everything gets settled." She turned back to him, "You don't want Felix to get to them first."

"Thanks." Tyler untied his horse which he had retrieved, mounted him, and then turned to the two women, "I owe you."

"Not if you get Felix. I want him, but stopping him is the priority," Maggie said.

"Get the bastard," Elsa said as she gripped Maggie's arm.

Tyler's eyes narrowed and he said, "Consider him stopped." He swung the horse around and dug his heals into his side. The horse sprinted forward and they moved into a gallop across the field with Jake at a dead run behind them.

∞

Summer paused every few feet to examine the tracks she followed, at least that was her excuse. The truth was she was exhausted. The run across the pasture, then the trek through the snow entrenched forest, took what little energy she had left. But she would not, could not stop to rest, at least not until she reached the girls.

There had not been a glimpse of Felix, or the girls, since she entered the forest, and it was eerily quiet. She strained to hear anything from them, but prayed not to hear her child scream.

Summer followed the trail until she found herself in an open field of snow. The tracks were easier to spot here, but she no longer needed them. In the distance she could see Felix. He was turned away from her as he screamed and waved a gun in the air. She whispered, "Oh, no," as she surged forward. His words were lost in the distance, but she strained to hear as she scanned the field for any sign of the girls. Then she saw a flash of movement across what looked like a deep canyon. "Shelly!" she shouted as she began to run.

As she moved closer she could see Shelly on the other side of the gorge as she hung for a moment from some sort of ladder, then scrambled up and over the cliff and plastered herself to the ground. Summer's breathing became labored, but she kept a steady pace with Felix's back as her target. When she was almost close enough to hear his maniacal rant, she saw Shelly reach over the cliff and extend her hand to someone—it was the teen girl who passed her the notes. The girl struggled but seemed to hang between the pulley and the rope ladder.

Her attention went back to Felix. He lowered the gun and pointed it toward the girls. Shots rang out. "No!" she screamed, but her voice was lost in the gun fire and distance. Her lungs burned, but she raised the pitchfork high above her head and pumped her legs harder.

The older girl broke free and scrambled over the side, then both girls scooted around a big rock. Felix kept firing the gun as wild shots hit the cliff and ricocheted off the rock. He was so focused on the girls, he didn't seem to hear her approach. Just as she prepared to drive the pitchfork into his back, he swung around in her direction.

Summer used all her strength and drove the pitchfork at his chest, but Felix jumped to the side as he grabbed the handle and pulled it from her grasp. She turned and charged into him, and he stumbled back a step, but then pushed her away with ease. He plunged the pitchfork into the ground and gazed at her. Then he started his insane laughter.

"You are frigging crazy!" she said as she back peddled away from him. He went quiet and raised the gun again, this time it was pointed at her head. Summer froze and placed one hand on her stomach. "No…" she whispered as Felix calmly smiled and pulled the trigger. The gun clicked, but there was no explosion. He looked at the gun then pulled the trigger repeatedly—click, click, click.

Silence, then they both heard a snap and loud clank. They looked over the chasm and there was no longer a rope that connected the two sides. The teen girl had cut it and was almost back to the rock. "Noooooo! You stupid bitch!" Felix screamed as he reloaded and began firing at the other side. It was as if she didn't exist. Summer jumped up and ran back toward the cover of the forest. Her breath came in gasps and her legs burned as she pounded through the deep snow. The woods looked very far away.

When the field became silent again, Summer glanced over her shoulder. Felix was no longer focused on the chasm or the girls, and ran in her direction. He gripped his gun and his eyes were locked on her like a hawk on a rabbit.

Summer placed her focus back on the woods, but she felt her stride get smaller and her lungs felt as if they would explode. She made it to the edge of the forest before she felt a blow to her back. She fell forward, and as the ground raced toward her, she tucked into a ball. She hit the snow covered ground hard, but her momentum kept her moving forward. The rolling stopped when she hit a deep snow drift at the bottom of tree. The snow bank all but encased her. A sharp pain in her ankle shot up her leg and her right arm felt numb.

She looked up from her cold bed. Felix stood above her and said, "Hello, little momma. You have spoiled my plans and destroyed your daughter's chance at achieving the ultimate greatness." He pulled out a clip and took his time as he reloaded his gun, "I should never have allowed you out of the cave. You belong below ground. You are unworthy and should not be allowed to gaze upon your deity." He raised his arm and pointed the gun at her face, "This time I have plenty of bullets."

He paused as a rustle in the bushes about a foot from them drew their attention. Their heads turned in unison toward the distraction. The bush gave a mighty shake, then the tree branches behind it moved.

The tree branches were high—at least seven feet tall. Maybe a horse and rider? Felix turned to her, placed a finger to his lips and smiled as he whispered, "Does someone want to save the little momma?" He turned his gun toward the bush, "I don't think so…"

"No, please," then she shouted, "Look out!" But Felix only laughed as he emptied his clip into the bushes.

CHAPTER TWENTY-SIX
FRIDAY

Yellow crime scene tape stretched from the tent to the barn. There were deep grooves in the snow under the tape where the firetruck passed through to extinguish the blazing plants. All that was left of the fire was some smoldering vines and wet ash. The firemen did a great job. They stopped the fire before it reached the bodies, but the field of plants was wiped out. Just as well; they would have burned it anyway.

Maggie gazed at the black plastic drapes that covered the bodies surrounding the picnic table. There were so many of them. Most of the snow was gone and had left a muddy field to work with. Soon the State Coroner would be there, and they could remove the bodies. To handle such a large number of dead, additional trucks from all the adjacent counties were called in. Two of the local officers now stood guard over the scene until the Coroner arrived. Maggie didn't envy their vigil.

Chief Anderson joined Maggie and shook his head as he waved his hand in the direction of what was left of the illegal crop and said, "If only we had known about the plants, we could have easily gotten a warrant, and we could have prevented this tragedy." He spoke through a mask, so his usual baritone was muffled.

Maggie pulled up her mask to speak, and then dropped it back down, suddenly grateful that the paramedics provided them. Not only was the stench from the bodies dreadful, but the fumes from the burned pot was pungent. Not a good combination. Besides, they needed clear minds, and the lingering pot smoke might change that.

"Ralph, there is no way in hell you can blame yourself for this. We value our privacy in this valley, and that means we also respect the privacy of our neighbors." She paused and wiped beads of sweat from her forehead. The day was cold, but the work was hard. All the horses had been rounded up, but they were skittish, and didn't want to return to the barn. With the strong smells of death and smoke that lingered, Maggie couldn't blame them, "It's not your fault we didn't get a break in the case until now." She gazed at him as she continued, "Most police work is to wait for the bad guy to screw up—you know that." He silently shook his head in a 'yes' motion. Maggie turned from him to gaze at the sky. It was overcast again, there would be more snow coming, "Glad the judge finally came through with the warrant."

He eased toward the picnic table, but backed away when his boots started sinking in mud. He said, "It was Elsa's car. Horrible that it happened that way, but she saved the day."

Maggie glanced toward the house where Elsa rested. The paramedics treated her injuries, and they said she was fine, but they wanted her to get checked out at the hospital. That was going be a battle.

Ralph continued, "Felix was really sloppy with her abduction. Left prints all over the driver's door and a rag soaked with chloroform got kicked under the car." He looked at her and said, "Sure glad she's okay, Maggie."

"Me too," she sighed, "Me too, Ralph."

"It could have easily gone another way. He must have lost it after

Billy's death. Did you see that man's face, or I should say what was left of it? I think it was downhill from there. With the way he must have freaked out, well, let's say we are lucky Elsa's injuries weren't worse than they are."

Maggie glanced at the sky again, "Speaking of Felix, I know you have the copter and some State Troopers on their way, but you and your officers are tied up here for now, and it will get dark early tonight, so I think I better go after Tyler."

He sighed, "We have search and rescue assembled, but I can't send them out there with Felix still on the loose—it's just too dangerous." He looked at Maggie and said, "Officially, I can't recommend you going; unofficially, I think that's a great idea." He glanced toward where they had tethered the last of the horses, "You know these woods and can handle yourself with Felix. Those are some good horses, let's get one saddled for you, and here, take my radio, I'll get another one from my officer."

She accepted the radio and said, "Thanks Ralph, after I go, will you make sure Elsa goes to the hospital to get checked out?"

He laughed, "You know that might be tougher than dealing with Felix?"

"Oh, I know that," Maggie said with a hint of a smile as they entered the barn for a saddle and some tact, "Believe me, I'm getting the better part of this deal."

∞

Shelly pulled her hair free of the cedar branch and tucked it under her knit cap. They moved through the forest to the east, or at least they tried to keep east, but the terrain was creating natural roadblocks. Ashley pulled out a pocket compass and checked it, then turned left in front of the massive tree that blocked their way, "Here, let's go this way."

Shelly sighed. No path now. They were making their own path through the thick woods, and it wasn't easy. Tangled underbrush and snow drifts made it impassable in some areas, and now it was almost dark.

Shelly wished she had her Grandma's snow shoes. She made fun of those ancient woven contraptions, but she wouldn't laugh at them now. Of course, with all the roots jutting out of the snow, and the deep drifts close to the tree bases, it probably wouldn't have helped that much. She gazed at her boots. They were soaked, and the hem of the coarse wool dress was wet, and getting heavier by the minute.

"Angel—uh, Ashley—sorry, do you have any idea where we are?" she asked.

"That's okay, you'll get used to it. It's been so long since I was called by my real name, that it sounds strange to me, too." She pushed a branch back and moved through before she continued, "No, I really don't, Felix never took me past the gulch onto Reservation land, but I told your Mom we would go east, so it's best to stick with the plan." The teen paused and stretched, "From what I remember from the map in Felix's office, we have to be well inside Reservation land by now."

Shelly smiled, "I'll be glad when mom finds us, I miss her."

"Don't count on connecting with her. We can't count on anything but ourselves right now."

"I know, I know," Shelly grumbled, then said, "How did you pick east?"

"I've studied the maps in Felix's office for a very long time, and east looked like the best and safest route to get help." She held a branch up for Shelly to pass under, "I hope we'll come across some tribal members, or that Felix doesn't want to follow too deeply into their territory. It would be risky for him. I know he was paranoid about getting the Feds after him."

Shelly pulled her coat tighter, "The sun is setting, I can barely see where we are going."

"Yeah, first spot where we can get some shelter, we'll hole up for the night."

Shelly shivered, "I bet it is going to get really cold." She shook her head, "But I guess we have no other choice."

"We don't. I don't want to fall off some cliff or run into wild animals in the dark."

"Wild animals?" Shelly turned her head back and forth, as she gazed at the shadows of the forest.

Ashley giggled, "It'll be okay, Shelly. I am not nearly as afraid of the four legged variety as the two legged ones."

Shelly quickened her step, but she mumbled, "Still, I would rather not meet either out here in the dark."

CHAPTER TWENTY-SEVEN
FRIDAY

The smell of gun powder hung in the air and the forest was deathly quiet. No birds chirped, no rustle of leaves, not even the wind blew through the branches. Summer stared at the bushes Felix had fired into, but they didn't move. She whispered, "You couldn't even see who it was. It could have been anyone."

Felix turned his attention back to her and grinned, "What does it matter? They shouldn't have joined our little party." He walked toward the bushes with his gun held loosely by his side. His boots crunched on the snow with each step. "Who is it? Anyone there?" he called out in a sing song voice, then looked at her over his shoulder and winked before he said, "Doesn't look like they can answer. Whoever it is, or was, they won't bother us anymore."

Summer cringed as he turned and took a step in her direction. She tensed, but then a loud crash shook the bush behind him, and a massive black bear charged through it headed straight for Felix. The animal had blood darkening his shoulder and side, and he tossed his head back and forth as he roared. Summer screamed as Felix swung around toward the bear, then froze. The animal stopped in front of him and rose on two legs to his full height. The beast towered above the man. The animal's mouth gaped open to expose huge teeth as he roared his rage and pawed at the air.

Felix raised his gun and fired once into the bear's chest before the animal crashed into him, then they both went down with a loud thump that shook the forest floor. Felix's gun flew into the air and landed a few feet away, but it was much too close to the pair for Summer to retrieve it.

White snow turned red as the bear ripped into Felix's upper torso. The sounds of flesh as it was torn from bone, combined with the guttural noises the bear was making as drops of blood landed at her feet, assaulted all of Summer's senses. She gagged and slapped her hand over her mouth to stifle another scream. As much as she hated the crazy bastard, it was dreadful to see him torn apart. The bear paused a moment, then used his huge front paws to pound on the blood soaked upper body. Felix moaned. God, he was still alive. The bear gazed at him, then bit savagely into his neck before he raised his head to roar over his kill.

Summer eased onto her stomach and crawled out of the snow drift toward the forest edge. She managed to pull herself forward with her one good arm as she dragged her injured leg. "Don't look back," she whispered as she focused on the break in the trees, instead of the sounds behind her. "Don't look back," she whispered again as she gulped at the air and tears ran down her cheeks.

She knew black bears were usually shy, but Felix and his wild shots had changed all that, so all bets were off. As she crawled forward she braced herself for the sound of his giant paws as he made a run at her. But it didn't happen, and as she crawled into the sunlight, she began to sob and make gulping sounds. She pulled herself up into a sitting position against the base of a tree. She couldn't seem to stop shaking or crying. Even in Afghanistan she had not felt this helpless.

Summer looked around for something to use if the bear decided to pay her a visit. Nothing but a few broken limbs and a lot of snow. She could plummet him with snowballs. Yeah, that should do the trick.

Laughter bubbled up from deep in her stomach, but she pushed it back down. She covered her mouth as she shook with laughter while tears still streamed down her checks. “You’re losing it, girl,” she mumbled, then hiccupped, which made her laugh again.

When the laughter stopped she sat very still and tried to think. What now? She gazed across the field toward the canyon. No sign of the girls. She would never catch them now, not with her leg this messed up. At least she didn’t need to worry about Felix catching them. Thank you for that Mr. Bear.

She stiffened as a sound came from the woods. She cringed and held her breath, but instead of the bear, it was a horse and rider that burst from the forest. They emerged from the woods farther away from where she had crawled out, and she didn’t think she had been seen. She had forgotten about Jose. He could have followed.

She attempted to stand and used the tree to make it to her feet. Summer shrank back against the tree as she tried to make herself harder to see. She squinted in the fading sunlight toward the rider and her heart quickened. She knew that silhouette—Tyler!

Summer raised her one good arm in the air and waved. She didn’t want to shout, but she moved her arm franticly. He saw her, waived back, and headed her way. “Thank you, God!” she whispered.

He pulled up next to her, jumped from the saddle, and embraced her in a big hug. She clung to him and laid her head against his chest. “Tye,” was all she could manage. A huge roar sounded from the forest, and the horse skidded sideways as Tyler held on to his reins.

“It’s a bear. He has the man who held us captive—at least what’s left of him.” Summer whispered, “The idiot shot him with a revolver and caused just enough damage to tick him off.”

Tyler nodded and encircled her waist with one arm as he gripped the reins with the other. The horse danced in place. “Can you walk?” he whispered.

"With your help."

He led the horse and supported Summer as they headed across the field until they were away from the woods. He soothed the horse, then asked, "Have you seen the girls?"

"Yes, they made it across the canyon." She pointed to the cliff edge, "I'll show you."

They continued until they were at the cliff's edge. Summer said, "This is where the girl's crossed. When I got here, our captor was on this side, he shouted and fired his gun at them, but they got away. She continued to gaze at the forest on the other side where the girls had disappeared, "He was a madman."

"Summer, did he hurt you?"

"Not really, no—not in that way—he was more interested in Shelly."

"Oh, God. Did he…"

"No, no—at least I am pretty sure he didn't touch her. There was an older girl, a teen, I think he's been abusing her." Summer dropped her eyes and sighed, "She seems to have been with him a while. The brave girl protected Shelly. She's the one who got Shelly out of there and warned me, or I would be dead." She shook her head and said, "A long story, and I want to tell you everything, but not now. Right now all I want is to find the girls."

He hugged her again, then touched her tummy and said, "I understand, but just one more question; what about this little one?"

She smiled up at him and said, "It's good. I think this is a tough one."

He smiled back and said, "Like its mom." He touched her face and said, "Oh, baby, I have been out of my mind."

"I know. I knew you would be, so have I." She leaned into his shoulder and said, "They kept us separated and I've been going insane not being able to protect her."

Tyler said, "Looks like they cut the rope for the gorge crossing. Smart girls, but that's going to complicate things a bit." He studied the canyon, "Did they see you?"

"No, he was shooting at them, so they had to keep their heads down as they escaped into the woods."

"So they don't know you're here, or that Felix is out of the way?"

"No, but the teen passed me a note that said they would head east, and I imagine they are still on the run." She turned and faced Tyler, "What do you think we should we do?" She looked over the cliff edge. The drop was steep and rocky. She couldn't see a way to make it safely across, especially with her bad arm and leg, "We have to find them."

"We can't cross here, maybe we can find another crossing?" A distant roar and bushes crashed. Tyler glanced toward the forest. "You said he was wounded. I should go finish him off," he said as he laid his hand on his rifle, "Are you sure Felix is dead?"

Summer placed her hand on his arm, "He is absolutely dead. But please, Tye, don't go after the bear. He is wounded and crazed with rage. Please, don't risk it. We need to get to the girls before they get too far away and get lost out there. We don't know how long it will take us to get to the other side of the gorge, so it will be hard enough to catch up to them."

He glanced at the forest, clearly torn, "I hate to leave a wounded animal, especially a dangerous one, but you're right. You and Shelly are my priority." He turned and faced the cliff for a moment, then turned back and put both hands on her shoulders, "Look, you're injured and I need to get you back to the ranch. The police are there, and Maggie. We can get help to find the girls."

"No." She stood straighter and looked him in the eye.

"Summer, please. You have our baby to think about. My God, when I think of all you have gone through it's a miracle you are still alive and you haven't lost the baby. If that madman wasn't dead already, I would kill him myself. Death by bear, though, is an appropriate end."

"No arguments on that," She turned toward the horse and said, "but I am going to find my daughter. Help me up, please." When he didn't budge she turned and looked at him with a steady gaze, "I am fine, really. The injury to my arm and leg is manageable. I can ride, and time is precious. If we go back to the ranch, the sun will be gone. I don't want my daughter—sorry, our daughter, to be stuck out in the forest once the sun goes down." Tears welled up in her eyes, "Please, Tyler."

He smiled and wiped a tear from her cheek, "Okay, you know I can't say no to you, so let's go find our girl."

He lifted Summer up into the saddle, then joined her. She felt one arm go around her waist and the other held the reigns. His body warmth engulfed her and she sighed deeply as he touched his boot into the horse's side and guided him along the canyon's edge.

∞

Maggie tugged at the reigns and tightened her knees. Her horse was young with a strong urge to run, and he was still spooked from the fire. "Whoa," she pulled the reigns hard, and brought him to a complete stop. She slid off his back and hit the ground with a thud in the deep snow. "Easy boy," she said as she placed a hand on his head and stroked his jaw. Something was getting him wound up. They were in a field between the forest and the gorge, and Maggie had spotted some new tracks around the opening to the forest. The horse's nostrils flared and he pulled at her hold on the reigns. "Easy now," She said as she eased the reigns around a sturdy limb and tied the leather tight before she headed for the tracks.

There were multiple tracks deeply imbedded in the snow. She walked around them, stood for a moment as she studied them, then went down on one knee to get a closer look. "This is not good," she mumbled as she raised up and gazed around the horizon. No movement, and the landscape was quiet, but the tracks told quite a story. There was an obvious struggle, possibly violent, that continued into the forest. There were a couple of specks of blood before what looked like a body rolled past the tree line.

Maggie pulled out her rifle and ducked through the break in the forest as she tried not to step in the tracks. Day turned to dusk, so she paused a moment until her eyes adjusted to the dim lighting.

Just inside the tree line, she found herself in a small clearing with a canopy of trees. Maggie's eyes roved the scene, then got out her flashlight and used it to follow the tracks. A body had rolled until it came to rest in a snow bank at the base of a large tree. The indentation where the body rested was deep, as if the person had struggled—perhaps injured? From there, the person, most likely Summer from the size, appeared to crawl through the snow, then exit the forest at a different point of entry.

Maggie sniffed at the air. A faint smell of cordite hung in the air. She frowned and swept the area around the tree base with her flashlight. Large boot tracks had stood in front of the body in the snow drift. Too small for Tyler, but too big for the girls—Felix? The boot tracks turned and moved toward a clump of bushes. Why? What drew him away from his injured victim?

Maggie eased forward and followed the boot tracks with her flashlight. She gasped. Scarlet carnage against a white backdrop. A mutilated body, or what was left of it, surrounded by large bear tracks.

She approached the bloody mess. Not Tyler. Right height, but the lower half was clothed in the same woolen pants and sturdy brown boots as the dead workers. Tyler wore cowboy boots and jeans. Felix? She smiled in spite of the gruesome discovery.

Maggie covered her nose and mouth and leaned in close. There was not enough left of the face for identification, but there was black hair, and a lot of it. She nodded her head and smiled broader, but she immediately quenched it at the reality of the grizzly sight.

No sign of the animal, but Maggie glanced around and gripped her rifle a little tighter. Thick bushes and underbrush bordered by closely spaced trees. She would be a sitting duck if the animal came back to finish his feast.

She returned to the snow drift and followed the other tracks out of the forest. Someone had crawled their way out. There was also a small amount of blood in some of the indentations, so there had to be some sort of injury involved. Maggie glanced up and tensed. The bear might have continued his temper tantrum after being shot.

She quickened her pace until she found a spot just outside the forest where the person had rested against a tree. There were more tracks close to the tree that looked like a horse and rider. Maggie glanced up. The rider came from a different section of the forest. She bent over and studied the tracks. This person wore cowboy boots—Maggie smiled—Tyler.

She turned and followed the tracks with her eyes as they disappeared toward the cliff. Maggie gazed across the field, but there was no sign of the pair, so she returned to her horse and mounted up.

She looked at her watch and noted her coordinates. That brought another smile. The watch was an anniversary gift from Elsa. She would have to remember to tell her how it helped with the search. That would please her. Maggie pulled out the radio and called the Police Chief.

"Maggie Littlejohn here, come in?"

Static, then, "Yeah, Maggie, I can hear you."

"Ralph, I found what I think is Felix."

"What you THINK is Felix?"

"Yeah—looks like he met a bear and the bear won. The tracks look like it was a big one, and it really tore into him. There's not much left of the face, but the hair and clothing match Felix."

"Damn—talk about Karma. Can't say I'm too upset. Where?"

"Just inside the forest before the clearing at the gorge crossing." She relayed the coordinates, then continued with, "Easy tracks to follow."

"Got it—I'll send someone out—I'm tied up here. Feds are on the pot and the murdered field hands, and the coroner is here with several of the transport vans."

"Ralph, tell them to be careful. Looks like the bear was wounded and he is still on the loose."

"Roger that."

"How's Elsa?"

"Mad as a hornet, but I got her in the ambulance and headed for the hospital with Jennifer." Static, then, "Those two make quite a pair."

Maggie nudged the horse to start him across the field as she spoke, "I saw more tracks leading away from the body. I think Summer might have been injured, but I think she got away, and now I'm on some tracks that look like Tyler's horse. It looks like they might be together on the horse from the deeper tracks."

"That's good news! Is there any sign of Shelly or the other girl?"

"Their tracks were the first ones that went through the forest. It looks like they were headed for the gully, and I think Summer and Tyler are headed in the same direction."

"Maggie, it's almost dark. I don't think we can send Search and

Rescue out now even with Felix out of the way. I don't want any more folks lost out there, especially with a pissed off bear throwing his weight around," he sighed.

"I know, Ralph, I understand."

"Guess we are going to have to send out Fish and Game after the bear, but that will be tomorrow. They are down a truck and don't have their bear cage. You heard about that driver who was moving the bear from town and went missing?"

"Yeah, we were talking about it at the Rez station yesterday."

"Well, they thought he took off, and the state police have a bulletin out for him. He was known as a stoner, and a bit unreliable, so they weren't too upset at first, but it's strange timing. Consensus was he freed the bear and kept going, but now I wonder. Keep an eye out for him, would ya? That might be where our killer bear came from."

"Good point. The bushes where Felix was attacked were shot up and some blood was sprinkled in the snow around the bear's tracks, so he may have clipped him pretty good."

"Damn. They definitely will have to put him down. And, after he did the community such a great service."

Maggie chuckled, then stopped her horse and shook her head before she continued, "Ralph, some more bad news, I just spotted more bear tracks in the field, and they are headed in the same direction as the horse trail."

"You said Tyler can handle himself, right? Does he have a rifle?"

"Yeah. I just hope he finds the girls before the animal does." They were both quiet a moment, then Maggie continued with, "I am going to keep at it. I feel like I'm really close."

"I thought you would, but please, be careful and keep me in the loop.

If something happens to you, Elsa would be on me worse than that bear was on Felix."

Maggie laughed, "Don't worry, Ralph, I plan on getting back safely, but I won't stop until I find them. Please let Elsa know, and give the word to the Tribal Police. Looks like the girls were headed toward the Reservation, so they need to keep eyes out on that end."

"You got it, but I am going to call Elsa not visit her—I value my own hide too much."

Maggie laughed again, "I'll call you later." She turned off the radio to save the battery. When she reached the cliff she slid off the horse and gazed at the wide gully.

The light was almost gone, but she could still see where the rope was cut on the zip line. It hung on the other side and grazed the gully floor.

Horse tracks lead along the cliff road parallel to the canyon. Tyler and Summer must have chosen to find a safer place to cross, one they could maneuver with the horse. Probably because of Summer's injuries.

Maggie gazed down the side of the cliff and spotted areas for hand and foot holds. The lighting was dim, but she had scaled canyons more difficult than this one. Once she was down this side, it would be a breeze to climb the rope up the other side. She would have to give up the horse, though.

As she looked around the area, she noticed there was something off to the side in the canyon floor. Even with the evening shadows she could tell it was a wrecked Forest Service truck and bear trailer. The one that Ralph wanted her to look for, but where was the driver? She needed to get closer before she reported it. A lot of snow was on it, so it had to have been there a while. Man, no wonder that bear was so pissed off, first he gets thrown in a cage, then thrown off a cliff, then shot.

She removed the saddle and her gear from the horse and slapped him on the butt. The animal took off at a gallop. Headed straight for the barn she wagered.

Maggie rolled the supplies she would need in the horse's blanket and used it for a makeshift backpack. She tucked her rifle in it, pulled on her gloves, and tied her flashlight to her right hand. She gazed across the canyon. It would take a little while to get there, but it was the way the girls had gone, and she could examine the truck. She might even get a head start on Tyler and Summer since they would have to backtrack after they found a place to cross. It would increase the possibility they would all meet at the same time.

Maggie smiled and started her decent. It felt good to be back on her land.

CHAPTER TWENTY-EIGHT FRIDAY

"This looks good," Ashley said.

Shelly stopped. It was getting dark and almost impossible to see even a few feet ahead, so she concentrated on the ground where she stepped. The only problem was the low branches, and she had gotten up close and personal with several of them. She looked up. A large tree with deep drifts was directly in front of them, "There? But the snow's so deep."

"No, silly, look to the right, over there, around the tree." Ashley pointed, "That big rock has an overhang. See how it kept the snow back? It's dry up close to the rock face. Looks like a good place to huddle up for the night."

Shelly gazed through the last light of the day and could barely see the carved out place under the overhang. It did look good, almost like a cave, and at least they would be out of this blasted snow. She felt something cold hit her nose and she gazed up at the sky. Millions of white dots. Shelly sighed and said, "Oh, man, here it comes again."

"It'll be okay, come on," Ashley took a few steps around the tree then disappeared from sight.

"ASHLEY!" Shelly screamed.

Where did she go?

A muffled cry, "Here, I'm down here." Then something unintelligible and, "careful—be careful of the hole."

Shelly moved forward as she extended her foot until she could feel where the ground gave way to nothingness. She dropped to her knees and edged forward a little more. A dark hole surrounded by gnarly roots and snow. "Where are you?"

"I'm here," she heard Ashley more clearly this time, but could not see beyond the top of the hole. It was a black void. "I think I broke my leg. I can't move it," silence, then, "Shit. Man that hurts."

"What can I do?" panic rang in her voice.

"Get a grip, kid, it's me in the hole."

Shelly laughed in spite of her fear, "What can I do to help you?"

"Well, short of a rope, blanket or hot meal, not much I guess."

"Ashley, please, this is serious. Tell me what to do."

"Look, it's actually warmer down here. Once you get past the hole at ground level, it opens up into a dirt cave. I'm okay, but don't try to come down. I can't see anything, but it was a long drop, and I know I landed on a pile of rocks." Shelly heard some movement in the darkened hole followed by a moan.

"What's wrong?"

"Nothing, but I just tried to move my leg again and it really hurts."

Some more rustling, "Yep, it's broken. Damn that hurts and I feel a stick coming out of it. I must have landed on a branch as well as the rocks."

"I'm coming down."

"No! All we need is for both of us to get stuck, and you would probably land on top of me. We can't do anything until daylight, so we can see what we're doing. You need to stay as warm as you can and out of sight. I don't think Felix will follow in the dark but he's crazy enough to do anything."

"Should I try to go for help?"

"No way. You would get lost, or worse. Crawl around the hole, but be careful. The ground felt solid then just gave way. Get against the rocks under the outcrop just like we planned."

"Let me throw you my coat so you can cover your leg."

"Are you crazy? You will be frozen stiff as a board by morning. Popsicle Shelly. It's going to be hard enough for you to stay warm without our combined body heat."

"Okay, but what about you?"

"Like I said, it's warmer down here, and there's no snow. If you can, find some dry grass or twigs and cover yourself as much as possible. Oh, and stay awake."

"Do you want me to go for help when it gets light?"

"Let's just make it through the night, then we can talk about that in the morning."

"Okay."

Shelly crawled around the hole then eased into the niche against the large rock face. It was relatively dry up close to the stony surface, so she pulled as much brush against her wet dress as she could manage. She pulled her knees up to her chest and yanked her jacket as far over them as she could, then watched as the snow piled up around her shelter. Her teeth chattered and her hands felt numb, so she tucked her hands under her arms in a self-hug. Stay awake. Stay awake. Stay awake. She thought as she yawned.

"Can you still hear me, Ashley?" she said.

A muffled reply, "Yeah." Ashley sounded as sleepy as she felt.

"You said you would tell me about the truck."

"Oh, yeah." Silence. "Some poor forest service guy was in it hauling a bear. Felix got his holiness on and wasted the dude."

"What?"

An audible sigh from the darkness, then "Felix thinks he is some kind of avenger and 'messenger of God'. He actually thinks he is God's son, when he's really more like the son of the devil. If he decides someone needs to be punished, he thinks it's his sacred right to do it. Of course, he has a whole litany of what he thinks are 'sins', and he adds to the list on a whim. You have to understand, the man is crazy, and I mean certifiable. He has his own rule book in his head and expects the world to operate by it. Like I said, totally bonkers."

"He killed the forest service guy?"

"Well, I think so. We came across him when Felix had me out on one of his 'nature walks'. He likes to take me out in the woods and spout scripture. I think he just likes the sound of his own voice as it echoes in the forest. Anyway, the guy was peeing by his truck, and to make matters worse, he had a lit joint in his mouth. Two major trespasses in Felix's mind, even though he sells and uses pot. What a giant, stinking hypocrite." She snorted, then continued with, "Felix started one of his sermons, and the guy was stoned, so it was intense. Felix told me to leave, so I did. I didn't see it happen, but with the truck wrecked at the bottom of the canyon, well, I can fill in the blanks."

"Ashley, I'm sorry. You have been through so much. I know he has hurt you in ways I can't even imagine."

"Doesn't matter, now. I am here, and Felix is not. One of the best things I learned about all this is to live right now, in the moment. I try not to think too much about my life before, or what will happen tomorrow. I tell myself 'you are alive today, make the most of it', and I do."

"You are so brave. I've learned a lot from you."

She heard Ashley laugh, then she said, "Oh, crap, don't learn from me. I just do what I have to do, and believe me, I am not proud of some of the things I have done to survive." Her voice trailed off at the end of her sentence.

"None of this is your fault. You didn't choose Felix, and you couldn't help what happened to you. If it weren't for you, I don't know what would have happened to me, but it wouldn't have been good. I'm amazed at how strong you are, and even that you are still alive. When I think about how good I had it, and I still managed to get an attitude over nothing. How do you do it?"

"Well. I guess the more we have the more we want. If you don't have much, very simple things like food, warmth, a kind word, those things become luxuries—now that, I have to say, I learned from my poor, stoner mom."

Shelly yawned, then said, "Do you remember when you got Felix to send me down to the cellar for the wine?"

"Yeah."

"Thank you for protecting me."

"I just gave him a little distraction. I didn't want you to get him all riled up, because it would have made it worse for both of us."

Shelly smiled, "Right—you were just looking out for yourself."

"Somebody has to."

"You're such a big fat liar."

"That I am, but not to you."

"Right." She was silent a moment, then continued with, "Ashley, I found something down there that night."

"Yeah? Wine?"

"Ha ha. No, a red suitcase."

"That wasn't any of your business."

"Well, maybe, but I looked anyway."

"That was private."

"They were the most beautiful drawings and paintings I have ever seen."

Silence for a moment, then, "Well, you haven't seen much, then."

"Oh, but I have. My grandma is an artist. She is kind of famous, actually."

"Really?"

"Yep. I think even she would be impressed."

"Stop," a yawn.

Shelly laughed, "You keep awake, too."

A voice, rose from the dark hole, low at first then it gained momentum, "This little light of mine, I'm gonna let it shine."

"Let it shine, let it shine, let it shine," Shelly responded.

"I learned that song when I was little and my mom took us to a shelter. They sang it before we could eat. You know it?"

Shelly started to sing the next line, and then Ashley joined in and they finished it together. Shelly smiled and thought about when Ashley disappeared. She said, "You know, after you fell into the hole, it looked like you disappeared. Poof, and you were gone. For just a moment, I thought the forest was magic, and the trees had grabbed you. You know—like in Harry Potter."

"You have quite an imagination."

Shelly laughed, "So I've been told. My mom said I should be a writer." The smile slipped away as she gazed into the darkness. There were monsters out there that were much worse than the ones conjured up in the books she had read. She looked up at the fat snowflakes as they floated in the night sky. "Let it snow, let it snow, let it snow," she sang out.

"Now that's just dumb. How about, it's going to be a bright, bright, bright, sunshiny day."

Shelly laughed again, "Okay, now I've got it, since you are doing oldies how about one of my Grandma's favorites, here comes the sun, dobby doobiė."

Ashley laughed, "That's it—if you don't know the words, just make them up." She laughed some more and said, "Keep em coming! We'll keep each other awake with bad singing."

Shelly smiled but pulled her coat tighter as the snowline around the rock face grew deeper.

∞

Summer could no longer feel her hands. She gazed at where they gripped the saddle horn, but it was too dark to see anything. Probably a good thing. She had a feeling they might resemble blue marble at this point, and it would be a little too freaky. She already felt like they belonged to someone else, so she didn't need to see Smurf hands to prove it.

Tyler walked in front of them and used a flashlight to lead the way. The gentle sway of the horse she rode made it hard to stay awake.

New snow covered the tracks, and darkness enveloped them, so they would have to stop soon. Summer didn't want to stop. She didn't care how cold it got, or how numb her hands felt, she wanted to find Shelly.

Jake's nose didn't seem to be fazed by the snow. He sniffed at the air and ground, then moved forward again. In and out of the light Jake held. On his mission. No hesitation, and he always moved forward. He was like a machine. A little grizzled, gray and black sniffing machine. Summer worried that he wasn't enough like a machine to protect his paws from the frozen ground. She hoped they weren't numb like her hands. "I feel like a baby up here while you two do all the work," her teeth chattered as she spoke.

Tyler stopped and turned the light on her face before he slid it down to her body and hands. Yep, Smurf hands. Without a word he moved to the horse's side, tucked the flashlight under his arm, removed his gloves, and reached for her hands. Summer felt pins sting both hands as he rubbed them with his, then he started to put his gloves on her.

"Tye, for God's sake, you need these more than I do. I am just sitting up here."

He smiled up at her, "You have the biggest job of all of us."

"Yeah, and what would that be?"

"Take care of the munchkin in your belly." He took off his knit cap and handed it to her, "You lose most of the warmth from your head, hands and feet. Keep our baby warm, honey."

She laughed, "Oh, good grief. You think you know how to play me." But she pulled the hat on over her wet head anyway. She felt an immediate difference, "You are so sappy." She sighed and said, "This is on one condition, we'll trade off, you get these back in an hour."

"Deal!" he turned and started forward again.

"What about Jake?"

He stopped again and looked at her, "What do you mean?"

"His paws, will they get frozen or damaged?"

Tyler gazed at the dog who was just ahead of them. Jake sat and looked from one to the other. He leaned forward a little and emitted a low chortle. They both laughed. Jake had voiced his impatience.

"We'll stop before then. I'm keeping an eye on him because he would go until he dropped once he picks up a scent, especially since the scent belongs to Shelly." He shined the flashlight further up the trail. The forest was getting thicker, and it had started to snow again, "We have to stop soon, but I want to keep at it a just little longer, before we completely lose visual on the tracks."

"I don't want to stop. I am ready to become a giant popsicle if we can find our girl, but I understand reality, and don't want to run Jake into the ground."

Tyler nodded and turned back to the trail, or what was left of it. Summer stayed quiet, and tried to keep alert as they moved on. With the added warmth of the gloves and hat, it was all she could do to stay awake. She jerked a moment later, just as she slipped sideways in the saddle, and thought, "Great. Not only am I unable to help, but now I'm about to fall out of the saddle. Fantastic."

Summer sat straighter and watched Tyler's back as he followed Jake. She started to play a movie in her head of their wedding day. What a beautiful day. She could almost smell the scent of the pink roses in her bouquet.

She smiled. She had Tyler back, the baby was fine, and they would find Shelly soon. Not to mention the boogey man was dead. Everything would be right, she just knew it. She whispered, "Hang in there, honey, we're coming for you. Stay safe, and we'll be there soon."

CHAPTER TWENTY-NINE
SATURDAY

"Snow stopped."

Chief Anderson grinned and nodded at the solitary volunteer, Chris, who was the owner of Noisy Water's town diner. You could always count on her for any community issue, from forest fires to parades; she would have refreshments available. She had set up a table in the barn, but he was her first customer. There were two large coffee dispensers and several trays of fresh donuts. "Yeah. Sun's almost up, too," he said as he accepted a steaming mug of coffee from her, then leaned over the donuts as he devoured each one with his eyes.

"Cold though," she said.

"Yeah, damn cold," he picked up a jelly donut. It had red goo oozing out of one end. Probably strawberry. Yum. He took a bite, then licked his lips. Yes, strawberry. So what if the cliché about cops and donuts was correct. Ralph Anderson liked them because they were easy, fast, and satisfying, "Thanks, Chrissy, you're the best." He still called her by her childhood name, even though she preferred the abbreviated form. He just couldn't seem to break the habit. He had watched the redhead grow from a tomboy toddler, to a beautiful, capable young woman.

He headed out of the barn as he munched his prize, then gazed at the sky. The snow had stopped, and the sun just peeked over the horizon. Red and gold streaks slashed the dark blue sky. He inhaled the coffee aroma, then took a sip of the dark brew. He closed his eyes and enjoyed the warm sensation as it slipped down his throat. If they could just locate everyone safely, the day would be perfect.

"That's not going to help your heart any, Ralph."

He cringed, "Jennifer, uh, when did you get back?" The cold made his words come out in a puff of smoke.

"Caught a ride with Elsa."

"Ah, she's back too?"

"That's right, Ralph. What are you all doing to find my daughter and granddaughter?"

He stuffed the rest of the donut into his mouth and held up a finger, then pulled a napkin from his parka pocket and wiped the rest of the strawberry jam from his lips. He wasn't about to give up his sugary treat, even for Jennifer. He watched her roll her eyes and cross her arms across her chest. He swallowed then said, "Maggie has been out all night. She reported in a couple of times. Last report she was on their tail, but had not caught up with them, so she was taking shelter until dawn. From the tracks she had followed, she thinks Tyler has Summer with him, and they are not far behind the girls."

"Thank, God; oh, thank God. Why didn't you tell me that right away?" she said as she glared at him, "Surely that bit of information was more important than a donut."

Ralph sighed and took another sip of his coffee before he continued, "I was about to call you, but I hoped you were able to get a little sleep, so I didn't want to disturb you too early." He shifted his weight and said, "Have you heard about Felix?"

"No, what? Did you catch the SOB?"

He smiled, "Uh, no, but he is no longer a threat. Maggie found his remains. Bear got him."

"What?"

"Apparently, the idiot took the bear on with a handgun at close range, and just pissed him off enough to enrage the beast. Maggie said it must have been a big one from the looks of Felix's body."

"Oh, my goodness." Jennifer clutched at her throat, "I have to admit I wished the man dead, but not like that."

"Damn shame, but the animal will have to be put down when they find him. As of this morning there have been no sightings. We think the bear is the one that the forest service was trying to relocate from town." He blew on his coffee and steam rose, but he continued before taking another sip, "Maggie found the missing forest truck that was hauling him, and unfortunately, the ranger's body. The truck went over a cliff and was hidden in a gully near where the bear attacked Felix. It was just off the National Forest access road that borders Felix's property. We aren't sure if the ranger died from the accident, or the bear killed him after they wrecked. Forensics will have to determine what happened. But it's everyone's guess that it is the bear that killed Felix."

"That's horrible! Ralph, what about my family? Are they in danger from the animal? They're still out there in the woods."

"Now, Jennifer, don't get all worked up. Maggie knows how to take care of herself, and Tyler strikes me as someone who can do the same, both are armed. Summer is most likely with Tyler, and I'm sure they will find the girls soon, so they should be all right." He glanced at the horizon, "Sun's up now, so they will be easier to find. Darkness stopped everything last night. The Fish and Game officer should be here soon, and he will take a group out to search for the bear. Search and Rescue will follow, and help with finding the girls."

Elsa joined them. Her color was back, but the bruises were darker than the day before, and they had yellow tinges around the edges. She walked on her own, but with a limp. Felix had really done a number on her. She was lucky to be alive.

Jennifer turned to her and filled her in on everything while Ralph gulped down more coffee. Elsa responded with, "Can't say it breaks my heart about Felix, and it saves the taxpayers a lot of trouble, but I don't like the situation with an angry, injured bear out there with our people. Not only did they have frigid temperatures to deal with last night, but that animal was prowling around." Jennifer shook her head in agreement and the two women turned and stared at him.

"What do we do, now?" Jennifer asked.

"Why don't you ladies go into the barn and get some coffee, then you can help serve the first group as they go out? Chrissy is by herself and could use the help. I have to get some maps from my truck so I can coordinate the search."

Elsa glanced at the burned field next to the barn. It was still roped off with yellow police tape, and lights were set up around the picnic table area, but the bodies were gone. "Looks like you all have been working all night. The Feds are still here?"

"Yes. They'll most likely gather evidence for days. They already collected a boat load of stuff from the barn. Pity, though, I'm not sure there is anyone left to prosecute, except Jose, of course. They hope they can get a line on some of Felix and Billy's contacts. They think this operation spread to Mexico and Los Angeles, and looks like it might include human trafficking as well as dope. They still haven't even gotten started on the house," Ralph said as they watched the forensic truck back away from the barn and head up toward the house, "I bet Jose will be singing like a bird, though. He was squawking about Tyler's dog until they carted him away."

"Can they give you air support and help on the search?" Elsa asked.

"We are good without them. They have a helicopter at the Noisy Water airport, and they offered it to us. It's on the way here now. We also have more state support on the way. Since both Billy and Felix are out of the picture, the Feds are happy to have Jose and will be interviewing him for days. They will also be interested in what the teen Felix claimed was his daughter has to say. Now that it's light, we will get everything underway. I really need to get those maps, ladies, and get a plan in action before they all get here."

"Okay, sorry, Ralph, you go do what you need to do. Has Maggie checked in with you this morning?" Elsa asked.

"No, but I'll let you know as soon as she does," he said.

"Good. I would like to talk to her when I can. I would just feel better when I hear her voice."

"Of course!" Ralph shifted on his feet as he gazed at the two women, "Maggie sounded fine when she radioed me just before she took shelter for the night, so she's okay."

"I'm not worried about her. If she comes across the bear she will put him down humanely. She won't stop until she has those girls safe, though," Elsa smiled, "That's just Maggie."

Jennifer glanced up toward the house, "Looks like they started on the house." They all turned and stared as federal agents exited the suburban and filed into the ranch house.

Ralph said, "It has been a long night, but it will be an even longer road ahead. What a mess. Just to establish how many crimes have been committed, and like I said, who is left to pay. What a nightmare."

"I don't really care about that, Ralph. I just want my family back safe. Go, do what you need to do, we'll help Chris," Jennifer said.

He smiled, "I'll let you know if I hear anything from Maggie, and the latest developments with the search." With that he turned and headed for his truck as the two women started for the barn.

∞

Shelly jerked awake. The snow had stopped, but there was a deep drift at the edge of the overhang. She leaned forward and called out, "Ashley?"

No reply. She kicked the snow away and shook off her leaf blanket. She crawled out of the protected area and tried to stand, but one leg was numb. How long had she slept with it tucked under her body? The last thing she remembered was the sound of night creatures as they rustled through the underbrush in the dark. She didn't think she could possibly sleep, but she must have, because the sun was now high in the sky. As she rubbed her numbed leg, she called again, louder this time, "Ashley, you awake?"

A weak reply, "Yeah."

She sighed and said, "You okay?"

A groan, then, "I must have fallen asleep."

"Me too," Shelly said as she held onto the rock outcropping and stood. She put some weight on the leg to test it, and the numbness had disappeared. "The snow has stopped, and the sun is out," she said as she edged closer to the hole.

Ashley said, "Still dark in here, but I can see the sun through the hole. Wish I had my flashlight, or even a match."

Shelly dropped to her knees and peered over the side of the opening. The hole was a little over a foot in diameter, but was crisscrossed with gnarly tree roots. The roots of the tree must have weakened the top of the underground cave, and when Ashley stepped on it last night, it simply gave way with her weight. Shelly hoped it was stable now.

She gazed past the dirt and tangled tree roots, but it was dark in the cave, so she couldn't see very much. "I can't see you, Ashley. How's your leg?"

"My leg doesn't hurt anymore, actually, I can't even feel it. I don't think that's good. I can see your silhouette, but not your face."

Shelly was about to respond when she heard a rustle from the bushes to her left. She jumped and whispered, "Shhhh—someone's coming." The noise was close.

"Oh, no—please don't let it be Felix. Hide, Shelly!" Ashley said in a fierce whisper.

A large black bear came out of the bushes and around the tree. It was only a few feet from where Shelly knelt. The animal stopped and stared at her for a moment, then raised its snout high, and sniffed at the air.

Shelly froze. The animal was enormous. He had dried blood on his mouth, and his shoulder was stained dark red against his black coat.

The bear rose to its full height and roared. "Oh, God," she whispered, then tried to stand, but her legs felt like rubber, and wouldn't cooperate. She opened her mouth to scream, but her voice was gone, so it sounded like "Ah, ah, ah."

The bear dropped to all fours, and bounced up and down on his front paws. Shelly felt the ground shake. Steam rose from the animal's hot breath in the chilly morning air.

"What is that? What's going on, Shelly?" Ashley called from the hole. The bear stopped all movement. His massive head locked in on Shelly and he turned it one way, then the other as he gazed at her. Saliva dripped from his mouth, then the animal's muscles tensed as he sprang forward in a blur of movement.

Shelly's body took over and she plunged head first into the hole. As she fell through the tangled roots, one of the limbs caught her right boot, and she dangled for a moment in total darkness. Finally, she felt her foot slip out of the boot, and she tumbled down a muddy slope until she hit something soft that broke her fall. A deep moan came from the cushion. Ashley.

She pushed into Ashley's side, and they clung to each other. Shelly whispered, "It's a bear." They were blanketed in darkness, but at the top of the cavern, the hole was a bright circle of light.

The bear appeared at the circle, then sniffed at the boot stuck in the roots. He grabbed at it with one giant paw and managed to tear it from the roots, then pull it into his enormous mouth. He chewed and growled, then shook his big head, and flung the boot through the air. It landed with a thump somewhere behind him.

Shelly wanted to close her eyes, but could not tear her gaze away as the animal dug and clawed at the opening. He couldn't get more than his big head and one paw past the top, but as he blocked the bright sunlight, Shelly moved closer into Ashley's side and hugged her tight.

The bear's roar filled the enclosed space, and his spittle and pieces of dirt and tree root sprinkled over them. Neither of the girls spoke, and Shelly could barely breathe. It seemed like hours, but was probably only minutes, before the bear quieted, and then disappeared. Only blue sky remained.

After a moment Shelly whispered, "Do you think he's gone?"

"I don't know, but I don't think you should stick your head up there and see. You saw what he did with your boot."

"Good point."

"Besides, I don't think you can get up there, even with two good legs. It looks too high and the slope is steep. Let's just stay quiet for a while and rest."

"Okay. I think that's a good plan." Shelly moved over a little to give Ashley more room, "I'm sorry I hit you when I jumped in—did I hurt you?"

"Honestly, I don't feel much right now. How about you? You fell hard—did you get hurt?"

"You broke my fall."

"Glad to be of service."

Shelly laughed, "Nothing rattles you."

"Felix does and now I guess bears do, too. I sure hope he can't get down here."

"Did you see the blood on his mouth?"

"No—All I could see were those huge teeth."

"When I saw him in the sunlight, he had blood all around his mouth—do you think he attacked someone else? Oh, wow—maybe it was Felix."

"Now that's positive thinking," Ashley laughed. "I will enjoy that thought," then she grew quiet, and her breathing deepened.

The girl was asleep again. Shelly felt her forehead, "Oh, Ashley, you're burning up." What do I do? She thought as she gazed up at the opening. The dark shadow of the bear moved around the hole, then stuck his head in for a moment before he moved away again. It looked like he wasn't going anywhere. Then a terrifying thought occurred to her. What if the blood wasn't Felix's? "Oh, God—not you mom, please, not you," she whispered to the dark.

CHAPTER THIRTY
SATURDAY

Warmth tickled at Summer's eyelids. She flicked them open and blinked. The sun danced as it reflected off the snow, so she shaded her eyes with one hand and shifted her position slightly. Nestled against her chest, a warm furry body was snoring—Jake. Her back was supported by Tyler, and he had one arm around her waist. What a comfortable sandwich. She sighed, but refused to enjoy the moment. How could she possibly feel cozy with Shelly still lost and alone? Well, at least she had the teenage girl with her. Hopefully, they were still together, but there was no way to know until they found them.

Where did they sleep? Was she hungry? Were they able to survive the frigid night? Summer was wrapped in a sleeping bag with two warm bodies, was Shelly lying somewhere in the cold snow? And what about wild animals? She saw firsthand what an angry bear could do. What if the girls had come in contact with something equally as ferocious? She made a small sound as a sob caught in her throat.

"Ummm—what's wrong?" Tyler mumbled.

Jake jumped up and crawled out of the sleeping bag. He stretched, then raised his nose to the air and ground before he circled the camp.

"It's light," Summer whispered.

"Okay," Tyler pulled his arm from around Summer and sat up, "Okay, okay." He rolled his head and neck in a slow circle, "Man, I slept too sound. I meant to stay awake, but it felt so good to be next to you again." He pulled her into his arms for a gentle hug and kiss, "I missed you so much."

Summer turned and kissed him back, then said, "I missed you too, I can't even tell you how much, but there will be time for that later—right now let's find our girl."

Tyler nodded, "Absolutely." He stood and moved to the horse, where he threw a saddle over the blanket on the animal's back. As he cinched the saddle around his stomach, the horse blew out air and snorted. Summer tried to stand, but wobbled, then eased back down. "Wait, I'll get you up as soon as I get the gear packed," he said.

"I am sorry I can't help more."

He laughed, "You're doing great, with all you've been through, you should be in a hospital, not out here in the cold."

Summer leaned back against a tree and watched him pack the blanket from the lean-to, and then their sleeping bag. He did it with clean, precise movements. In minutes he had the camp almost completely dismantled and the horse ready to go. It was wonderful to watch him work. She could almost pretend everything was normal. Almost.

When she was in the cave cell, she had too much time to think, and her thoughts had strayed to very dark places. Her biggest fear was to die in the cave and leave Shelly to spend her life with that madman, Felix. She shivered. Unthinkable. And what about Tyler? For him to deal with their disappearance with no answers. Simply vanished. Not to know what happened to her and Shelly after all he had been through, that would have taken him over the edge. And her mother, oh, God—it would have ruined all their lives. She gazed up at Tyler and said, "I love you."

He turned to her with a question in his eyes, then his face softened, "I love you, too." He moved over to her, bent and picked her up in his arms, then kissed her deeply before he lifted her onto the horse. They touched hands and smiled, then Tyler gave her the reins and whistled to Jake. The dog's head snapped toward him, then he jumped forward and sniffed at the snow and bushes until he found something he liked. Jake took off at a fast pace into the forest. Summer couldn't see the tracks, but it was Jake's nose not their eyes, that led the way.

∞

Ashley felt like a hot blanket by her side. The older girl was very still as they lay side by side, and she hadn't spoken in a while. Shelly listened to her breathing. It sounded shallow and ragged. "Ashley?" she whispered, but there was no response. She touched her friend and said, "Ashley, can you hear me?"

A dark shadow moved across the sun at the top of the cave. Shelly stared intently at the hole until the shadow erupted into an ear splitting roar. She cringed. The bear moved his head away and an arm plunged through the opening and clawed at the roots and dirt.

Debris rained on them, so she covered her and Ashley's face as much as she could. When it finally stopped, she coughed and shook her head, then she gently brushed the dirt off Ashley's face. The older teen had not moved during the assault.

"Ashley?" Silence. Tears welled up in her eyes and she said, "Please, Ashley, you've made it this far, don't slip away from me now. I need you to be here. I don't think I can do this by myself."

Shelly gazed up at the hole. She could smell the earthy dirt mixed with the stink of the animal. The hairy arm disappeared and his head jammed through, this time deeper than it had before. "Go away!" she yelled at him, then she belted out a loud, long scream. She knew it would only anger and entice the beast, but she couldn't seem to help herself. Shelly felt tears flow across her cheeks and into her hair and ears, but she didn't try to wipe them, she simply let them flow. They felt warm as they traced across her cold cheeks and tasted of salt where they hit her lips. "Enough!" she growled as she swiped at her eyes, then propped up on one elbow. She touched Ashley's face again and whispered, "Please…" It was all she could manage.

Debris began to rain on them again, so she looked up and gasped. The bear now had his head and one shoulder through the opening and the hole was much bigger. She watched in amazement as he scratched and pulled at the roots which loosened the dirt.

Damn smart animal, or just very determined. Shelly squeezed her eyes shut and mumbled, "Go away, please." This time she felt a hand pat her arm. Her eyes flew open and she put her hand on top of Ashley's. It felt hot and dry, "You're awake, and burning up!"

"Yeah—it's hot in here," so low, Shelly could barely hear the mumble. She watched the teen lick at dry, cracked lips in the dim light.

She felt her forehead again, "Oh, Ashley, you need water but I don't have any down here."

"Well, don't start blubbering again," the mumbled reply.

That made her smile, at least until a big piece of root landed on her shoulder. She looked up to see the bear had moved even deeper into the opening. She turned back toward her friend, "Ashley?" No reply this time. "Are you still with me?" she asked, but the girl had slipped away again. The teen twitched and then lay very still. Shelly couldn't hear her breathe, so she leaned close to her lips, and listened. Small, shallow breaths. Shelly sighed. It was just as well. If that bear got all the way in, she hoped her friend would not be present for what would come next.

CHAPTER THIRTY-ONE SATURDAY

Maggie placed the rifle sling over her shoulder and climbed to a lower limb of the tree, then jumped. She landed in the snow, then stood for a moment and listened to the quiet. Snow both muffled and magnified sound, but not much stirred in the morning forest. Even Mother Nature slept in on a cold morning like this.

She pulled some beef jerky out of her pocket and popped it into her mouth. The dried beef was spicy and had the texture of leather. She squatted while she chewed and stared at a slight depression in the snow. Last night it was a more distinctive bear track. The overnight snow filled in the depth and made it appear as if the animal was much smaller. Maggie wondered if the bear searched for a place to hibernate, or if he was still on a rampage. The snow covered the blood drops she originally saw in the tracks. Now there was only a slight rust color, and it was dim, but she knew the animal was injured, and that made him dangerous.

When the night had grown dark, and the snow began to fall, the tree became her home. Bears can climb trees, but they make a lot of noise doing it. She just hoped Tyler, Summer, and the girls had also found a safe refuge to wait out the dawn.

Maggie stood. Her warm boots kept her feet from feeling the cold, but the deep drifts would make her movement slow. She thought longingly of her snow shoes hanging in the tool shed at the cabin. She glanced at some of the saplings around the area. It wouldn't be too hard to come up with a makeshift version, but it would steal precious time.

She moved out of the tree's deep root ring and her head snapped up. Sound carried well in the frozen, silent morning, and she had heard the noise she had been dreading. Maggie moved her rifle around to her side, but paused. There it was again, and it was very clear, but this time the roar of the bear was accompanied by a human scream as it cut through the calm morning air.

Maggie gripped the rifle and charged due east. No time for snowshoes, the boots would have to carry her at a faster pace than they normally would.

She warmed quickly as the sun climbed in the sky, and she soon worked up a sweat. The trees became thicker as she headed farther into the forest, but she kept the same pace, ignoring the branches that slapped against her thighs and arms. The scream was a girl's and the bear sounded enraged.

∞

Summer leaned into the horse's neck as they edged through the tightly spaced trees. The animal felt warm in spite of the cold. He kept tossing his head and his eyes were wild. She had to hold on tight and press hard with her knees to move him forward. Tyler was on foot a few feet in front of the horse. He could move much faster through the thick woods, so he had to stop often to wait for them to catch up.

There it was again, the roar of a bear. It sounded much closer this time, and like it had something cornered, but maybe that was just her imagination. Then Summer felt chills grip her spine and she cursed into the horse's neck. The roar had been followed by a muted scream. She knew now she should have let Tyler finish the wounded animal off when he had the chance. She never imagined it would travel this far and be a threat to her child. What was she thinking when she called him off? An extra hour would have prevented this. She choked on a sob and gripped the reigns tighter.

This was all her fault. She knew bears, since she grew up in the area, so there was no excuse. If this was the same bear that attacked Felix, it was a threat to anyone it came into contact with. The animal was yanked out of his territory, wounded, and had killed. He was unpredictable and should have been put down immediately. Each time she heard it roar, she felt as if her heart would burst.

The horse stopped and danced in place as he tossed his head from one side to the other. Summer raised her head and shouted, "Tyler!" He paused and turned in her direction. His face was contorted with urgency, "Go! Don't wait for me—go!" He shook his head in a 'yes' motion, then turned and ran. Within moments he was swallowed by the forest.

Summer held the reins with a strong hand, squeezed her knees tight into the animal's side, and guided him toward the area where Tyler disappeared. The horse was skittish, probably from the same sound that made her heart race, and he could most likely smell the beast by now. She reached down and stroked his neck and said, "Easy, boy, easy."

Silence. The wild roars stopped as abruptly as they had started, and the only sound was the snow as it crunched with each of their steps. Her horse calmed a little, so she relaxed her knees and her hold on the reigns. Summer ducked her head as she spied a large limb weighted down with snow just ahead. When she looked up again, Tyler was in front of them. He was at the edge of a small clearing and stood in a shooting stance with the rifle pointed to his right. Summer gazed in that direction. The bear.

It looked like the same huge beast that killed Felix. It had its back to Tyler as it dug in the ground close to a big snarly tree. How odd.

What was it after? A rabbit in a hole? She held her breath and tightened her hold on the reigns as Tyler eased closer. He raised the weapon and tensed. Summer couldn't see the animal's head and he needed a head shot to put him down.

The bear suddenly looked up and twisted toward him. Tyler had his shot, but the animal was quick and charged as the rifle blazed. The sudden movement of the bear caused Tyler to barely graze its shoulder before it was on him. The bear skidded to a stop as he slashed out with his giant paw.

Summer looked on in horror as Tyler fell back and landed on the ground as the rifle flew from his hand. She could see the front of his jacket was shredded where the animal's claws had found contact. The bear hovered just above him as he threw his head back and roared at the sky. Tyler attempted a back pedal motion and visions of the attack on Felix flashed in Summer's mind.

A sudden flurry of movement to her right as Jake flew through the air at the massive bear. The bear swatted the dog away like a fly, but it gave Tyler a moment to get to his knees. Jake landed in a snow drift close by, but lay motionless. "No!" Summer screamed as she gripped the reigns and dug her heals deep into the horses flanks, but instead of a surge forward, he reared up and kicked at the air. The bear turned and looked at the horse. He rose to his full height and growled at the new adversary that was so much bigger than the man on the ground.

Summer dug her heals in once more, this time the horse bucked hard enough to dislodge her from the saddle, so she slid backwards off its hind quarters and landed on both feet. As she landed, the damaged leg gave way and she went down fast. The horse bolted in the opposite direction of the bear. Summer just missed being trampled in the process. "Sure, now you can move fast," she thought as she watched the horse disappear through the trees.

Tyler no longer held an interest for the bear as he moved toward Summer. When he got close, he sniffed at the air, then at her boots. She heard Tyler as he yelled, "No, no—here, come back, I'm over here!" His voice sounded as if it came from a great distance as she stared up at the bear. Damn he was big. This was the second time she was close to him, but this time she had his full attention. He raised one big paw in the air, as if prepared for a curious swipe at her, when several shots rang out. The animal froze and its eyes glazed over. Summer gasped as it began to fall in her direction. She couldn't seem to move as the animal crashed toward her, but at the last moment, she felt a hard pull on her arm, and she slid sideways. The beast fell next to her with a loud thump that shook the ground and one of his huge arms hit her left shoulder. She struggled to move, but found herself pinned from the weight on her shoulder. She stopped struggling and turned to look at him. All she could see were his massive claws and huge head. His eyes were wide open, but unseeing, and blood ran from two holes in his head. Summer gagged. The smell was overwhelming; it was somewhere between wet dog, blood, and mold. She struggled again, but this time felt the weight of the bears arm lift off of her, so she rolled free and retched violently in the snow. When she gazed up, she was shocked to see an Apache woman in a Tribal Police uniform, instead of Tyler. She managed to say, "Thank you."

"You're welcome," the woman said as she put her rifle in a sling over her shoulder.

Tyler moved in and put his arm around her waist and helped her stand. They moved away from the bear and he asked, "Are you alright?" But before she could answer he continued with, "What were you thinking?"

She frowned and replied, "Well, I was thinking I didn't want you to become a bloody spot on the ground like Felix."

His face softened and he enveloped her in a hug, but she flinched as they made contact. He pulled back and said, "I'm sorry, thank you, but don't ever do it again!" They both laughed and Tyler turned and stuck out his hand, "Thanks Maggie—Thank you so much," he said as he pumped her hand, then he turned to Summer and said, "Summer, this is Maggie Littlejohn. She's the one who figured out Felix was the one who took you. It's the reason we were here so quickly."

Summer extended her hand and said, "We owe you a huge amount of gratitude."

Maggie said, "Not necessary. I can't tell you how glad I am to see you."

Summer knew she didn't say it, but "and still alive" was implied. She smiled back, "Not nearly as glad as I am to see you, and your rifle."

Maggie nodded, then moved over to the bear and squatted by his enormous head. She placed a hand on the animal and whispered "he-ay-hee-ee!" in Apache, then turned toward them and said, "He was a young one." She shook her head, "A shame. He just followed his nature when he was threatened."

Not so unlike Felix, but I am glad they are both dead. Summer thought, then turned when she heard a muffle cry. It came from where the bear was digging.

"Was that one of the girls?" Maggie said.

"Oh, God, please?" Summer said as she leaned toward the noise, "Listen, there it is again!" She looked around and said, "But, where?"

Jake rose from the snow drift and limped toward the sound. Summer smiled. That was one tough little dog. Jake stopped suddenly and stared at the ground. He sat, raised his head, looked at them and barked, then returned his gaze to the ground.

A muffled, "Hello?" They all heard it that time and Tyler rushed closer to Jake, but then stopped as his foot slipped into the top of a hole.

"What the hell?" he pulled his leg out and dropped to his knees, "Shelly? Is that you, Honey?"

Maggie moved in beside him and gazed down into the hole, "Damn," she said. Jake whined and barked, then raised his head and bayed.

"Tyler! It's me!" Shelly yelled up at them.

"Shelly, Oh my baby!" Summer tried but couldn't stand, so she began to crawl in their direction. Tyler returned and lifted her into his arms, then carried her close to the hole before easing her to the ground.

"Mom?" They heard a sob, then, "My friend Ashley is here with me and she's unconscious. She has a fever and I think her leg broke in the fall."

"Don't worry, Honey, we're here now, and we'll get you both out. Are you okay?"

"I am now."

Maggie stood and pulled out the police radio. When she tried to call the Chief, they heard only static. She looked at Summer and Tyler and said, "Looks like we are on our own on this one."

CHAPTER THIRTY-TWO SATURDAY

"Can you reach a little higher? Come on, Shelly you can do it—that's it, I almost have you!" Tyler's voice coaxed. He lay flat on his belly with his upper torso in the hole and his legs spread out on the ground behind him. Maggie sat on his calves and gripped his jeans while she braced her feet against the roots that circled the hole. Summer hovered just behind Maggie with Jake close by her side. If she weren't so worried, Summer would have laughed aloud at the comical sight. She itched to help them, but with her arm and leg injuries, she could only sit and watch.

Maggie tightened her grip as Tyler's legs slipped forward an inch. Summer whispered, "Can I help?" The back of Maggie's head shook from side to side, then her back tensed and she slid forward a little more. Summer held her breath, but Maggie shoved hard against the roots and gave a pull on Tyler's legs.

A grunt from Tyler, then, "Go, you've got it!" he yelled from the hole. Shelly's head popped up and she groaned as she reached over the side and pulled at the roots, then she scrambled up and over Tyler. She was free of the hole, and other than being filthy, she looked unharmed.

"Shelly!" Summer called.

"Mom!" the girl yelled as she ran forward. Maggie scooted backward and pulled until Tyler's upper body appeared, then he swung around and sat on the edge of the hole. Shelly plopped down in front of Summer, hesitated a moment, then fell into her lap. Summer held her daughter and stroked her hair. Teen to toddler. Shelly lifted her head and said, "Mom—we survived." Then she buried her face in Summer's shoulder and sobbed.

Summer murmured into her daughter's hair, "Yes, Honey, we did, we sure did." Jake moved in and sniffed at the girl, then licked at her hands and her face.

Shelly's sobs quieted and turned into giggles. She raised her head and said, "Okay, okay, Jake. I missed you too!" She rubbed her hand down his back and he yelped. "Oh, sorry, Boy." The dog whined in reply. She turned to her mother and asked, "Did he get hurt?"

Summer shifted her daughter's weight and winced, "He had a run in with the bear and it was quite heroic." She gazed at the bear carcass, "Just look at the size of that animal. Jake is lucky to be alive. We all are for that matter. We'll get him checked out with a vet as soon as we get back to civilization."

Shelly touched her mother's arm, "You're hurt, too? Did the bear attack you?"

"No, he tried, but Maggie shot him. My injuries came from Felix, but I'm okay." She smiled at her child, and pushed the blonde hair off her forehead. "You got dirty down there, Pumpkin," she said as she glanced at Shelly's clothing, "I have to say I am not too fond of this fashion statement, either."

That made Shelly laugh, but she sobered and said, "Did that horrible man hurt you very much? He did awful things to Ashley." She frowned and shook her head, then gazed into the forest, "Is he still after us?"

"Not any more, Sweetie. He will never bother you again."

"They got him?"

"In a manner of speaking—the bear got him."

"You're kidding?"

"No, very serious."

The corner of Shelly's lip twitched, then she said, "Hmmm, I guess the bear wasn't all bad."

Tyler broke in with, "Shelly, is your friend, uh, Ashley, still unconscious? We haven't heard anything from her."

Shelly looked up at them and her eyes widened, "She is in and out of consciousness, and she's burning up with fever, even her breathing sounds bad, like a rattle. She was completely out when I started my climb. She said she hurt her leg in the fall and thinks it might be broken. I couldn't see it, but I think she was in a lot of pain." Her eyes glistened and she said, "She saved my life more than once, please help her."

Maggie and Tyler gazed at each other, then Maggie said, "I'll go down, I'm smaller and will fit better. The cave wall isn't stable and we don't want the sides to come down on her."

Tyler said, "I had a rope on the horse, but with the way he ran from the bear, it might take a while to round him up."

Maggie moved over to the hole and leaned over it as she shined her flashlight around the space below, "I can't see much from here. If you can help me get down there I'll try to stabilize her leg enough to lift her up to you." Maggie glanced around the clearing, "We should find something to use as a brace for her injured leg."

"There are a lot of broken limbs where we fought with the bear. They look strong enough to work if you can find something to strap them to her," Summer said.

"How about your belts?" Shelly asked.

Maggie and Tyler looked down at their pants. Each of them had on a sturdy belt. Tyler laughed and said, "Perfect! That's good thinking, Kiddo." Shelly jumped up to help Maggie and Tyler gather some limbs. Once they cleaned the smaller branches off, they placed them beside the hole with the belts.

Tyler sat at the edge of the hole with his legs dangling just below the surface. He wrapped his hands deep in the roots then nodded at Maggie. She used his legs like a ladder to lower herself as she held her flashlight in her mouth. It did very little to illuminate the dark cave as the arc of light swung around the underground space.

Summer and Shelly scooted closer to the hole and gazed down from above. When Maggie was close to the bottom she let go and jumped, landing close beside the girl. She moved her flashlight around the tight space and over the girl's body. They all gasped in unison. The light played over an unconscious Ashley. Her leg was twisted into an odd angle. It looked like a stick had stabbed her in her shin. Summer leaned forward, gazing at the girl and a small sound bubbled up from her throat. It wasn't a stick, it was her bone. The poor girl must have been in agony. Maybe it was better she had slipped into unconsciousness.

Maggie looked up at them and said, "Hand me the branches and belts."

Tyler moved around until his upper body was in the hole again and held each branch at arm's length until Maggie could reach and retrieve them. She laid them by the bad leg while she brushed some of the dirt away from the wound area, then she said, "I have to straighten it out a little before I can strap the braces to it." As Maggie leaned down and began to move the leg, but the girl awoke with a scream. "It's okay, Ashley, I'm here to help," Maggie said.

"Who are you?" Ashley asked.

"I'm Maggie Littlejohn and I'm with the Tribal Police."

"Thank you." the girl fell back and closed her eyes before she mumbled, "That hurts like hell, by the way."

"I'm sorry to say that it will hurt even more, so scream all you want. I have to get your leg as stable as I can before we get you out of this hole. I'll tie these branches to it, but I have to move it a little straighter before I do. We don't want to damage it even more as we lift you."

"You had me at 'get me out of here.' Do what you need to do," Ashley said.

Maggie handed the girl one of the smaller branches and said, "You can bite this if you like."

Ashley opened her eyes, looked at the branch and said, "You've got to be kidding?"

Maggie smiled, "No. Honestly, it will help." The girl sighed and took the branch as she clasped it in both hands and hugged it to her chest.

"Okay. But I'd rather have some drugs. Good old modern pharmaceuticals."

Maggie chuckled and said, "Are you hurt anywhere else?"

"I don't think so—just my leg."

"Ready?"

The girl placed the stick in her mouth and nodded. Maggie nodded back, then in one swift movement, yanked the leg straight. Ashley screamed and Summer heard the branch she held in her mouth snap, then the girl's head fell back as she again slipped into unconsciousness. The bone had disappeared, but the wound looked ragged and swollen.

"It's for the best, but she will be harder to lift," Maggie spoke over her shoulder. She took off her jacket and gently wrapped it around the girl's leg. Then she placed a branch on either side of the leg and strapped the belts on it. She turned and looked up at them and said, "We need to be as gentle as we can when we lift her. The wound is very dirty, and the area around it is swollen and looks like it is tinged with some yellow pus."

Summer drew in a quick breath and Tyler said, "No wonder she has a fever. We need to be gentle, but we also need to get this done, and fast. She could lose the leg—or worse."

"We're ready," Maggie said.

Tyler lay on his stomach, with his upper body dangling into the hole, while Summer and Shelly each held onto his legs. Maggie grasped the unconscious girl under her arms and lifted her. Tyler couldn't quite reach her, so Maggie edged up the slope of the cave, and pushed the girl higher. This time Tyler was able to get a grasp, and began to inch backward until the girl's upper body was free of the opening. Shelly moved in, and together they somehow got Ashley out of the hole.

Tyler reached back into the hole to help Maggie, but instead she shook her head and said, "Let me try." She grabbed at the biggest dangling root, pulled on it, and when it didn't give way, she used it like a rope. She climbed it hand over hand as she walked up the side of the cave. The dirt wall began to crumble, so she moved faster until she was nearly at the top, then reached for Tyler's hand. She grasped it, and the next moment, she was above ground.

"Thanks," Maggie said.

"No problem," Tyler replied, then they all laughed as Tyler realized what he said, "Okay, maybe it was a little problem." He glanced at a still unconscious Ashley. She was pale but her cheeks were red with fever. They could hear a rattle as her chest moved slowly up and down. "What now?" he asked.

"Why don't you see if you can find the horse?" Maggie said, "We'll need him to get her out of here." She turned to Summer and Shelly and said, "You two keep an eye on Ashley, and I'll get some more branches. As soon as Tyler gets back we can make a litter with the rope. We need to get help before dark, so let's move."

"I can take care of Ashley," Shelly said.

"No, you can move and I'm pretty immobile. It makes more sense for you to help Maggie. She can tell you what to look for and I'll take care of Ashley." Shelly gazed at the girl lying so still in the snow. Summer said, "I'll take good care of her. You gather some strong limbs so we can get her to some real help." She touched her daughter's arm and they locked eyes for a moment, then Shelly jumped up and turned to Maggie.

"Tell me what you need."

∞

Summer shifted her good foot in the stirrup. The branch from the litter rested underneath it, and she didn't want to put more pressure against the horse's side. He was still a little skittish. Tyler had finally gotten him back to the clearing, but he tried to bolt again as soon as he smelled the dead bear.

They had to move farther away from the giant carcass before they were able to attach the litter to the horse. Maggie and Tyler worked together to quiet the horse while Shelly eased the litter into place. It worked, but it took precious time that they didn't have. The sun would soon slip behind the mountain, and they would be stuck for another night. Another night that Ashley didn't have.

Summer turned in the saddle to look at the girl. She could still lose her life, or at the very least, her leg, even if they made it to a hospital before dark. The teen protected her daughter at the compound, and without her help, she doubted if either one of them would have escaped that madman, Felix. She didn't want to think about what would have happened if Ashley had not been there to help Shelly from the start, not to mention how much abuse the girl must have suffered over the years from him. Summer shook her head. She really wanted to save this child.

After Tyler found the horse, they assembled the litter, or travois, as Maggie called it. They were able to use the rope, branches, and Tyler's sleeping bag to put it together. It looked sturdy, and Ashley was tied down and swaddled in Tyler's sleeping bag. Her skin was almost the color of the snow that surrounded them and she had not moved recently, but Summer could hear her labored breathing, so at least she knew she was alive. "Please God, let this child live," she murmured. Shelly leaned over the litter and tucked her friend in a little tighter. Summer smiled. She liked this maternal side of her daughter.

Shelly stood and her voice rang out very clear in the still afternoon, "Where are we going?" The air was chilled and crisp. It would be a perfect day if a life didn't hang in the balance, and the fear of another frigid night in the woods loomed.

Maggie answered before Summer could say anything, "There is a plateau a few miles to the southeast. Reception on our radio, or one of our cell phones, should work there. At least I hope it will. It's also the only place in the area that a helicopter can land, and we need a medevac." She glanced at the girl on the litter, then continued with, "The sooner the better."

Shelly moved alongside the horse and looked up at Summer as she asked in a low voice, "Is Ashley going to die?"

Summer drew in a quick breath. Shelly had a slight tremor in her tightly clasped hands, and her upper lip quivered as she asked the question. "I hope not. We're going to do our best to make sure that doesn't happen."

Tyler moved toward them and pulled something from his pack on the horse's back, then turned to Shelly and handed her a small, stuffed bear, "I brought this from home because it was your favorite and I knew I would find you." He glanced at the bear as he handed it to her, then said, "I didn't know you would get so up close and personal with a real one, so it may no longer be your favorite."

Shelly laughed, "It does change one's perspective." She pulled back and gazed at the bear then hugged it close to her chest, "It's still my favorite—it was a gift from my dad before he met me, and now it came from my new dad." She hugged Tyler, then said, "Thank you."

Tyler returned the hug and said, "We'll get through this."

Shelly tucked the bear in beside Ashley, put one hand on the litter, and said, "What are we waiting for? Let's go."

Summer smiled, wiped her wet cheeks, and turned forward on the horse. She picked up the reins and said, "You heard the girl, let's do this."

Maggie was at the front of the group, so she headed forward first. Tyler moved in beside her as they used their knives to cut branches to fit the horse and travois.

Summer couldn't help but think about the primitive people who probably followed this route in much the same way. Possibly with an old or injured loved one on a litter. But they didn't have hopes of a medevac when they reached their destination, only their wits and experience to get them through. We can do this, she thought. This child has been through too much not to make it now. We will save her.

CHAPTER THIRTY-THREE SATURDAY

The open plateau was a white blanket framed by mountains and massive pine trees. A vast expanse of pristine snow. Gray and white clouds danced over the mountain range bursting with the promise of more snow. The wind was still at the moment, so the helicopter would be able to get to them before the weather turned—if they could only contact someone.

Summer turned to Shelly and asked, "How is she?" Her daughter's hand brushed over Ashley's forehead, then she leaned over the litter and placed her ear close to the girl's mouth, "Her head is really hot and her breathing sounds even more like a rattle." She gazed up at Summer with troubled eyes.

Maggie took several long strides into the field. The snow was only ankle deep, but her tracks were the only ones in the vast expanse. She pulled out her cell phone and held it up as she turned in a slow circle. She frowned and said, "No bars," but tried it anyway. She cursed softly and pulled out the radio. Silence, then Summer grinned when she heard static, and finally the welcome voice of Chief Anderson booming from the radio as he said, “Copy? You there?”

Maggie grinned and nodded at them as she said, “This is Maggie. We are on the southeast plateau, approximately ten miles from you. Ralph, do you copy?” Summer eased the horse forward so she could hear the conversation more clearly.

“Yes, thank God—yes! Do you have everyone with you?”

Maggie glanced up at them as she spoke, “Yes, we are all here. Summer is injured, but not seriously. Shelly and Tyler are fine, but the teen girl, Ashley, is critical. Bad leg, and possible infection. She is running a high fever. We need a medevac ASAP—can you get us help?”

“The copter is already in the air and ready to go. We have EMT’s and a doctor standing by, I’ll send them your location now. Maggie, there will only be room for the girls and Summer. The winds are picking up here, so we will need to scoop them up fast. Can you and Tyler last out there a little longer?”

“Of course, the main concern is the girl. She needs medicine and fluids.”

“Good. Maggie, the BIA have people closer than us on the Rez, they’ll help you guys make it out that way. I’ll radio them next.”

“From which direction? After we get the girls and Summer on the helicopter, Tyler and I will head their way.” She held her hand up to the group. Even though she could hear every word, Summer began to cry when she saw the thumbs up signal.

“From the east, Maggie, head east.”

“Got it! Thanks, Ralph, tell Jennifer and Elsa we are on our way.”

“They are right here, Maggie. We have all been waiting for your call. This is great news!”

"Maggie? You stay safe and get yourself back here. You took too long!"

They all laughed when Elsa's voice rang out of Maggie's radio over Chief Anderson's. The helicopter sounded in the background and a cheer went up from the group. Maggie said, "Okay, we're on our way as soon as they're loaded." Maggie signed off and disconnected the radio, then turned to the group and said, "You heard the man, let's get that litter off the horse. Shelly, why don't you take Jake with you? He's one of the injured and he doesn't weight much."

Shelly turned to her mother and asked, "Can I?"

Summer looked at her daughter and said, "Of course, now let's get Ashley ready. We're headed home." She grinned then gazed up at the sky and whispered, "Thank you."

CHAPTER THIRTY-FOUR

A little more to the right," Summer narrowed her eyes, "No, that's too far, back to the left just a smidge."

Tyler sighed, "Can you tell me in inches how much a smidge is?" He scooted the tree over a couple of inches. He was crouched on his knees with his hands around the trunk of the large cedar tree, "There, is that a smidge, your highness?"

"Smart ass," Summer said then laughed as she sat on the couch with her leg propped up on the coffee table, "Okay that's perfect."

Tyler raised up and gazed at the tree, then turned to Shelly, "You hear that? She said perfect! We did good, kid."

Shelly grinned back and said, "Yes we did!" She gave him a high five then bounded over and plopped on the couch next to her mother. She leaned on Summer's shoulder and said, "Mom, I picked it out myself, Tyler only cut it down."

"Listen to you? No mention of how I also hauled it all the way back to the house," he added.

"Ok, maybe, but I helped pull it into the truck."

Summer pulled at a sticky spot in her daughter's hair, "I can tell you helped, this sap in your hair will not be easy to get out. Think you might want a pixie cut?"

"Moooom!"

Oh how Summer had missed that three syllable 'mom' when they were separated, heck, even before they were separated, and Shelly had turned into a teen monster. Her sweet girl was back. It might not be forever; Summer knew she would slip back into teen angst again, but that was okay, it was all part of the process. A process she thought she might lose for a while, so now it was welcomed as a part of this sweet life. Summer shifted her position and her weight before she reached down to scratch at the top of her cast, "I will be so glad to get this thing off."

"When is your appointment?" Shelly asked.

"Next Monday—thank goodness it will be before Christmas!"

"And before Grandma and Ashley get here."

"That's right—did you get the trundle bed ready?"

"Yep—all set to go, and I made room in my closet for her. Grandma will have the guest room all to herself. Besides, the wheel chair will fit through my door easier than the guest room door." She sighed and fiddled with the tinsel she held in her hand, "I wish they could stay longer than just for the Christmas break."

"Well, you know she will be here longer once school is out for the summer." Miss Elsa is strict about her not missing school. She has a lot of ground to catch up with on her studies, and she needs to keep up her physical therapy."

"I can help her with her physical therapy and Tyler is a teacher for goodness sake."

Tyler joined the two on the couch and gazed at the tree, "I can get the lights strung, and if you make popcorn, we can decorate it."

"All right—I'll do it, but you are not fooling me one little bit. I know when you try to change the subject, and I want you both to know we aren't through with this argument." Shelly jumped up and headed for the kitchen, then turned and said, "Oh, I guess mom could make some of her famous cookies. You know, the ones that were the envy of all the other moms at the last bake sale? No wait, the bakery is closed today."

Summer's mouth fell open, "What?"

Tyler and Shelly both laughed and then Shelly eased into the kitchen.

Summer turned to Tyler, "You both knew?"

He smiled, "Of, course. We thought it was cute."

"Cute?"

"Ah, I think I better change the subject before I wind up in the doghouse with Jake."

"What makes you think you're not already there?"

Tyler rubbed Summer's protruding belly bump, "How's the little one, today?"

"Active—this one is already kicking, and I am much bigger then I was with Shelly at this point. I think it's a boy." She rubbed her stomach and her hand brushed Tyler's, "Talk about changing the subject."

He laughed and said, "Are you sure you don't want to find out?"

"Well—we'll see, but right now I still want to be surprised."

"Me too."

They both settled into the couch with their hands barely touching between them. Summer sighed and said, "You know she isn't about to give up on Ashley spending more time here."

"I know, but Shelly is a smart girl, and in the end she will want what's best for Ashley. Ashley needs stability and a sanctuary, and time to regain some of the childhood Felix stole from her. Another move would be too much right now."

Summer nodded, "You're right, I know." She hiccupped, then reached for her water and took a sip before she said, "I am so glad mom decided to take Ashley as a foster child. She was too young when she had me and she was such a free spirit. I think at this point in her life the girl is just what mom needs, as well as what Ashley needs." Summer smiled, "And there is the art connection. Ashley has a lot of talent and mom can help her develop it."

"Or the fact that it will get your mom off our backs a little."

"Tyler!" Summer said as she gently punched his arm.

Tyler laughed and said, "Elsa and Maggie will help with her education and when she needs someone younger, and did I mention it will get your mom off our backs? You know it's true, especially with another grandchild on the way!"

Summer laughed, "Okay, okay. All true, but that's just the icing on the cake, it really is a good fit."

"What is that saying? It takes a village."

'Look at you, Mr. Philosopher." Summer turned and gazed at Tyler, "Thank you."

"For what?"

"You came for me."

"Babe, I will always come for you."

"I know."

"I didn't get it right with marriage the first time, but when I was in my dark time, an old cowboy at a bar gave me the best advice of my life. He said, 'son, don't be with the person you can live with, be with the person you can't live without.' I followed that advice and I will never let you go."

Summer had tears in her eyes as she said, "My own personal stalker."

Tyler laughed, "You got that right, little missy."

Shelly walked into the room and said, "Hey, here I am with the popcorn and I don't see any lights on the tree." Jake jumped up from his place by the door and scooted over to Shelly. He parked himself at her feet.

"I think someone smells the popcorn," Tyler said as he got up and headed for the tree. On his way by Shelly he grabbed a handful of popcorn and tossed one kernel in the air. Jake jumped up and caught it before it hit the ground. They all laughed and Tyler picked up the string of lights and wrapped it around the tree.

Summer's heart swelled. Life was good.

The End

Made in the USA
Middletown, DE
20 January 2016